D0429708

Miss Dimple Rallies to the Cause

Miss Dimple Rallies to the Cause

MIGNON F. BALLARD

St. Martin's Minotaur
NEW YORK

MISS DIMPLE RALLIES TO THE CAUSE. Copyright © 2011 by Mignon F. Ballard. All rights reserved. Printed in the United States of America. For information, address St. Martin's Press, 175 Fifth Avenue, New York, N.Y. 10010.

www.minotaurbooks.com
An imprint of St. Martin's Publishing Group

Library of Congress Cataloging-in-Publication Data

Ballard, Mignon Franklin.
    Miss Dimple rallies to the cause : a mystery / Mignon F. Ballard.—1st ed.
        p. cm.
    ISBN 978-0-312-61475-1
    1. Women teachers—Fiction.   2. Elementary school teachers—Fiction.
    3. Georgia—History—20th century—Fiction.   I. Title.
    PS3552.A466M59   2011
    813'.54—dc23
                                                                    2011026760

First Edition: December 2011

10 9 8 7 6 5 4 3 2 1

*With gratitude to all the "Miss Dimples,"
and especially to our fourth-grade teacher,
Mrs. Eddie Mae Lang, who read
to us and loved us*

Acknowledgments

Again, to Hope and "both Lauras," with a million thanks for holding my hand!

Miss Dimple Rallies to the Cause

CHAPTER ONE

*D*arkness was an ally and trees don't tell. How deep was deep enough? The shovel struck a stone, a root, but the earth was softer here. Soon leaves would blanket this secluded spot. Oh, God, forgive me!

"Virginia?" Miss Dimple Kilpatrick stood in the doorway of the Elderberry Library and looked about. On low shelves beneath leaded casement windows, open now in early September, worn volumes tumbled against one another, waiting for the next reader, and Miss Dimple hesitated before rejecting the urge to straighten them. Cattus, the gray-striped resident cat, slept curled in the rocking chair by the empty stone fireplace, and a vase of wilting pink roses shed petals on the dark, glossy surface of the piano in the corner. Probably left over from the Woman's Club meeting earlier in the week, Miss Dimple thought, stepping closer to inhale their dainty fragrance. Cattus, so named by the librarian, Virginia Balliew, who had taught Latin years ago before she married Albert, jumped down and curled around her ankles, and Dimple stooped briefly to stroke her. If she didn't love teaching so, Dimple Kilpatrick thought she would be perfectly happy spending her days in this blissfully peaceful place, and she'd have to admit she was sometimes a little envious of her librarian friend.

"Virginia?" she called again, noticing the half-filled mug of coffee on the large oak desk where a stack of books waited to be checked in and her friend's familiar blue raincoat on the coat rack behind it. Probably taking a restroom break, she thought, or chatting with a patron in the tiny nonfiction section in the rear. Virginia didn't run what Dimple considered "a tight ship" and was more relaxed in her routine than she herself could possibly endure, but the tiny log building everyone called "the cabin" was the hub of their town, with people constantly drifting in and out to browse through books, catch up on local news, or stretch out on the old cracked leather chaise lounge to read. It wasn't unusual to find somebody belting out the latest tune on the piano, and Virginia herself was known to entertain listeners with "Take Me Home Again, Kathleen," when the mood struck her. It was the only song she could play all the way through.

The room smelled of old books, old wood smoke, and new fall apples heaped in a wooden bowl on the window sill, and Miss Dimple basked in the comfort of it. She added the two Christie mysteries she was returning to books that had come in earlier and stuck her head in the back room just as a figure darted between the stacks. She was just in time to glimpse the top of Virginia's once-red hair over the row of fraying *World Book Encyclopedias*.

"What in the world are you doing back here, Virginia? I've called to you two times. You might want to consider getting your hearing checked," Miss Dimple demanded.

"Oh, thank goodness it's you!" Her friend emerged sneezing. "I really have to dust back here . . . I thought you were Emmaline. She's supposed to be headed this way, and I'm just not in the mood to deal with her today."

"What about tomorrow?" Dimple suggested, smiling.

"Then, either." Virginia followed her back into the larger room and switched on an ancient electric fan in the window. "Must be almost ninety in here. I was hoping that shower this morning would cool things off."

"I don't suppose that new Eberhart book's come in," Miss Dimple said, frowning as she checked authors under *E.* "And what's all this about Emmaline? Is she still after you about the War Bond Rally?"

Virginia held up a copy of *Wolf in Man's Clothing.* "Came in just this morning. I hid it behind Gibbon's *Decline and Fall of the Roman Empire.*" She sighed, scooping Cattus onto her lap. "You know how Emmaline is—won't take no for an answer. She's been after me to ask her nephew to promote the rally, and I really don't need the help, but Buddy's between jobs again and she thinks it might be a good idea to give him something to do."

Miss Dimple accepted the book with halfhearted dismay. "I know you shouldn't have held this for me, but I'm so glad you did," she said, setting the book aside with her bottomless handbag embroidered with multicolored yarn flowers. "Now, Buddy, he's her brother's son, isn't he? Used to sell insurance."

Virginia nodded. "And farm equipment . . . wholesale groceries . . . even furniture, if I remember right. Must be in his forties now, and too old for the service—thank the Lord—although I understand he drills with the Home Guard." She laughed. "God help us if we have to depend on Buddy Oglesby to stand between us and the enemy!"

"But this is strictly volunteer. You're not being paid to be in charge of the rally, and he certainly couldn't expect compensation," Miss Dimple pointed out as she selected a Lord Peter Wimsey mystery for Virginia to stamp.

"Emmaline thinks it will boost his confidence, and heaven knows he needs it." Cattus leapt to the floor in pursuit of a shadow, and

Virginia stood and studied the wisteria vines outside the window behind her. "She's due here any minute for that meeting, and there's no way I can avoid her, so I suppose I'll just have to think of *something* to keep Buddy busy." She sighed. "You know I'm glad to do whatever's asked of me for the war effort, but if I had known Emmaline was going to take charge of entertainment for the rally, I might've had second thoughts."

"What meeting?" Miss Dimple gathered up her books and started for the door.

"A planning meeting for the entertainment." Virginia smiled. "Are you interested?"

She didn't expect an answer, and she didn't get one. "According to the *Eagle*, there's to be some kind of pageant at the high school," Dimple said, referring to the town newspaper. "I wondered who would direct it."

"Well, wonder no longer," Virginia said, shaking her head. "And I understand there will be a parade as well."

Dimple Kilpatrick nodded, thinking of the reason for the rally. "I think we could all use a bit of festivity. You can put me down for ticket sales."

The country was winding up its second full year in a war against the Axis, which included Germany, Japan, and Italy, and although the British Eighth Army had landed in Southern Italy, German troops still occupied Rome.

"Did I hear somebody mention a parade? That oughta liven things up around here!" Delia Varnadore, who had just turned twenty and looked even younger, maneuvered a baby carriage containing her six-month-old son through the doorway and wheeled it to one side. "Wonder if I could still remember how to twirl a baton," she said, giving the carriage a jiggle.

Miss Dimple doubted if she could've forgotten in the three years since she'd graduated from high school and married Ned Varnadore. "We were discussing the upcoming bond rally," she whispered, peeking at the sleeping child. "I believe he looks something like your father." Charles Carr, if she remembered correctly, had that full lower lip and hair the color of daffodils.

"Oh, you don't have to whisper," Delia told her. "Tommy . . . well, we call him Pooh . . . can sleep through anything. Even the train doesn't bother him. Remember when you used to read us about Winnie the Pooh, Miss Dimple? Doesn't my little baby bear remind you of him?"

Miss Dimple didn't see the resemblance but she smiled and agreed just the same.

"Charlie's on the way," Delia said, referring to her older sister, who was beginning her second year teaching the third grade at Elderberry Grammar School, where Miss Dimple Kilpatrick had been shaping first graders for so many years she'd almost lost count. "She stopped by Mr. Cooper's to pick up a few things for supper. Jesse Dean called to let us know they got in a couple of bushels of sweet corn, and that's probably going to be the last of it till next summer."

Miss Dimple looked forward to enjoying some of the same at Phoebe Chadwick's rooming house, where she stayed. She had walked part of the way to town with the Chadwick's cook, Odessa Kirby, who was on the same mission. Jesse Dean Greeson, the grocer's young clerk, usually notified their regular customers when something special came in, and with wartime rationing, many foods were in short supply.

"I'm here to learn more about that pageant," Delia added, dropping into a chair. "Maybe that will give me something to do."

"I'd think you'd have your hands full with this little elf," Virginia said with an admiring glance at the baby.

"He keeps me busy, all right, but his conversational skills leave something to be desired. Most of my friends are away at college and Charlie's teaching all day." Delia shrugged. "With Mama working part-time at the ordnance plant over in Milledgeville, I miss having somebody to talk to."

"And what do you hear from Ned?" Miss Dimple asked. Ned Varnadore had been a bright child, but a bit impulsive. She'd never forget how he'd nearly frightened her to death when he came close to being hit by a car while chasing a ball into the street, and hoped he had become more cautious.

Delia's face brightened. "I just came from the post office. I try to write him every day, but it's been a while since we've heard anything . . . he's in Italy, you know." She stood abruptly and turned away to examine the titles at hand, and Dimple exchanged knowing looks with Virginia. Hardly more than a child herself, Delia Varnadore was lonely, frightened, and primarily responsible for a tiny life while her young husband risked his in a foreign land.

"Hope I'm not late!" Delia's sister, Charlie, appeared in the doorway and paused to shift her bag of groceries to the floor before stepping in front of the fan. "I've had enough of this rain! Humidity's awful out there, and it's not much better in here. Aunt Lou promised to drop by later with a churn of peach ice cream, but it looks like we might have to drink it."

As refreshment chairman of the club, Louise Willingham took advantage of that fact to miss much of the business part of the meetings, and everyone looked forward to the good things she would bring. Today she was using some of the last of the summer peaches for a favorite dessert.

"Let's hope it holds off until after they get the cotton in," Virginia said. "I understand they're letting the schools out to help pick this Thursday if the fair weather lasts." Everybody knew you couldn't get a good price for wet cotton and a few days of sun should help to dry out the fields and the crop.

Charlie wasn't sure how much actual picking to expect from her boisterous third graders, who considered the outing a good excuse for a picnic, but with most of the young men away at war, local farmers had to rely on whatever help they could get. She laughed. "Some of the mothers had the class making their own child-size cotton sacks this morning out of whatever they could find in the rag bag, and I wish you could see the results!" She looked about. "They haven't started the meeting, have they? Annie's not here yet, and I know she promised to help choreograph some of the dance numbers."

Virginia looked at her watch. "Emmaline should be here soon, and I believe Reynolds Murphy has agreed to help organize the parade."

Charlie was glad. The owner of the local ten-cent store where just about everyone traded seemed glum since his wife ran off with that notions salesman a few years before and left him with their ten-year-old son. She hoped this would help him focus on something positive.

Delia tucked a receiving blanket around little Tommy's toes, although the day was still summertime hot. "Who else is coming?" she said.

"I believe Mr. Weaver mentioned something about it at dinner," Charlie told her. Sebastian Weaver, the new chorus director at the high school, had taken up residence at Phoebe Chadwick's rooming house, where Charlie's friend Annie and Miss Dimple lived, and Charlie and several others from the community took their midday meals there as well.

"He seems awfully quiet, don't you think, Miss Dimple?" she continued. "Maybe this will give him a chance to get to know people."

"I expect he's shy," Miss Dimple said, "and probably a bit overwhelmed. I hear he's a gifted musician."

"We're lucky to have him, then," Virginia said as she put a handful of books back on the shelves. "I don't think that woman they had before could carry a tune in a bucket.

"Have you met the new coach yet?" she asked Charlie. "The one who took Frank Carver's place when he left for the army. I hear he and his wife are living with your aunt and uncle."

"Not *with them* exactly," Charlie explained. "They're renting that little garage apartment behind them. Aunt Lou said his wife told her he caught malaria on some island or other and was wounded in the war. That's why he walks with a limp, but he doesn't like to talk about it. Nobody's used that apartment in years, but there aren't many places available here."

"Oh, it's the cutest place!" Delia chimed in. "Uncle Ed had it cleaned and painted and Aunt Lou has the kitchen fixed up nice. They're supposed to move in sometime this week."

"We'll have to do something to welcome them. A party, don't you think?" Virginia suggested.

Charlie nodded. "Aunt Lou's already a jump ahead of you," she said. "I think she plans some kind of shindig in October."

"Maybe his wife would enjoy being a part of the pageant," Virginia suggested. "Why don't you mention it to her, Delia? It would be a good way to introduce her to the community. After all, there's no reason one can't contribute to the war effort and have fun as well."

Delia agreed wholeheartedly. After all, didn't everybody say she should be in the movies when she had the lead in her class play? Maybe there would be a good part for her in the pageant. It wouldn't hurt to suggest it to the director.

But when Emmaline Brumlow arrived a few minutes later, she had other things on her mind.

One didn't have to know Emmaline well to know the woman bore no nonsense. She was almost as tall as Delia's sister, Charlie, who at five feet ten towered over her friend and fellow teacher, Annie Gardner. Bright circles of rouge made Emmaline look as if she had a fever, and since the war she'd taken to wearing tailored suits that had been cut down from her late husband's extensive wardrobe. Today's was a lightweight tan wool with the ever-present shoulder pads and a hint of a peplum. Delia thought her green felt hat looked a lot like a sand bucket turned upside down on her head with a bunch of feathers sticking out and, biting back a smile, avoided looking at her sister. Charlie had been keen on Emmaline's son, Hugh, before he enlisted in the navy the year before. Having finished the medical part of his training to become a navy corpsman, Hugh had since completed his instruction at Pendleton marine base in California and was now serving somewhere in the Pacific. Although the two still corresponded, her sister claimed they were just good friends. Privately, Delia hoped Charlie wouldn't burn that bridge behind her. Not only was Hugh Brumlow good-looking, but his family owned the biggest dry-goods store in town, where before the war you could buy clothing almost as stylish as anything you'd find in Atlanta. If the two of them married, she might even get a family discount there. Delia had mentioned this once to her sister, who fell into an uncontrollable fit of laughter at the notion.

Now Emmaline set her bulging briefcase aside and instructed Charlie to position the club's lectern in front of the fireplace. "We'll begin as soon as everyone arrives," she announced, glancing at her watch, and Miss Dimple took that opportunity to discreetly leave. Glancing back at Virginia, she felt a pang of pity, but it was of brief duration. She exchanged pleasantries with the Weaver fellow, Phoebe Chadwick's new boarder, as he passed her along the walkway, and paused to speak to Annie, who hurried along behind him.

"Please tell me I'm not late!" Annie implored, stopping to catch her breath. "Emmaline will have a conniption fit, but I just couldn't go off and leave Miss Phoebe in such a state."

Miss Dimple frowned. The hostess of their rooming house had seemed fine when she left there an hour before. "Why, what's the matter? Is she ill?"

"It's Harrison," Annie explained. "You know, her nephew—or great nephew, I guess. Her niece's son—the one she talks about all the time . . ."

Miss Dimple nodded. Phoebe Chadwick doted on the boy to

9

the point where people were beginning to roll their eyes at the mention of his name. "What's wrong with Harrison?"

"He's been drafted into the army." Annie shrugged. "Phoebe must've known it would happen sooner or later, but she just went to pieces when her niece telephoned with the news. I thought I was going to have to call Doc Morrison, but she calmed down a little when I got her to drink some hot tea and elevate her feet. I didn't know what else to do, and Odessa had already left for town."

Miss Dimple patted the young woman's shoulder. "You did just fine. Odessa should be along shortly, and I'll be on my way as soon as I see if Mr. Cooper has my order in. I'd like to make my Victory Muffins tonight, but I'm almost out of soy flour and a little low on molasses as well."

Leaving Annie to face the disapproval of Emmaline Brumlow, Dimple Kilpatrick opened her umbrella to ward off the sun and continued on her way. The umbrella was large enough for three and had once been purple, in keeping with most of her wardrobe, and, in addition to shielding her from the elements, was used to spear and dispose of unsightly litter along the way.

In time, she hoped, Phoebe Chadwick would come to terms with her nephew's military duty, as had so many others. Several young men she had taught and loved as children had lost their lives in defense of freedom, and others were in danger of doing the same. Newsreels, radio, and newspapers brought the fighting close to hand, and learning of death and defeat was constant and unavoidable. It gnawed away at her heart, but Dimple Kilpatrick had not one doubt that her country would be victorious.

"Well . . . perhaps now we can get started," Emmaline Brumlow announced as Reynolds Murphy quietly took his seat and Annie slid into a place next to Charlie. Charlie Carr sensed her friend tensing beside her. How in the world, she wondered, could Emma-

line remain calm and collected in a wool suit when it had to be close to ninety degrees in the room? What a witch the woman could be! And as if she could read her thoughts, Annie Gardner whispered aside to her, "Eye of newt and toe of frog . . ."

Seated at her desk in the background, Virginia Balliew longed to become invisible, but because she was heading up the War Bond Rally and was a member in good standing of the Elderberry Woman's Club, Emmaline expected her to take part in the meeting. Her first announcement, however, came as a shocking revelation.

"Most of you are aware that Virginia Balliew, our capable librarian, has agreed to be in charge of the rally . . ." She paused for modest applause. "Because of her many duties here at the library, Virginia has enlisted the help of my nephew, Buddy Oglesby, to assist her in this cause." (Only two people applauded this time, she noticed: Delia and the new chorus director, who didn't know any better.)

"Buddy has several ideas for promoting our rally," Emmaline continued, "and I expect him to arrive shortly to share them with you."

Virginia bit her lip until it hurt. *Strange, but she didn't remember asking Buddy Oglesby's help with the rally.* She wanted to leap to her feet and make that known to all, but her small salary as librarian was paid by the local Woman's Club, and Emmaline Brumlow reigned as the current president of that group. The extra income, although slight, supplemented the meager pension she received as the widow of a Methodist minister.

Charlie kept an eye on her sleeping nephew as the meeting progressed and hoped it wouldn't go on too long. Naturally, she wanted to be a part of helping to ensure that the rally was a success, and had convinced her sister to attend, hoping she might contribute as well. With her young husband serving in Italy and most of her friends away at school, Delia seemed unsure of her place in an unsettled world. Maybe, Charlie thought, if she just helped a little more with the housework . . . and then she felt ashamed of herself. She knew the fear that consumed her sister whenever she saw the boy on the black bicycle who delivered telegrams, some of which contained tragic news from the War Department. Her mother had received such a telegram about their brother, Fain, the year before, and the memory of that day was still so painful she flinched to think of it. *Deeply regret to inform you . . .* it began.

Her brother was missing in action with General Patton's army somewhere in Algeria, a blue area on the map of North Africa, rich in petroleum and iron, that her third graders had studied in geography. He was injured over there, possibly dead, and the army didn't know where he was. It might as well have been a million miles away, and they couldn't do one thing to help him. It had been almost unbearable to see her mother suffer, but Josephine Carr was a strong woman. She cried her share of tears, and then threw herself into the war effort with even more purpose with her work at the munitions plant in Milledgeville.

The letter arrived in January.

CHAPTER TWO

*T*he earth was black with burning and smoke hung like a
dark veil in the air. The new ground would be ready to
plant in the spring. Soybeans the first year, then cotton,
robust and green in the rich bottomland. And then the waters came . . .

"... most people seem to enjoy a womanless wedding, and it should
be easy and inexpensive to put on."

Charlie was jolted to the present to see that Annie had the floor
and everyone's attention as well. Reynolds Murphy squirmed in his
seat.

"I've canvased several merchants," Annie continued, "and most
of them have agreed to take part—especially for the cause." Now
she directed her gaze at Reynolds, who gazed longingly out the
window while mopping his brow. "I think Mr. Murphy would make
an absolutely beautiful bridesmaid, don't you?"

Of course everyone laughed, including Reynolds, when Virginia
offered a hand-me-down gown once belonging to her late cousin
Ethel.

The poor man blushed. "I'm afraid I'd be much too large for that," he said.

"Oh, but you didn't know Ethel," Virginia countered.

And so it was decided that Reynolds would be in charge of getting the wedding group together. Charlie suggested they ask the various clubs in the area to contribute ideas for the pageant and schedule a joint meeting at the high school auditorium the following week. Emmaline had brought along a book of short, humorous skits they might choose from that she turned over to Delia, and Buddy Oglesby finally arrived, looking flushed and sheepish, with several designs for posters and banners that Charlie found surprisingly clever.

Many of the others agreed, and Buddy blushed as he received their praise over Lou's peach ice cream after the meeting. "I thought I'd have to get down on my knees and beg Amos Schuler for the extra cream," Lou told them, and most nodded in understanding. Just about everyone was familiar with the milkman's curdled disposition, but Charlie was surprised he would deliver to her aunt at all after her outrageous stunt the year before.*

"Aren't you going to stay for ice cream, Reynolds?" Lou asked as he prepared to leave.

Reynolds shook his head and smiled. "Looks tempting, Lou, but I overindulged as a child and haven't been able to enjoy ice cream since."

"I can't say that I'm sorry," Annie told him. "That just means there's more for me!"

❧

"I think Buddy's been hiding his light under a bushel," Charlie told Annie as the two walked home together after the meeting. Delia had stopped by their aunt Lou's with the baby to visit the new coach

*Miss Dimple Disappears

and his wife, who had recently established themselves in the garage apartment.

Buddy Oglesby had revealed plans for a large banner showing a clock with hands pointing to the scheduled time of the rally. In bold letters it read: *Time to unite and win the fight!* Charlie had agreed to make several posters using Buddy's suggested slogan: *Help boost the tally! Come to the rally!*

"We should've started on this sooner," Annie said as they waited to cross the street. "We have less than three weeks to get this thing together."

The parade was scheduled to begin at four in the afternoon on the first Saturday in October, to be followed by the War Bond Rally on the courthouse lawn and a pageant that same night, with proceeds going to the war effort.

"Thank goodness this has given Delia something to look forward to!" Charlie said. "She hasn't heard from Ned in a while and she lives for the mail to come."

"Don't we all?" Annie's voice was somber. "Heard anything from Will?"

"Just a short letter yesterday. How about Frazier?"

"Still helping train recruits at Fort Benning, but he's dying to get into the fight." Annie shook her head. "Crazy, isn't it? Frankly, I wish they'd keep him there for the duration of the war, but I hate to see him so unhappy."

"At least you get to *see* him once in a while," Charlie said. The two had gone to Brenau College with a girl from Columbus, Georgia, where the fort was located, and Annie had arranged to stay with her friend a couple of weekends during the summer in order to spend time with her young lieutenant. She had met Frazier Duncan the year before when the people of Elderberry entertained the recruits on his troop train with an early Thanksgiving dinner, and since that time, Annie Gardner hadn't had eyes for anyone else.

"I have enough on my mind with Joel up there zooming around

the 'wild blue yonder,'" Annie added, speaking of her brother. "Do you realize it won't be long before he and Will move on to advanced flight training at Craig Field? And then they'll be off to who knows where!"

"That *is* why they signed up," Charlie reminded her. "Can you imagine them anywhere else?" Of course she was concerned for the two men as well, but they were doing what made them happy, and all those in combat risked their lives every day, no matter where they fought.

Annie's brother Joel and his friend Will Sinclair would soon complete their basic flight training at Courtland Airfield in Alabama, and their letters were filled with enthusiastic accounts of their time in the air. The two cadets had been guests of Charlie and her family for a few days the Thanksgiving before, and because she thought her friend was interested in him, Charlie had tried to suppress her attraction to Will Sinclair. Drawn irresistibly to his clean-cut looks, intelligence, and keen sense of humor, she had attempted to put as much distance as possible between them, but on the day after Thanksgiving the foursome stopped for lunch at a rustic drive-in and found they had the dance floor and the jukebox to themselves. While Annie danced with her brother to "The Pennsylvania Polka," Charlie had no choice but to accept Will's offer and follow them onto the floor. "Just one more," Will had insisted when Glenn Miller's "At Last" began to play, and Charlie Carr found herself between heaven and, if not hell, some place that was equally agonizing. With the closeness of his arms around her, his lips inches away, she had never felt so right, and yet so wrong.

Later, when Will confessed he felt the same way, he had trouble convincing her that he and Annie were good friends and nothing more, until, reluctantly, she abandoned herself to his kisses. It was soon after that that Charlie's brother, Fain, had gone missing, and Charlie felt she was being punished for being disloyal to her best friend. Annie, thank goodness, put an end to that! "Of course I'm fond of Will, silly," she assured her, "but I thought you knew from the beginning how I felt about Frazier!"

That had been almost a year ago, and much had happened since. They walked past the post office on the corner with the recruiting poster out front: *Uncle Sam Wants YOU!* The wicker baby carriage that had once held Charlie as well and Fain and Delia was parked by the front steps of their aunt Lou's Gothic Victorian cottage with its gabled roof and wide, welcoming porch. Across the street at the gray stone Baptist church, evening bells rang in familiar cadence as they had for as long as Charlie Carr could remember. Would her brother ever hear them again?

Parting with Annie at the corner, she strolled down Katherine Street for home. She had been just across the street the day she saw the boy from the telegraph office on the dreaded black bicycle turn into their driveway to deliver the news about Fain, and Charlie wasn't sure she would ever see her brother alive. But there were no such doubts for her mother, Jo. Her son was *alive*, and she wouldn't allow herself to believe otherwise.

Charlie would never forget the January day the letter arrived. The telephone was ringing when she reached home after school that gray winter afternoon, and she snatched the day's mail from the box on the porch and hurried inside to answer it. Her mother was calling to let Charlie know she had stopped by Aunt Lou's after their shift at the ordnance plant where the two sisters worked three days a week and to ask if she needed anything from the store. Charlie said she thought they could make do with leftover Spam and potatoes for supper, tossed the mail on the hall table, and lit a coal fire in the sitting room grate. It wasn't until she started to the kitchen a few minutes later that she picked up the mail and recognized her brother's familiar handwriting on the envelope.

She didn't remember running all the way to her aunt's, but the Baptist minister, who happened to be on his way to visit a sick member at the time, said Charlie never even paused for the traffic light on the corner and sprinted past him so quickly her feet hardly touched the ground.

The letter, while brief, was written in mid-December by Fain himself from a British hospital ship as he was being evacuated to the United Kingdom, and Josephine Carr almost ripped the paper in her haste to read the message.

Dear Mama,

Just want to let you know I'm ok, so don't worry! Am unable to walk because of leg injury and will probably need some surgery on shoulder, but nothing that can't be fixed and the doctors are taking good care of that. Am told dog tags were lost or destroyed but I'm here and should be as good as new in time.

My love to all of you,
Fain

A few days later a telegram arrived from the government confirming Fain's report, and by the end of March he was able to rejoin his regiment in Tunisia.

By the time Charlie reached home that afternoon her green cotton shirtwaist dress was sticking to her, and once inside she quickly traded it for shorts and an old shirt of Fain's. The local school board frowned on its teachers sporting such scanty attire in public, but what they chose to wear in the privacy of their own homes was their own business, and Charlie, along with most of the younger members of the faculty, had even purchased overalls at Murphy's Five and Ten for the scheduled day in farmer Emmett Hutchinson's cotton patch.

Would Miss Dimple follow suit? Charlie Carr smiled at the image. Most definitely not, she told herself. Besides, she was pretty sure overalls didn't come in purple. As far as Charlie knew, Miss

Dimple Kilpatrick had arrived in this world some sixty years before fully dressed in a long-sleeved purple print dress with a plain gold bar pin at her throat and a lace-trimmed hankie peeking from a pocket of the bodice. Her graying hair, gathered neatly in a bun in the back, was held in place by tortoise-shell combs. Heavens, no! Miss Dimple would never be caught dead in a pair of overalls!

⟡

Miss Dimple Kilpatrick stood in front of the mirror in her small bedroom in Phoebe Chadwick's rooming house and adjusted the straps on the faded blue overalls once worn by her younger brother Henry. The straw hat, however, was new, recently purchased at Clyde Jefferies Feed and Seed, and at the risk of being immodest, she thought it rather becoming.

The thought of picking cotton again didn't distress her. She and Henry had done their share of that as children on their father's farm, and she wasn't afraid of hard work. She was afraid, however, of her irresponsible first-grade charges running off on their own and perhaps even getting into deep water in the creek that ran through the property. That was why she had invited several mothers to go along and help keep an eye on the group.

The sun lay gently across the grass and small clouds drifted in a blue-washed sky as they boarded one of the borrowed buses that would take them to the farm. Dimple Kilpatrick inhaled the fresh, clean air and looked forward to the autumn days to come. She was fond of September, of course, because it brought a whole new bouquet of uncharted minds and fresh faces to her beloved classroom on the first floor of the old brick building with its dear, familiar bell. October, however, swept away the heat of summer with crisp, clear nights and patchwork days. It would be soon be time, she decided, to have her young charges begin memorizing "October's Bright Blue Weather," a favorite poem of hers by Helen Hunt Jackson.

Buddy Oglesby, who had been commandeered, probably by his aunt Emmaline, to drive the bus, led the children in that silly new song, "Pistol Packin' Mama," that had become so popular that year, and of course the children found it hilarious and shouted it over and over during the six-mile ride to the Hutchinsons' farm. Miss Dimple was glad when they arrived.

Long tables, made by laying planks over sawhorses, waited in the shade of large oaks that bordered the fields, and Emmett Hutchinson's wife, Lucy, had made sure there was plenty of lemonade and cold well water for the thirsty workers. Watermelon was keeping cold in the spring for the children to enjoy that afternoon, she told them.

A small area of the cotton field had been marked off for the first- and second-grade children, and Miss Dimple shouldered a burlap bag and ventured forth to oversee her energetic six-year-olds, who spread out into the rows, each equipped with a small bag of their own making.

"Just lift the fluffy cotton out of its cup," she told one overly enthusiastic picker who was snatching entire bolls and cramming them into his bag. Her father, she remembered, had referred to that as "lazy man's picking."

"This way," she continued, demonstrating to her class, "somebody won't have to come behind you and separate the bolls before the cotton goes to the gin."

Distributing the children among four rows, she suggested a game to determine which row could be picked cleanest in the fastest time. The winners, she promised, would not only get to choose for an entire week the story that she read to them after their noon break but also to have an extra ten minutes to draw, paste, and color during what Miss Dimple referred to as creative time.

In spite of this, scarcely fifteen minutes elapsed before two of her charges had to go to the bathroom, three were "just dying of thirst," and a fourth cried from a scratch on her arm. While some of the mothers took care of those needs (the "bathroom" being a secluded spot screened from view by a tangle of honeysuckle and spindly pines), Dimple Kilpatrick blotted her moist brow with her ever-present handkerchief and concentrated on her own row, her fingers automatically snatching the cotton clean from its brittle brown husk and crossing over to shove it into the sack. Pull . . . cross . . . shove . . . pull . . . cross . . . shove . . . The motion seemed natural as the old rhythm came back to her and brought a satisfaction she had almost forgotten.

It also brought a backache she would have *liked* to forget. The children had been busily running back and forth to empty their small bags into a large basket where Emmett Hutchinson weighed the cotton before it was loaded onto a wagon to haul to the gin. Now Miss Dimple hoisted in her hefty burden to do the same. Ordinarily workers would be paid according to the number of pounds they picked, but in this case the farmer gave whatever he could to the school. Many of the teachers, Miss Dimple included, hoped it would be enough to replace the wooden stairs to the second-floor auditorium as the passage of years and hundreds of small feet had taken their toll on the existing steps, wearing a smooth dip in the middle.

Nine-year-old Willie Elrod ran bare toes through the rich, loamy soil at the edge of the cotton field. He had shed his shoes immediately upon arriving, and the moist river bottomland felt cool to his feet. Willie couldn't make up his mind which of his teachers was prettier. Miss Charlie, who had taught him the year before, had hair almost the same color as that yellow hat she wore, and didn't she always wave and smile when she saw him? But Miss Annie, his fourth-grade teacher, had short dark curls all over her head and lived right next door in Miss Phoebe Chadwick's rooming house. He had brought her a bunch of zinnias from his mama's garden on the first day of school, and she'd made a big fuss over them, too.

After a morning in the fields, the children lunched on lemonade and sandwiches brought from home, except for the few who either had forgotten or didn't have any, and some of the mothers had brought extra for them. Willie talked Junior Henderson into trading his peanut butter and jam for the pimento cheese his mama had made him bring, but he had to throw in the plastic whistle he'd found in a Cracker Jack box. Some of the older children had already gone back to picking, while the younger ones played quiet games in the shade until the Hutchinsons brought the watermelons up from the spring. Willie could hardly wait. He spit on the scratch on his foot and rubbed it in real good. It sure was hot, and that creek looked inviting. They were *absolutely not* to go wading, Miss Annie had told them, and this was reinforced by their principal, Oscar Faulkenberry. Willie wondered if the man knew that almost everybody, including some of the teachers, referred to him as Froggie because he sure did look like a first cousin to one.

"I don't reckon it would hurt if we just sorta stuck our feet in a little way," Willie suggested to Junior after they tired of chasing each other through the browning cotton stalks. Because of recent rains, the creek had overflowed its banks, and the two made a game out of racing through the sticky mud and laughing at the sucking noises their feet made as they ran. Willie knew there was an unspoken dare between them of who would reach the water first, but the creek was swollen with rushing reddish brown water, and he didn't like the sound of it as it leapt and foamed over fallen logs and boulders in its path.

"Let's make boats," he suggested, throwing a stick into the turbulent stream. "See which one's the fastest." That way they could keep a safe distance and still play in the creek.

"Aw, you're just chicken!" Junior taunted, but he took a step backward and looked about for a suitable "boat."

They had found a good launching place from an overhanging

sweet gum tree when their teacher, Annie Gardner, demanded in no uncertain terms that they come down at once.

"I told you boys you weren't supposed to go near that creek! What if you had fallen in? Why, it could carry you all the way to the Oconee River before you knew what was happening. What am I going to do with you two?"

Miss Annie sure sounded mad! Willie hoped that didn't mean he wouldn't get any watermelon, but he and Junior climbed reluctantly from their perch and slogged their way to join the others. And that was when their teacher screamed.

CHAPTER THREE

*W*hy was Miss Annie making such a big fuss about an old pile of rags? Willie turned to go back to where his teacher and several others gathered at the edge of the woods. Miss Moss, the sixth-grade teacher, was crying and hollering so that one of the mothers had to lead her away, but then she was always carrying on about something. He hoped she'd retire before he got that far—if he ever did.

"It's probably just an animal," one of the teachers suggested.

"That's no animal. Somebody call the sheriff!" another shouted.

The sheriff? Wow! This was getting interesting. Willie edged closer for a better look. And that was when a hand came down on his shoulder. "William Elrod! You have no business down here. Now hurry on back with the others where you belong."

Willie sighed. You didn't argue with Miss Dimple Kilpatrick.

Miss Dimple had been helping to distribute wedges of watermelon when she heard the cry and thought immediately of a snake. With the creek close at hand, it wouldn't be surprising to encounter cottonmouth moccasins as well as the nonpoisonous variety, and she had warned the children in her care to be careful where they stepped. Instructing her excited charges to stay seated, she hurried to see if she could be of help. Years ago a hired hand on her father's farm had been bitten by a water moccasin, and he had to be taken by wagon eight miles into town to see a doctor. Dimple was told to try to keep the man calm along the way, and she had never been as frightened. She remembered her father splinting the man's leg to keep it immobile and below the level of his heart, but it had begun to turn dark and swell by the time they got there. The doctor did manage to save his life, but he was one sick fellow for a while.

And of course there was that rascal, Willie Elrod, right in the middle of all the commotion! If asked, Miss Dimple would deny ten times over that she favored one child over another, but little William would always hold a special place in her heart, and she was grateful to see that he was all right as she sternly sent him away.

"Has someone been hurt?" she asked Geneva Odom, who was hurrying away from the scene. Geneva taught second grade in the classroom next to hers and was stalwart and calm in most emergencies, but she looked a bit unsteady on her feet and was almost as white as the cotton they'd been picking all morning.

"More than that, I'm afraid, Miss Dimple. It appears that human remains were exposed when the creek overflowed its banks. I think we should get these children away from here as soon as possible."

Dimple Kilpatrick agreed. The skeleton, partially shrouded in dark mud, lay in a shallow grave inches deep in foul water in a wooded area several yards from the edge of the creek where the water had now receded. Fragments of rotting fabric clung to the pathetic remains of what had once been a human being. Miss Dimple turned away. Even after all this time, she could still discern bits of color in the cloth. How long had the body been there? The area had been deluged with an unusual amount of rainfall the past summer, but the year before, farmers had complained of near-drought conditions.

"Do you think this might've been part of a family cemetery?" Geneva asked.

It wasn't unusual for people in the country to use a section of their land for that purpose, but there was no evidence of other grave sites or markers of any kind. The older teacher didn't want to alarm her, but she was very much afraid this poor soul had been buried without benefit of a casket, or even a decent service, and probably not all that long ago.

"Has anyone seen Buddy Oglesby?" she asked Annie as the teachers herded their young flock away from the grisly scene. "I'd like to get these children on the bus right away."

"He was here just a while ago," Geneva said. "Maybe he went up to the house with Mr. Hutchinson to phone the sheriff."

But Annie shook her head. "I saw Mr. Hutchinson take off in that direction in his truck a few minutes ago, but Buddy wasn't with him. Frankly, Buddy didn't look so good to me. I've eaten collards that weren't that green."

Geneva groaned. "Poor thing! I know how he feels. We'll probably all have nightmares—and I'd just as soon you hadn't mentioned collards, either!"

Miss Dimple thought Lucy Hutchinson, whose family owned the farm, looked as distraught as anyone would who'd had a skeleton discovered on her land, but she deserved an A for accountability, thanking each child for their help with the cotton as she collected watermelon rinds for disposal. The Hutchinsons had owned that acreage since the mid-eighteen hundreds, the woman confided, and although they did have a small family cemetery on the hillside across the road, no one would have considered using that low area for such a purpose.

"I can't imagine who that person might've been, or how he—or she—got there," she whispered aside to Miss Dimple, "but the devil had a hand in it. You can be sure of that! I don't think I'll ever be able to come near that place again."

With the aid of a few bars of soap and several large containers of water hauled from the well, Miss Dimple and the other teachers did their best to see that the younger children washed at least the first layer of dirt from their hands and faces before starting for home. She wished she could wash away the memory of the day's grim discovery as well.

But Willie Elrod was not of the same mind. "I sure wouldn't want to come around here after dark," he announced. "You know what that thing is, don't you?"

"That's enough of that, Willie Elrod," Annie Gardner told him. "Now, wash your hands and face and try to think of something more positive—like the rally parade coming up. Your Scout troop will be taking part, won't they?"

"Yes'm." Willie dashed water on his face and head, shook the excess on Lee Anne Stephens, who stood next to him, and received a kick in the shins for his efforts. "Ow! Miss Annie, did you see what she did? Old Raw Head and Bloody Bones will get her for sure. That's who that is, you know. He lays in wait near the water . . . that's what's he's doing, just waiting there for somebody bad to come along, somebody just like you, Lee Anne! Then he's gonna come up outa that slime and drag you into the creek—"

"If that's the case, I'd hate for you to get left behind," his teacher said. "If I were you, I believe I'd get on that bus right now."

Miss Dimple, standing by the bus as he boarded, did her best to look disapproving. What would become of this child, she did not know, but she hoped to be around to find out.

Because Annie Gardner had been the first to discover the exposed remains, the sheriff had sent word by Mr. Hutchinson asking her to stay behind. Miss Dimple agreed to take her place on the fourth-grade bus while one of the mothers took charge of the smaller children during the ride back to town.

"Are you going to be all right?" Miss Dimple asked Buddy Oglesby as he waited for the children to board. The man looked unwell, and she certainly didn't want to take a chance with the lives of her children if he wasn't fit to drive.

But he made an attempt to smile. "Oh, yes, ma'am. I'm fine, really. I think I had too much sun and that watermelon didn't agree with me. I feel much better now."

"And what about you? How will you get home?" Miss Dimple asked Annie, who was checking to be sure the children had cleaned up their litter from lunch.

"I suppose the sheriff will bring me." She smiled. "I guess everybody will think I'm under arrest. At any rate, it looks like I'll be here while he looks into 'this thing of darkness,' and the sooner, the better."

Miss Dimple knew that Annie, who had a passion for the theater, was fond of quoting Shakespeare. "I'm afraid I'm not familiar with that one, dear," she said.

"I'm not sure, either, but I think it's from *The Tempest,* and what we saw today really is a thing of darkness, Miss Dimple. Such an awful sight for the children—or for anyone—to see. I hope they'll be able to get to the bottom of this soon."

❦

Having made certain that Willie Elrod and Lee Anne Stephens were situated as far apart as possible, Miss Dimple took her seat where she could keep an eye on the former and encouraged the children to sing a round they had learned in music class. She had much rather they try to outshout one another with "Frere Jacques" than to dwell on the appalling discovery that had taken place on what was supposed to have been a day of work and fun. Although most of the children hadn't actually seen the skeletal remains, she had no doubt that the few who had would be eager to share the experience.

Who could have done such a hideous thing? The Hutchinsons' son, she'd learned, had enlisted in the navy the year before and was now serving somewhere in the Pacific Theater. Their daughter was beginning her junior year at Wesleyan College in nearby Macon. Did someone in the family harbor a monstrous secret?

"Stay in your seat, Martha. You can talk with Joanne when we get to the school." It was sweltering in the bus, and Miss Dimple removed her hat and dabbed her damp brow with a handkerchief that had somehow managed to stay crisp and white. Anyone could have had access to that area near the creek, she thought. Although it was screened from view by a wooded hillside, it was only a short distance from the road and convenient *to anyone who knew it was there.* Her heart went out to the person who apparently had been dumped unceremoniously into a crude grave. What had she—or he—done to deserve such callous treatment? And although she couldn't be sure, Miss Dimple believed the unfortunate victim had been a female. She had only a brief glimpse of the sad thing the rains had exposed, but it was enough to see what was left of the clothing had once been bright blue and red, such as something a woman would wear.

*   *   *

"So what did the sheriff want to know?" Charlie Carr asked her friend Annie the next morning as they stood on the back steps of the redbrick building that housed the first through fourth grades of Elderberry Grammar School. The first bell hadn't rung yet to summon the children inside, and they watched as a cluster of third-grade girls jumped rope on the red clay ground, chanting, *Cinderella, dressed in yella, went to the station to meet her fella . . .*

The day was already warm and Charlie stepped back into the

shade of the building. "I tried and tried to call you last night, but the phone at Miss Phoebe's was always busy. Did you find out anything about who was buried out there?"

"So many people called, we finally had to take the phone off the hook," Annie told her. "And if they know anything, they didn't share it with me. Sheriff Holland just asked when I first noticed it and if anybody had disturbed the area before he got there. I told him I didn't know why anybody would want to do that, and that what he saw was just the way I found it. Of course there were a lot of footprints in the mud all around it where we'd been standing, but that was all."

"I guess he was asking to find out if somebody had tried to . . . you know . . . dig it up or something before we got there yesterday." Charlie shivered in spite of the heat.

Annie shook her head. "I think it's obvious the creek did that when it overflowed. They took some pictures and then somebody came and put what was left of whoever it was in some kind of ambulance and drove away. I couldn't watch."

"I can't stop wondering whatever happened to . . . whoever that was and why. *Somebody* had to have put him there, Annie, and for all we know it could be somebody we know," Charlie said. "I guess we'll read all about it in the *Eagle*," she added. "I'm surprised Bo Albright didn't turn up with his camera and notepad five minutes after you screamed." The paper's editor was a notorious ambulance chaser.

Charlie had an uneasy feeling in her stomach. "I couldn't go to sleep last night for thinking about that person being buried there all that time, and there we were eating sandwiches and watermelon, not knowing it was there."

"*You* had trouble sleeping! What about me?" Annie lowered her voice. "At first I thought it was a dog or something . . . Believe me, I wanted it to be, but I could see that it wasn't." She turned away. "I thought I was going to be sick."

30

"How did you get home?"

Annie flushed. "One of the deputies brought me. When I left, the sheriff was still talking to the Hutchinsons."

"Why are you blushing? What happened?"

Annie shrugged. "He asked me out."

"The deputy? Really? Are you going?"

"Of course not! He's old enough to be my father! And you know I wouldn't do that to Frazier." She smiled. "He tells me it would be okay, but I know he doesn't mean it, and besides, I don't want to see anybody else."

Charlie frowned. "What's his name? The deputy, I mean."

"H.G. something. Can't remember his last name, but I wish you could see his boots. They look like the kind cowboys wear."

"No kidding! With spurs and everything? Maybe he's trying to look like Gene Autry or Roy Rogers."

"No spurs—or I didn't notice any. It doesn't matter anyway as I don't plan to see him again . . . Sandy, be sure and bring in that ball when the bell rings. If we lose this one, we can't get another!"

"Has Miss Phoebe come to terms yet with her nephew's being drafted?" Charlie asked as the children lined up after the second bell.

"Doesn't seem like it to me. You'd think Harrison was already over there in the middle of a battle. I've never seen her so jumpy."

"Well, she'd better get used to it," Charlie said. "It doesn't look like this war's going to be over anytime soon."

❧

"You'll never believe what Emmaline Brumlow asked me this morning!" Charlie's aunt Louise stormed into the house, plopped into the platform rocker that had belonged to Charlie's grandmother, and began rocking at top speed.

"Keep it down, Lou!" her sister Jo looked up from the notebook where she was writing up a wedding for the next week's *Eagle*. "The baby's asleep."

Charlie, who had just come in from school, unloaded a stack of workbooks on what had been her father's old rolltop desk. She wouldn't be surprised at anything Emmaline would ask, but she had a good idea what her aunt was referring to and tried her best to keep a straight face. "And what was that?" she asked.

"Wanted me to let them use my wedding dress for that woman-less wedding they're planning!" Lou Willingham's hefty bosom heaved in indignation.

"Why not?" Jo asked. "You aren't planning to wear it again, are you?"

"And do you know who's going to be the bride?" her sister demanded. "That fool Delby O'Donnell, that's who! Big as the broadside of a barn! My Lord, the man's got a behind like a Tennessee walker! I just told Miss High and Mighty to use her own damn dress!"

Jo Carr paused with her pencil in midair. "You didn't! Tell me you didn't, Louise." She hoped Delby, who was known to frequently overindulge in the "demon rum," could stay sober long enough to make it down the aisle.

"I'm telling you I *did*—and about time, too! The nerve of that woman! Emmaline Brumlow has gotten entirely too big for her britches."

Charlie thought it might be a good thing she and Emmaline's son, Hugh, had decided to remain just good friends. "We're meeting at the high school next week. Maybe somebody on the committee will know of one they can use."

"If Delby O'Donnell's wearing it, you'll be better off just to stitch together some bedsheets," her aunt announced.

"Tell me," she added, her expression serious, "have they learned any more about those remains you all found? It must be terrible for the Hutchinsons, having something like that turn up on their own farm! I wonder who it might be."

"If the police have learned anything, they're not sharing it with us," Charlie told her. "Annie's having a hard time dealing with it, and so am I. It's like a bad dream. I wish it were."

"It's been on my mind all day," Jo said. "I hope they'll get to the bottom of this soon."

"A gruesome thing for the children to see," Lou added. "I wouldn't be surprised if all of you don't have nightmares, and I'll have to admit, it makes me want to look over my shoulder."

Most of the children didn't see the remains, Charlie assured them, but that didn't stop them from talking about it.

"I hear Buddy Oglesby's in charge of publicity for the rally," her mother said, obviously eager to change the subject.

"Yes, and he's doing a great job of it," Charlie said. "He came up with an idea for a poster contest for the children and they're all excited about it. The whole town will probably be covered in them by Monday."

"Maybe this will be a good thing for Buddy," her mother said. "I can't help feeling a little sorry for him. He always seemed to kind of wander through life."

He seemed to be wandering as well through the school that day, Charlie thought. She had met him in the hallway as he was leaving the principal's office after presenting his suggestion about the poster contest, and he walked as if he were in a daze.

"Buddy, are you feeling better?" Charlie had asked. "I was afraid you might be coming down with something yesterday."

"Yes, yes, much better, thank you," he mumbled, and practically knocked her down in his rush to the door. The poor man looked as if he was going to be sick. Charlie knew how he felt.

CHAPTER FOUR

It had to be her! And he was almost certain he knew who had put her there. How long had it been? A lifetime, it seemed, but the pain was as fresh as if it were yesterday. What if they found out? Or maybe they already knew!

The Elderberry High School Auditorium felt cool after the heat of the day, and Charlie, sitting in the second row in front of the stage, felt right at home with the scuffed floors and hard wooden seats that sounded like gunfire when students slammed them up or down. It had been only a little more than five years when she herself had been here as a student, and by the look of things it hadn't changed a lot. After what her aunt Lou had said about the wedding dress, she had dreaded coming face-to-face with Emmaline Brumlow, but the woman had either decided to forget the comment, ignore it, or was letting it simmer until it came to a boil. Probably the latter.

Murmurs rose and fell in waves as the group tossed about theories and speculations on the recently exposed skeleton in the Hutchinsons' cotton field as they waited for the meeting to begin.

". . . could've been a Union soldier—you know, like the one Melanie shot in *Gone with the Wind*," Delia offered. She had read the novel five times.

"Maybe it was an old graveyard," someone else suggested. Another thought it was probably a long-ago tenant whose family couldn't afford a cemetery plot.

They were interrupted by Emmaline, who had given in to the heat by shedding her suit jacket. Clearing her throat for all to hear, she rose and stood in front of the stage to get the meeting under way and to introduce Sebastian Weaver, who would be in charge of music for the production. Thin and lanky with a neat salt-and-pepper beard, Phoebe Chadwick's new roomer, with his sad face and quiet demeanor, reminded Charlie of Abraham Lincoln. He sat alone at the end of the first row of seats and rose briefly when acknowledged.

Delia had brought along Millie McGregor, the new coach's wife, whom she said had once been an extra in a movie with Judy Garland, and the two of them took time about telling the group about a couple of skits they'd chosen from the book Emmaline had passed along earlier. Millie was one of those people, Charlie thought, who could be anywhere from thirty to fifty. She wore her curly blond hair swept up in a pompadour and tied back with a bright green ribbon, and her dark red lipstick was almost the same color as her dress and matching wedge-heel shoes. Delia and little Tommy had been spending a lot of time with Millie since the couple moved into their aunt's garage apartment, and Charlie was glad her sister had a new friend to keep her company, but it seemed she was always there when she needed help in the kitchen.

Charlie had noticed that the new coach walked with a pronounced limp, and Delia said that Millie told her Jordan had been wounded in the war when he lost part of his foot serving with MacArthur's Forty-first Infantry Division. "And he came down with malaria, too, during the fighting at Buna in New Guinea," Delia added, "but Millie said not to talk about it."

Reynolds Murphy, with Annie's help, had begged, coerced, and threatened enough of the remaining men in town to make up a thoroughly disreputable wedding party, and Louise Willingham's husband, Ed, one of the town's two dentists, would be playing the father of the bride—complete with shotgun.

A group of fifth- and sixth-grade girls, calling themselves Victory's Voice, with help from Annie and Sebastian Weaver, were rehearsing a song-and-dance number as part of the entertainment, and several students from the high school had agreed to a couple of dance numbers as well, Annie told them.

Virginia Balliew spoke up from her seat a few rows back, where she sat with Bessie Jenkins, Charlie's next-door neighbor, who had volunteered to help with costumes. "Are you telling me the *boys* are dancing as well?" she asked Annie.

"That's right." Annie grinned. "We have six couples—maybe seven if Susie Hamilton gets over her ear infection by next week."

Virginia shook her head. "How on earth did you manage that? You must've had to threaten them."

Millie McGregor raised her hand and smiled. "No, but my husband did—made it a requirement for the football team—at least for those who don't have two left feet."

Virginia laughed. "In that case, we're lucky to have seven."

Now Emmaline drew herself up to her full five feet nine and a half inches and laid aside her notes. "I'm sure you've noticed all the wonderful publicity about the rally that has been circulated around town, and you'll soon be seeing more. We have Buddy Oglesby to thank for that. Buddy, would you like to let us in on some of your other inspiring plans to spread the word?"

Poor Buddy! Tall and gangling with graying blond hair, he seemed ill at ease in front of the group, and his face turned watermelon red. Charlie could see he wanted to crawl under his seat and disappear, but at least he had more color in his face than he had when she saw him last.

Buddy shared some of the posters he'd received from the government that would be displayed in public places around town. One showed three small children standing in the shadow of a large swastika. The caption at the bottom warned: *Don't Let That Shadow Touch Them. BUY WAR BONDS.* Another, picturing a wounded soldier, read: *Doing all you can, brother?* A third featured a look-alike mother and her young daughter pasting defense stamps in a booklet and advised: *Even a little can help a lot—NOW.*

After giving out the posters to those who volunteered to help distribute them, Buddy told them about the contest he'd suggested for the children, depositing a large stack of them on the stage. "We've had a huge response, as you can see," he added, "and a prize will be awarded on rally night. It would be nice, I think, if some of the members of the rally committee would help select a winner."

"I don't think it would be fair for me to be a part of that since I teach some of these children," Charlie said, and Annie agreed on the same grounds, but Millie McGregor volunteered to help, as did Emmaline and Delia.

"Charlie, I'd like you to write an article for the *Eagle* about the womanless wedding and the other entertainment we're planning," Emmaline directed. "Since your mother is society editor, she should be able to finagle a featured spot.

"Rehearsals begin at seven thirty Wednesday," she reminded them, "and I'll expect all of you to be here, especially you, Bessie, as you'll need to get measurements for those who'll need costumes."

Charlie, who said she'd be glad to write the article, wondered if Emmaline had found a wedding dress for the bride. Annie must've been thinking the same thing because she looked for all the world like she was trying not to laugh.

"I heard you were there, Charlie, when they found that poor soul buried out in the country," Millie said as they walked outside together. "It must've been awful!"

Charlie admitted it was something she'd just as soon forget.

"And you were, too, weren't you, Buddy?" the woman persisted. "Somebody said the thing had hair, and it still had scraps of cloth sticking to it. Could they tell if it was a woman or a man?"

"I really don't know." Buddy walked a little faster.

"Well, it sure didn't get in that grave by itself," she continued. "Do you think they'll ever find out who did it?"

But Buddy Oglesby had hurried away into the night.

"I've brought you some of my Victory Muffins," Miss Dimple said to her friend Virginia during an afternoon lull at the library. "I know you don't take time to eat the way you should, and"—she lowered her voice—"they provide a lot of the necessary fiber we all need at our age to aid in digestion."

Virginia fluffed a feather duster over the piano. "I'll have you know I'm perfectly regular, thank you."

Dimple smiled. "Because you eat my muffins. Now, promise you'll have one at least every other morning."

Virginia crossed her fingers and promised. She loved her friend, but was of the opinion that if you built a wall with Dimple's Victory Muffins, which were intended to make one regular and healthy, as well as patriotic, you could hold off the enemy indefinitely.

"Emmaline held her first rally meeting at the high school last night," she said, "and I declare, Dimple, that woman could give Mussolini himself a run for his money. She has all the makings of a dictator."

"It doesn't look as though we'll have to worry about him anymore," Dimple said. The Fascist Grand Council had turned against their defeated leader only the summer before and imprisoned him on the island of Ponza.

"Well, we still have to worry about Emmaline. I just hope I can get through this rally without committing murder or mayhem."

Virginia shoved a stray book into place and stooped to stroke Cattus, who ignored her.

"Since you're speaking of that subject, I see Bo Albright has a front-page story about the remains of the woman uncovered on the Hutchinsons' farm," Dimple said.

Virginia frowned. "How do they know it was a woman?"

A copy of the *Eagle* lay on the massive oak table by the windows where students sometimes did homework, and Miss Dimple folded it neatly into fourths to read. "Bo quotes the coroner as saying the skeleton belonged to a woman who had been dead for approximately two years." She sighed in disapproval. "This is most unnecessary, and on the front page, too. Did you see this, Virginia? It sounds like a circus barker: *Floodwaters uncover shallow grave! Who was the mystery woman buried there? What secrets did she hold?*

"Secrets indeed! It's not only sensational, but disrespectful as well. There's just no excuse for it."

"I haven't had a chance to read it yet." Virginia reached for the paper. "It should be easy enough to find out," she said after studying the article. "Who went missing about two years ago? Of course it could've been someone who wasn't from this area."

"I can't think of anyone right offhand, but I do hope they'll find out soon so the unfortunate person can be properly laid to rest," Dimple said.

"But whoever put her there could still be close by." Virginia tossed the newspaper aside. "The Hutchinsons' son would've been here two years ago—about high school age, I imagine . . . and the war would have given him a perfect excuse to leave."

Miss Dimple nodded. She hoped it wasn't true.

❦

"You all better eat your fill of this here fried okra. Ain't gonna be no more till next summer." Odessa Kirby, Phoebe Chadwick's longtime cook, set down a bowl filled with the crisp vegetable, dipped in buttermilk, seasoned cornmeal, and fried in bacon drippings, and watched it disappear. Today was vegetable day at the rooming house, and no one seemed to mind. In fact, they happily devoured the green beans, tomatoes, cucumbers, and field peas that had come from the Chadwicks' victory garden.

Dimple Kilpatrick helped herself to Odessa's delectable corn pones, golden brown and crusty on the outside and moist and flavorful on the inside, restricting herself to one. Miss Dimple's brother, Henry, kept Odessa supplied with the water-ground cornmeal he ordered from a mill near his vacation home in the North Georgia mountains, and everyone agreed the texture couldn't be equaled. Miss Dimple didn't deny it.

"I hear Harris Cooper's going to be the groom for the womanless wedding," Geneva Odom said, spooning field peas onto her plate. Although Geneva didn't room at Miss Phoebe's, she took her noon meal there during the week, as did Charlie. The school had no cafeteria, and the students who didn't bring a bagged lunch went home for dinner in the middle of the day.

Harris Cooper, a local grocer, was so short he had to stand on a box to see over the counter. He wore his thinning hair slicked down with Wildroot Cream Oil, and a gold pocket watch usually peeked from his vest pocket.

Charlie laughed. "Why, Delby O'Donnell could pick up Harris Cooper and toss him over his shoulder!"

"I suppose that's the point," Geneva said, "but how are they going to find a dress large enough for Delby?"

"Bessie's making one from some of her old dotted Swiss curtains," Charlie said. "I believe the wedding party is complete—or I hope it is. The first rehearsal's tonight."

Ignoring Phoebe's frown, Lily Moss blotted her mouth with her white linen napkin, leaving orange smears of Tangee lipstick. "Well, I think the whole thing's silly! Grown men dressing up in women's clothing. You'd think they could find better ways to spend their time."

The room came to attention as Miss Dimple rested her fork on her plate. "I don't believe any effort to support our country could be considered a waste of time."

Silence like a blanket of snow descended on the diners as Lily flushed and reached for her water glass with a trembling hand. Charlie wanted to stand and cheer for Miss Dimple's stand, but she couldn't help feeling a little sorry for Lily, who never seemed to think before she spoke.

To her relief, Velma Anderson spoke up. "Well, I can hardly wait to see it. That new coach, Jordan McGregor, has talked our own Froggie Faulkenberry into being the maid of honor."

"That I have to see!" Geneva said, thinking of their stuffy school principal parading down the aisle in lace. She turned to Annie. "What do the younger girls plan to sing?"

"We're working on a little dance routine to 'Praise the Lord and Pass the Ammunition.' I think it should be fun—if Sebastian has the patience to put up with us," Annie said.

Sebastian Weaver, who was the lone man at the table, folded his napkin and stood. "If I can tolerate seven high school couples . . . how do you say it . . . jitterbugging . . . to 'The Two O'Clock Jump,' I don't think I'll have a problem with that little group."

Odessa thumped a tray down on the sideboard. "You not leaving now, are you? You gonna miss dessert."

Even with sugar being rationed, along with just about everything else, Odessa continued to work miracles in the kitchen and usually managed to provide a sweet of some kind.

"I hate to miss that, but I have a class in half an hour and will have to hurry to make it." The high school was almost a mile away, and almost everyone walked to save on gas. Eyeing the dessert, Sebastian hesitated on his way out. "Looks good. What is it, Odessa?"

"I found this here recipe for War Cake in one of them ladies' magazines. Here, you can take a piece with you."

"Why do they call it War Cake?" Velma asked as Sebastian left, happily munching.

"'Cause it ain't got no sugar in it," Odessa explained. "Just honey. Be a lot better with a good lemon sauce, but we don't have enough sugar for that, either."

Charlie found the dessert delicious even without the sauce. The new choral director had seemed to enjoy it, too. She wondered how he got along with the rowdy teenaged boys under his supervision as he was basically shy and had been raised in Austria, so his accent was sometimes a handicap because of the war with Germany.

Sebastian Weaver had been gone only a minute or two when he reappeared with a handful of letters. "The mail just came, so I thought I'd bring it in," he said, depositing the small stack by Phoebe's plate.

Annie jumped to her feet. "Oh, is there anything for me?"

"Just some old letter from a Cadet Frazier Duncan, but you wouldn't be interested in that," Geneva, looking over Phoebe's shoulder, pretended to toss it aside.

Miss Dimple received a letter from her brother, Henry, and Velma, one from her sister in Augusta. Charlie finished her dessert and excused herself from the table, intending to wait on the porch for Annie to read her letter before walking back to school together, but Phoebe brushed suddenly past her, dropping several pieces of mail in her hurry.

Charlie stooped to collect what appeared to be a water bill, a postcard from a former roomer who had moved away, and an advertisement from Rich's department store in Atlanta. "Wait, Miss Phoebe. You dropped something!" she called after her.

But her hostess had already disappeared down the hall to the back of the house, and there was only one word for the look on her face. *Fear.*

CHAPTER FIVE

*D*imple Kilpatrick seldom worried. It did no good to dwell on conditions one could not change, but if there was something she could do to improve a situation, she believed in doing what her father had referred to as "stepping up to the plate."

When the other teachers left for school after the midday meal that day, Miss Dimple gathered up her leather handbag decorated with colorful yarn flowers, along with her umbrella, just in case she spied litter along the way, and left them in Phoebe's front parlor. According to the porcelain clock on the mantel, she had more than enough time to get back to school before the first bell rang.

And then she made her way down the long hallway, knocked on Phoebe Chadwick's bedroom door, and "stepped up to the plate."

❧

Phoebe opened her door only a few inches to see who was standing there, but it was enough for Dimple to notice the woman had been crying, and although she quickly brought up a hand to hide her mouth, it wasn't soon enough to conceal her quivering lips.

Dimple spoke softly and calmly, as she would to a sobbing first grader. "Phoebe, dear, I don't mean to intrude, but it's obvious that you're upset, and I want to help if I can. You haven't received bad news about Harrison, have you?"

Phoebe shook her head silently, but she didn't step back and continued to hold the door barely open. Miss Dimple didn't see how the young man could be in danger this soon after his induction into the service, but casualties didn't just happen on the battlefield. Also, she doubted if Phoebe had a chance to read the contents of a letter before she ran from the room. Yet *something* had arrived in the mail that day to cause her friend such distress, and it had to have been something she would immediately recognize as trouble.

It was obvious that Phoebe wasn't going to confide in her or invite her into her room, and Dimple Kilpatrick wasn't the barging-in type. She stepped back to assure Phoebe of that. "We've been friends for a long time, and I hope you know you can count on me—" she began.

Phoebe fumbled for a handkerchief and blew her nose. "Thank you, but I'm all right, really. Must've eaten something that upset my stomach."

Then we all did, Dimple thought, since everyone at the table had eaten the same thing, but she only smiled and said she hoped her friend would soon be feeling better. Phoebe thanked her and closed the door, but not before Dimple saw the envelope on the table behind her, and that it didn't have an address on the front at all—only a name.

Josephine Carr and her sister, Louise, along with their neighbor Bessie Jenkins and several others from the area, worked three days a week at the ordnance plant in Milledgeville, where munitions were processed for the war, and Charlie knew if her mother wasn't there when she got home after school on Mondays, Wednesdays, and Fridays, she had probably stopped off at her aunt Lou's.

That afternoon she found the two of them in her aunt's kitchen drinking iced tea and nibbling on something that smelled heavenly.

"Spiced icebox cookies," Aunt Lou explained as Charlie sniffed her way into the room. She offered a heaping plate. "Made with molasses and a little brown sugar. I thought I'd give them a try. Might make some for that little party we're giving for the McGregors next month."

"Mmm . . . good!" Charlie reached for another. Unlike her sister, Jo, Lou Willingham was a fantastic cook, and Charlie managed to stop in for a visit and a snack as often as possible.

"Did you get the cologne for Bessie?" her mother asked. Their neighbor was celebrating her birthday the next day, and Jo had invited her to join them for supper.

Charlie patted her handbag. "They only had one bottle left at Lewellyn's." Bessie was fond of Yardley's Old English Lavender and had hinted to Jo that she was almost out. "Sometimes it makes me feel kinda funny to go in there," she added. "I can still see Daddy in the back filling prescriptions with Phil." Her father, Charles Carr, and Philip Lewellyn had been partners in the local drugstore before he died of a heart attack when Charlie was in high school.

Her mother nodded. "I know. I just try not to think about it."

"So, what's going on at school, Charlie?" Lou Willingham, noticing, no doubt, the look of sadness on her sister's face, poured a glass of tea for Charlie and replenished the others. "I know you must've picked up some news at Phoebe's."

Charlie smiled. If her aunt didn't know about something, it probably hadn't happened. She told them how Miss Dimple had set Lily Moss straight about the womanless wedding. "And guess who's going to be the groom? Harris Cooper!"

Her aunt laughed. "At least he won't have to wear a dress. I guess

I'd better dust off Ed's old tuxedo since he's to be father of the bride. I hope he can still get in it."

"Annie tells me she tried to bribe Willie Elrod into being the flower girl," Charlie said. "Told him he could be the pitcher for a whole month when they choose teams for softball during recess, but Willie said he'd rather wrestle an alligator than wear a dress! Heck, he usually ends up pitching anyway." She shrugged. "They'll probably have to use one of the younger boys who hasn't started school yet."

"Has Phoebe heard any more from her niece's son, Harrison?" Jo asked. "I understand she took it pretty hard when the boy was drafted. He can't be more than eighteen."

"Nineteen, I believe," Charlie said. "Too young, but then so many of them are. She hasn't mentioned him lately, but something came in the mail today that seemed to upset her a lot."

Lou frowned. "Do you know what it was?"

"She left the room in a hurry, and I didn't know quite what to do. I think she just wanted to be left alone." Charlie sipped her tea and made a face. "Ugh! Is there saccharin in here?"

"Well, there *is* a war on, you know," her aunt reminded her, but she smiled when she said it. People used the expression so much it had become sort of a joke to help ease the reality that, because of the war, scarcity was a fact of life.

"I remember when Phoebe married Monroe Chadwick," Lou said. "It was the first big wedding we'd ever been to—I must've been about sixteen. Her gown was made of Brussels lace, and her hat looked like it had yards and yards of tulle on it. I thought she looked like a princess!"

"I'll never forget it," Jo said. "Phoebe told me later that her mother had made that dress. Like most of us she came from a family of modest means."

Her sister snorted. "I don't think Phoebe ever felt accepted by Monroe's clan."

"Isn't that Monroe Chadwick's brother who owns the bank?" Charlie asked.

Her aunt made a face. "Hubert. Heart as cold as a well digger's butt."

"Louise!" Jo gasped. "What would Mama say if she could hear you talk like that?"

Louise Willingham laughed. "I reckon she'd say I sounded just plain *common,* but it's the truth, and you know it, Jo. Both Hubert Chadwick and that wife of his act like the Baptist church would dissolve into dust if they weren't there every time the doors open."

Charlie reached for another cookie. "I can't imagine why anyone wouldn't love Phoebe," she said.

"Oh, well, they supposedly have important relatives in Atlanta—a judge or something," her mother explained. "Served in the state legislature for several years."

"Monroe was into politics, too," Lou said. "Lord, he was mayor here forever, and ran for Congress a couple of times, remember? I never understood what Phoebe saw in him. Always seemed a bit of a stuffed shirt to me. And now I hear Hubert's son—you know, the tall one with the receding chin—is thinking of running for governor."

"Phoebe's been a widow almost ten years, hasn't she?" Jo said. "I thought maybe she'd marry again, but she never seemed interested in anybody else."

"Too bad they never had children. She should've had a houseful," Charlie said. "She absolutely dotes on Harrison."

"She was that way about his mother, too—her sister's daughter. Remember Kathleen, Jo? I always thought she was such a pretty child. Her mother used to bring her here for visits in the summers, and Phoebe would always entertain for them."

"I don't suppose we heard from your brother today," Jo asked her daughter as she glanced at the clock and gathered up her belongings.

"You know I would've brought it along if we had," Charlie said. "And we did get a long letter from him last week."

"But that was last week." Josephine Carr knew all too well that during wartime, a lot could happen in a week. "Anything from Will or Ned?"

Charlie shook her head. She and her sister raced to the mailbox every day for news from Delia's young husband, Ned, who was serving in Italy, and Will Sinclair, whose greatest fear was that the war would be over before he completed his training as a fighter pilot.

Annie was onstage with the fifth- and sixth-grade girls when Charlie arrived at the high school auditorium for rehearsals that Friday night. In fact it seemed that all of those involved in the entertainment were present on time and had been marked accordingly by Emmaline, who sat in the front row, notebook in hand. It was surprising what fear could do to a person, Charlie thought as she slipped into a seat to wait until she was called. She, Delia, Millie, and Geneva were to portray fairy-tale characters in a brief sketch, and she hoped they would be able to run through their part soon, as she had a stack of papers to grade when she got home.

"I guess we'd better take a few minutes to look over these posters the children made, as I know Buddy wants to get them circulated," Delia whispered to Emmaline during a lull in the rehearsals. Most of the contestants had colored or painted their entries on pieces cut from cardboard, and Buddy Oglesby had stored them as neatly as possible in a box beside the stage.

"I have already made my selection, and I'm sure you'll agree it's the best one by far," the woman replied.

Delia exchanged glances with Millie, who stated calmly that she was sure the poster was good, but preferred to make that judgment for herself.

"Go on then," Emmaline said with a wave of her hand. "See for yourself, but I'm sure you'll find I'm right."

"Oh, dear Lord, help them!" Geneva, sitting beside Charlie, muttered under her breath as the other two judges took the box of posters to the other side of the aisle and began to go through them. Charlie darted a look at her uncle Ed, the father of the bride, who sat behind her and bit her lip to keep from laughing out loud. Thank goodness she hadn't agreed to help with the judging!

As soon as the younger girls left, Emmaline called for the cast of the womanless wedding, and Bessie Jenkins, tape measure dangling, did her best to outfit them all. Cast-off evening gowns had been donated by some of Elderberry's older (and larger) matrons, and four of the bridesmaids lined up to see if any of them would fit. Everyone laughed as the Presbyterian minister held up a ruffled pink organdy; Reynolds Murphy slipped into a gold taffeta number with billowing skirt, and Froggie Faulkenberry struggled into an apple green gown with a huge purple sash. The new coach, Jordan McGregor, flushed as Bessie pinned him into a pastel flowered dimity with flowing sleeves, and confessed that he'd made a promise to the players on his team. "If they can get up there and dance, I guess I can be part of the wedding party," he admitted.

Bessie peered over her bifocals into the audience. "We're missing a fifth bridesmaid. Isn't there supposed to be another?"

"Here I am. Sorry I'm late, but I couldn't get away from work." The voice came from the back of the auditorium, and Charlie turned to see a man she didn't recognize approaching the stage. Annie, who had slipped into the seat beside her, gasped.

"What? Do you know him?" Charlie whispered, but Buddy took that opportunity to remind everyone to help get posters up as soon as possible. "We have less than three weeks before the rally, and if anyone wants to buy tickets in advance, they'll be on sale at the library."

Emmaline shooed the newcomer onto the stage to be measured

while at the piano Sebastian Weaver ran through a few bars of "The Wedding March." "Try to be on time from now on," she commanded. "Can't have you holding up the wedding, you know."

The man looked as if he wanted to say something else, but he took a deep breath instead and told Emmaline he would do the best he could, but in his line of work, the job had to come first.

"Oh, I know who you are. You're one of the deputies who works for Sheriff Holland." One of the high school girls called out from the wings, where the group had been waiting to practice their dance. "Did they ever find out who that woman was who was buried out there?"

Her dance partner spoke up before the deputy could answer. "Aw, she was probably just one of those tramps that come through here. I don't reckon they'll ever learn who she was."

"That's not true!" Buddy Oglesby, his face red, threw his notes to the floor and jumped from the stage.

"Hey! Wait a minute!" the deputy yelled. "If you can identify that person, you should notify the sheriff."

"Maybe he put her there," someone said.

Buddy looked about, his face grim. "No. I'm not the one who did that, but I can imagine who did," he told them before walking up the long aisle and out the door in silence.

CHAPTER SIX

*S*omething was going on. He just knew it. The signs were there, but he didn't dare mention it or he'd start another war, and he couldn't bear that. Just this once, maybe he was wrong . . . maybe things would be different. Life was full of maybes, and he could hope, couldn't he?

❦

"Can I offer you ladies a ride?"

The truck slowed alongside them as Charlie, Delia, and Annie walked home from rehearsals, and Charlie, recognizing the driver, waited for Annie to respond.

"Thanks, but it's not that far and we need the exercise," Annie said, walking a little faster.

"Are you sure?" Deputy H. G. Dobbins continued to shadow them. "It's mighty dark on this side of town."

"We'll be fine," Charlie told him, sensing Annie's reluctance.

"Okay. Suit yourselves, but you all be careful now." And with a roar of his engine, he was gone.

"Sure doesn't seem like *he* was keeping to the speed limit," Annie said, watching his taillights disappear.

"Why didn't you let him give us a ride?" Delia asked. "We could've been home in five minutes."

"And how do you think he was going to squeeze all three of us into the cab of that truck?" her sister asked. "Besides, he was only interested in Annie."

"Well, I'm not interested in him! I thought I made that clear last week," Annie said. "I was shocked out of my socks when I saw him there tonight. I had no idea he was going to be in the womanless wedding."

"Speaking of being shocked, do you think Buddy Oglesby *knows* who was buried out there on the Hutchinsons' farm?" Charlie asked. "If he doesn't, he's certainly been acting peculiar."

"From what he said tonight, it sure sounded like he knows something," Delia said, "but he didn't hang around long enough to answer any questions."

"By the way," Charlie said, elbowing Delia. "Did the judges reach a decision on the poster contest?"

"Huh! Millie and I did. One of the fifth-grade boys did a fantastic drawing of a fighter plane with a ship below it, and the slogan said, 'In the sea and in the air, let them know how much we care! Buy Bonds!'"

"Sounds great," Charlie said. "What did Emmaline have against that?"

"Only that it wasn't submitted by a relative," Delia answered. "The one she liked had pictures of soldiers and sailors cut from a magazine and pasted on cardboard and it just said, 'Help them win the fight!' I think somebody in your class made it, Charlie."

"Really? Who?"

Delia thought for a minute. "Linda Ann . . . somebody. Orr . . . Linda Ann Orr!"

"You're right! Her grandmother and Emmaline are first cousins." Charlie laughed. "What now? How will you decide without starting World War Three?"

Delia shrugged. "Millie knows a lot more about art than Emmaline Brumlow. She told me she used to be a commercial artist, and some of her work has been in national magazines, but we'll just let the cast choose between the two of them tomorrow night. Even Emmaline won't be able to argue with that."

"Wanna bet?" Annie said.

Miss Dimple froze as the floor creaked under her feet. Could whoever was out there hear it? And what on God's green earth *was* anyone doing on the front porch in the middle of the night unless they were up to no good? In the past, Phoebe had left a small lamp burning on the hall table during the night, but she had discontinued that since the war began. In the event of an air-raid drill, it would be one less light to extinguish, and tonight Dimple was grateful for the darkness. A few steps more and she would be able to look through one of the windows on either side of the door, and if the person seemed suspicious, she would immediately call the police.

Whoever it was certainly wasn't very tall. Maybe it was an animal. Willie Elrod's dog, Rags, was forever getting loose and running about the neighborhood, and she always coaxed him home when she found him. Dimple Kilpatrick frowned as she peered through the glass. But this wasn't Willie's dog crouching on the porch tonight. It was Willie himself!

Miss Dimple quietly opened the door before speaking. "William Elrod, just what in the world are you doing out here in the dead of the night? Do you realize what time it is? I'm sure your mother has no idea where you are."

"Oh, lordy, Miss Dimple! You ought not sneak up on a person like that. You just about scared me half to death!" The child jumped to his feet and began to back away.

"You haven't answered my question, William." Miss Dimple spoke in her no-nonsense classroom voice. "What were you doing out here? It appears that you've been looking in Mr. Weaver's window. Just what did you expect to see?"

Willie shrugged. "I was just looking for Rags. He got away from me when I went to put him out on the screen porch."

Miss Dimple knew that Willie, who lived next door, smuggled his dog into his bed at night and moved him to his box on the porch before his parents woke in the morning. She also suspected that Willie's mother was aware of his nocturnal activities. She looked at the boy without speaking until he began to stare at the floor and shift from one foot to the other. "And what makes you think Mr. Weaver has Rags inside with him?"

"I was just lookin' after things," the child mumbled. "Somebody has to, you know." He looked up at her and his face seemed almost angelic in the pale glow of the streetlight, but of course she knew better. "You said yourself you don't know what you would've done without me when those bad things happened last year," he told her.

There was nothing Dimple Kilpatrick wanted more than to gather this little boy into her arms and kiss his freckled cheek, but she knew such an act would probably embarrass him for the rest of his natural life and cause awkwardness on both sides in the pleasant relationship they shared.

"And I meant every word of it," she said, "but that doesn't explain why you were looking in the window."

"Because . . ."

"Because why?" she insisted.

"Well, because he talks funny—scary, like those Nazis in the movies. And he used to live there, you know. Germany, I mean."

"Mr. Weaver came here from Austria," Miss Dimple explained.

"Same thing, ain't it? Aren't we fighting them, too?"

"*Isn't it!* And indeed we are, but I doubt if some of them had a choice." Miss Dimple sat in a rocking chair in order to face him on his level. "William, Mr. Weaver came to the States before our country was even involved in the war with Germany. He had nothing to do with any of that."

The child's expression was doubtful. "But how can you be sure? They might've sent him here to spy on us, you know."

Although not infallible, Dimple Kilpatrick considered herself an astute judge of character, and the gentle nature of the shy musician was discernible even through his often sad countenance. It was possible that *someone* in this house had slipped a message for Phoebe into the mailbox, and it might have been Sebastian Weaver—or it could've been anyone. It was most distressing to contemplate. "I understand your concern, William, but I don't believe you have to worry about Mr. Weaver," she said, "and it would do him a great disservice to spread hurtful rumors when we have no reason to believe they're true. How would you feel if someone did that to you?"

"But I'm not German," Willie said.

"The man can't help where he was born, William, but he's here now and contributes to the community *and* to the war effort in a meaningful way. Why, Miss Annie tells me he's being a great help with the entertainment for the rally."

Willie sighed. He would rather eat cold oatmeal with turnips in it than give up seeking out spies. After all, wasn't it up to him to help defend his town and his country? And he had done a fine job of it, too! But Miss Dimple . . . well . . . she understood things better than most grown-ups, and he knew he could trust her.

"I'm right here in the same house with Mr. Weaver, and if anything suspicious takes place, I'm sure I would notice it," Miss Dimple persisted as she looked into his brown eyes with her keen blue ones. "I want you to go home now and get some sleep. Tomorrow's a school day, you know, and let's keep this little adventure our secret."

"But you will let me know if he starts doing anything weird—like talking in code and stuff like that?"

She nodded. "That I will, now off with you, and remember, this is just between the two of us."

"Yes, ma'am. I promise." Willie yawned. He would just have to spy on somebody else.

"I don't know when chicken has tasted so good to me," Bessie said as she cuddled Delia's little Tommy on her lap. "And that sweet-potato cake just hit the spot, but you shouldn't be using your precious sugar rations on me. I insist on paying you back." She paused to kiss the back of the baby's plump neck.

"You'll do no such thing!" Jo told her. "As many times as we've borrowed from you! And Jesse Dean at Mr. Cooper's saved us that small plump hen especially for you."

"Well, bless his heart! That's just like him, and it's a treat to have something besides that everlasting Spam!" Bessie rescued her glasses from Tommy. "I think I've had it fried, baked, battered, and just about any way I can think of except in ice cream. And I can't thank you enough for my cologne. How did you know it was my favorite?"

Charlie avoided her sister's eyes. They had been supplying their neighbor with English Lavender for as long as she could remember. "I hate to run," she said, "but Delia and I better be off to rehearsals if we don't want to suffer the wrath of Emmaline Brumlow."

Bessie reluctantly surrendered the baby to Delia, who took him upstairs to bed. "I don't see the need for me to go tonight, but I'll check back later this week to take care of alterations and to see if they have anyone new who needs to be fitted." She paused. "You know, I was in Peabodys' Cleaners this morning and Hiram Peabody told me *he* was supposed to be one of the bridesmaids but that Dobbins fellow talked him into letting him take his place."

Jo Carr pulled her chair a little closer. "That's strange! Why would he want to do that? Most of these men had to be dragged into it kicking and screaming."

Charlie thought she knew why but decided it was best to keep it to herself. "Reynolds Murphy told me he had to practically beat the bushes to line up the cast. And now Buddy Oglesby's trying to back out of helping with the rally. Said he didn't mind being in charge of publicity but he'd rather we'd find someone else to take his place."

Bessie lowered her voice. "I suppose the girls told you what he did last night—got all upset over that poor skeleton they found," she said to Jo. "I don't know what's going on with Buddy, but as the old man said, it's gettin' curiouser and curiouser!"

But that night at rehearsal it appeared that Buddy had been persuaded to remain in the group. Probably, Charlie thought, because he was afraid of his aunt's displeasure, but it was obvious that he was uneasy.

"I can't imagine what came over you to say what you did last night," Emmaline told him. "How could you possibly know who was buried out there on that farm? Talk like that gives people the wrong idea."

"I didn't—don't . . . of course I don't, but we don't know it was a tramp, either. I guess—well . . . I just took offense to the supposition, that's all." Buddy flushed and took a seat next to Charlie, who patted his hand in commiseration.

Delia, she noticed, seemed glad to let Millie take over the voting for the winning poster and was relieved that the newcomer was tactful enough not to recommend one entry over another. "We've decided on two posters that, in addition to being creative, we believe show the great need for supporting this rally." She held them up for everyone to see and propped them on a couple of chairs. "I'm going to leave these here for a while so you can all have an opportunity to look at them, and later we'd like you to choose between them. The winner will receive a five-dollar prize from the Woman's Club during intermission the night of the rally."

"I don't need time to look at them," Charlie's uncle Ed muttered. "That one with the plane on it is the best by far."

Emmaline, much to Charlie's surprise, managed to keep her mouth shut, but if looks could kill, Uncle Ed would have been up there in the family plot on Cemetery Hill.

The rest of the evening seemed to go smoothly except for Emmaline's long-winded direction and H. G. Dobbins's obvious attraction to Annie. Charlie was glad to see Harris Cooper's young grocery clerk, Jesse Dean Greeson, there to help Buddy with the props. Jesse Dean had tried several times to enlist in the military but had been turned down each time because of poor vision. In addition to serving as an air-raid warden, he was always eager to help with the war effort.

After the younger girls and high school dancers had rehearsed to her satisfaction, Annie slipped into a seat beside Charlie while Emmaline took center stage to supervise the womanless wedding.

"Tomorrow, and tomorrow, and tomorrow creeps in its petty pace . . ." Annie whispered under her breath as the woman barked endless instructions to the weary cast. "I wonder if the military is aware they're missing out on a drill sergeant."

Everyone laughed as Ed Willingham herded the diminutive groom protesting all the way down the aisle of the auditorium at the business end of a shotgun and as mother of the bride, the *Eagle*'s diligent editor, Bo Albright, wept and wailed appropriately. The bridesmaids tried to upstage one another, some racing and one even loping as if he wore combat boots, and the vocalist sang an off-key rendition of "At Last," a song made popular by Glenn Miller. Sebastian Weaver, as accompanist, seemed to take it all in stride.

"I believe Reynolds is the clumsiest of them all," Annie whispered as the reluctant "bridesmaid" stumbled onto the stage. "I didn't know he was that much of a ham."

"I doubt if he had to try," Charlie said. "He and Uncle Ed played on the same baseball team for the Home Guard last summer. You oughta see him run."

"I've heard rumors that the bride will be in the family way the night of the wedding, but don't let on to Emmaline," Charlie said under her breath. She wondered if her friend was aware that Deputy Dobbins had been eyeing her the entire time he was onstage, and as soon as the wedding scene ended, he headed in their direction.

Fortunately, Millie suggested they had better vote on the poster before everyone left, and it took only a minute for the cast to decide on the one she and Delia had chosen. "But we do think we should award a dollar to our wonderful second-place winner," she added, obviously seeing Emmaline's reaction.

Millie, Charlie thought, should one day run for office.

Almost everyone had left, including the deputy, much to Annie's relief, and the four women, under Annie's direction, were reading through their ridiculous fairy-tale skit when Ed Willingham interrupted them. "Has anybody seen my shotgun?" he asked. "I left it backstage on the prop table."

"Are you sure you didn't leave it on the other side of the stage?" Emmaline asked. "Ask Jesse Dean. Maybe he moved it somewhere for safekeeping."

But Jesse Dean denied ever touching the weapon. "The last time I saw it, it was right there on the prop table like Doctor Ed said."

"Well, look on the floor under the table, Ed," Emmaline insisted. "Maybe you put it down there to get it out of the way."

"No! No, of course I didn't. I know very well where I left it," he said, and Charlie could tell he had just about run out of patience with Emmaline Brumlow. "That gun was given to me by my father, and one of these days I plan to pass it along to Fain. What in tarnation would anybody want with my shotgun?"

Chapter Seven

*S*omebody knew too much, and he thought he knew who that somebody was. If only the bitch had stayed buried! Soon now they would learn her identity, and although he thought he had covered his tracks, it wouldn't be long before they came sniffing around, and that wouldn't do. No, that wouldn't do at all!

News of the missing shotgun was all over school the next day, and during the noon meal at Phoebe Chadwick's, it was all anyone could talk about.

Lily Moss put down her fork in mid-bite. "It had to have been somebody in the cast," she said, and it seemed to Charlie her look was directed at Sebastian Weaver. Thank goodness he was too engrossed in his macaroni and cheese to notice.

Annie spoke up. "Then it could've been any of us. I stayed behind to help Charlie and the others run through their skit, and just about everybody involved in the womanless wedding had left by then."

"But whoever took it could have done it earlier," Lily insisted.

Odessa Kirby paused as she served the corn muffins. "How come they needed a gun in you all's weddin' anyway?"

Everyone laughed as Geneva explained the humor of the situation, adding that of course the shotgun wasn't loaded, and Odessa shook her head. "If somebody gonna go to the trouble to steal a gun, they'll *know* where to find the ammunition."

"But why?" Velma Anderson looked up in concern. "If somebody steals a weapon, I assume they plan to use it, and I'll have to admit, that makes me uneasy. I hope it wasn't one of our high school group."

"Perhaps it was just mislaid," Miss Dimple said. "Let's hope it will turn up soon." Phoebe, she noticed, had been quiet during the meal and had hardly eaten a bite.

Odessa was aware of it, too. "How come you not eatin'?" she asked her. "You know you like my macaroni and cheese, and you haven't even touched them spiced apples. You just gonna waste away to nothin'!"

Phoebe managed a smile. "I'm sorry, Odessa. I'll confess, I'm getting a little tired of apples, but everything's good as usual. I guess I'm just a bit under the weather."

Dimple thought her eyes looked a little teary, but it could have been because of an allergy. After all, this was September. "What do you hear from Harrison?" she asked in an effort to evoke a positive response.

Phoebe's eyes brightened. "The dear boy is so exhausted, he hardly has time to write, but I did hear from his mother today, and Kathleen says he's doing fine. I just wish they wouldn't drive them so hard. These young people need more time to rest."

Dimple could only imagine that the other diners were thinking the same thing she was: *Harrison and his fellow recruits were being toughened up to fight,* but of course no one wanted to point that out. And while it was obvious that Phoebe was worried about her nephew, she was certain that wasn't the only reason for her peculiar behavior . . .

"Would you pass the peach preserves, Miss Dimple, please? . . . Miss Dimple?" Sebastian smiled patiently. He had obviously been waiting for her response for some time, but Dimple's thoughts were occupied elsewhere. She apologized and offered him the familiar cut-glass dish. Dimple Kilpatrick had known Phoebe Chadwick since she first came to Elderberry more than forty years before and had lived in the small room on the second floor of this rambling frame house for over a quarter of a century. She felt as at home with the rose-patterned china, the brass umbrella stand shaped like a heron that stood in the front hall, and the Victorian love seat in the parlor as if they had belonged to her.

To keep her company when her husband, Monroe, went into the service during World War I, Phoebe began accepting boarders and saw no reason to stop upon his return. She had confided to Dimple once that Monroe stayed so busy with his political goings-on, she would have been at her wit's end without her "other family" to look after. Dimple Kilpatrick had that thought in mind on her return from school later that afternoon and was pleased to find Phoebe alone making applesauce in the kitchen, Odessa having gone for the day. Of course she knew that Odessa sometimes left early to attend a prayer meeting at the Gates of Heaven Baptist Church.

Selecting a paring knife, she quietly joined her friend at the table and began peeling an apple from the gnarled tree that shaded the back steps. And then she waited.

"I know what you're doing, Dimple Kilpatrick," Phoebe began, "but there's nothing wrong with me. I'm fine."

Miss Dimple nodded. "I'm glad to hear that." She cored her apple, sliced it into fourths, and tossed it into the blue-striped bowl with the others.

"It's not that I don't welcome your help with the apples," Phoebe said after a few minutes of silence. "That old tree just seems to go on bearing until I'm afraid we're all going to grow stems on our heads . . . but I've just had a little indigestion. That's all."

"Have you seen Dr. Morrison?"

"I still have some of those powders he gave me last time. I feel much better now," Phoebe said.

"I know you're concerned about Harrison," Miss Dimple continued, but Phoebe interrupted.

"Of course I worry about Harrison, but that's not . . . well, it's *nothing*, Dimple. Really"

Miss Dimple was quiet for a minute as she selected another apple from the pail. "This all seemed to begin when that skeleton turned up the day we picked cotton." Dimple Kilpatrick's exacting blue-eyed gaze had been known to make the most dedicated liar confess, and she fastened it now on her friend. "Is that what's been responsible for making you feel this way?" She hoped her voice didn't reveal her emotions because Dimple Kilpatrick was truly alarmed. "I don't like seeing you like this," she said, "and if there's anything—"

Phoebe held up a hand. "It's not that . . . it's not anything. I expect I just need a tonic."

"You might consider easing up some on all you do in this town, Phoebe dear. Elderberry will get along just fine if you let someone else fill in once in a while. I'm afraid you're wearing yourself out."

Phoebe laughed. "You're a fine one to talk!"

"Ah, yes, but I limit my obligations. You know very well what I mean—all these committee meetings, doing this and doing that, and going here and there all the time—and *that's* in addition to taking care of all of us. Monroe's been gone for a good while now. Don't you think it's time to slacken the pace?"

Phoebe began on another apple. "I never thought of that, but I suppose you're right. I just got in the habit when Monroe was alive . . . he liked me to stay in touch, you know."

"And I'm sure he would like you to stay healthy as well." Miss Dimple pared an apple in a series of continuous curlicues and, with a sigh of satisfaction, tossed the unbroken peeling over her left shoulder, where it landed with a plop on the green Linoleum floor.

Phoebe looked on in amazement. "Now, why in the world did you do that?"

Dimple Kilpatrick smiled. "Why, didn't you know? If you don't break the peeling, and toss it over your left shoulder, it's supposed to tell you the initial of your sweetheart."

"You surprise me, Dimple. I didn't know you were interested in anyone." Laughing, Phoebe tried to get a look at the coiled peeling on the floor behind them. "Mind telling me who's the lucky fellow?"

But Dimple hastily scooped up the peeling and threw it into the trash can. "You'll be the first to know," she said, "but for now, I have papers to grade."

She smiled to herself upon leaving. Not only had Phoebe laughed for the first time in ages, she could have sworn she was actually trying to pare an apple without breaking the peeling.

To keep her students on their toes that warm September afternoon, Charlie Carr devised a game of multiplication "baseball." She had found that third graders would work harder to memorize their tables if a competition was involved, so improvised bases were determined on each of the four walls of the classroom and the children divided into two teams: red for the army and blue for the navy. After about fifteen minutes of play, the red team was ahead by two runs when Freddie Myers came up to bat for the blue team and soon had two "strikes" against him. Arithmetic was not one of the child's better subjects, so to boost his confidence Charlie asked him what she considered an easier question, the product of five times five.

Five, the magic number. Charlie smiled to herself. Will had written earlier that he would attempt to telephone her at *five* that afternoon. He had something to tell her, he said, something he didn't want to put into a letter . . .

"Miss Charlie, make Freddie sit down!" Harold Shugart complained. "He said five times five was twenty and he's done struck out. It's our time now."

"But I *meant* twenty-five!" Freddie wailed. "Please give me another chance, Miss Charlie."

"I'm sure your intentions were good, Freddie. However, your answer was wrong," Charlie began, startled into the present. How could she allow her mind to wander in the middle of an exercise?

"My daddy says the road to you-know-where is paved with good intentions," Linda Ann Orr said primly.

School had been in session less than a month, and Charlie had already learned to ignore some of Linda Ann's comments. She did so now. "If all of you promise to study hard, we'll schedule another game in a week, and both teams will have a second chance to win," she told them in what she hoped was her best don't-argue-with-me voice she'd learned from her own former teacher, Miss Dimple Kilpatrick.

This was one of the days her mother worked at the ordnance plant, and she and Delia would have to have supper ready early if they were to get to rehearsal by seven. Phoebe's cook, Odessa, had shared a recipe for tuna croquettes that were not only inexpensive but surprisingly good and, if you added enough mashed potatoes to the canned tuna, it would go a long way.

"If you'll have the potatoes ready, it won't take long to put them together when I get home," she'd told her sister at breakfast, but Delia was nowhere around when Charlie got home that afternoon, and she found the potatoes still in the bin in the pantry. She had peeled and sliced the last of the tomatoes and cucumbers from their small victory garden and was rolling the croquettes in cracker crumbs prior to frying when her sister breezed in the front door, crying baby in tow.

"Oops! I forgot to cook the potatoes—sorry! Millie called and wanted to rehearse the skit, and she has some great ideas for our costumes. Wait till you see them." Delia transferred a fussy Tommy into Charlie's waiting arms. "Here, see if you can calm him down while I heat his oatmeal for supper."

Charlie held her hungry little nephew against her shoulder and kissed his wet cheek. Would she and Will ever have one of their own? The thought brought a happy surge of warmth that began in her toes and settled comfortably in her heart. She glanced at the clock. In twenty minutes he would call.

"Why don't I change Pooh's diaper while you warm his supper and set the table?" she suggested. "Mama should be home any minute, and we can have an early supper."

But Jo Carr had been home only a few minutes before the telephone rang, and Charlie, still struggling to pin a wiggling baby's diaper, heard her mother answer from the hallway.

"Yes, Lou, I know . . . I won't forget. It's on my list. She said *what*? Well, how does she know? My goodness, Lou, you should know by now you can't believe . . . yes, I remember . . ."

Charlie looked at the clock. In five minutes Will would call, and her aunt Louise could go on and on forever. Panicking, she took the windup alarm clock into the hall where her mother had settled comfortably for an extended chat.

"Wait a minute, Lou, Charlie's trying to tell me something . . . yes, Charlie, I know what time it is . . ."

Sighing with frustration, Charlie set the dry-diapered baby in his grandmother's lap and scrambled to find a piece of scrap paper on which she hastily printed: "WILL IS GOING TO CALL AT FIVE. PLEASE GET OFF THE PHONE!"

But although her mother quickly made her excuses and hung up the receiver, the telephone remained silent. At five thirty, her stomach in turmoil, Charlie went back into the kitchen and heated shortening to fry the croquettes for supper.

"Do you want me to heat up a can of corn?" Delia asked as her mother settled Tommy in the high chair that had belonged to his mother, and to Fain and Charlie before her.

"I guess." Charlie wanted to cry. She didn't care what they ate, or even if they ate. Will had said he would call at five and that was thirty minutes ago. *Over* thirty minutes ago. She didn't think she would care if she ever ate again.

"Charlie, you told me yourself, Will said he would *try* to call at five," her mother reminded her. "He might not have been able to get to a phone. Just be patient, honey, you'll hear from him in time."

But like some of her grade school students, Charlie Carr had no patience with patience. She longed to hear Will Sinclair's warm, distinctive voice with more than a suggestion of his rural North Carolina upbringing and an endearing hint of humor. And she wanted to hear it *now*.

They had just sat down to supper at a little after six when the telephone rang again. Charlie answered on the second ring.

"Hey," Will said. "Do you think you could just squeeze yourself through the telephone wires and pop out here on my end? I'd sure like to hold you, Charlie Carr."

Charlie smiled. If only it were possible! "You're the one who can fly."

"I'd be standing at your door right now, but your Uncle Sam's downright selfish about sharing his planes—especially the B-13s we're flying now—gets kinda testy about it." Charlie could picture him standing there with a funny little half smile on his face. "I'm glad I caught you," he continued. "Had to stand in line for the phone, and there are a bunch of fellas making ugly faces at me right now, so guess I'd better hurry . . .

"Listen, is there a chance you might be able meet me in Rome this weekend? I've an opportunity to fly with a buddy to Gadsden, and he has an uncle there who'll let us use his car to get over to Rome. His girl's in school there."

Charlie knew of Shorter College in the northwest Georgia town because that was where Delia was slated to go before she decided to marry right out of high school.

"Elaine—that's Don's girlfriend—says you can stay with her in the dorm. I only have a twenty-four-hour pass, but it would give us at least a few hours together."

The few seconds of silence on the line were heavy with longing from both directions. "Charlie? If I could only see you—even for a little while! Please say you'll come." His voice was husky with emotion, and Charlie Carr felt her heart dissolve into warm mush. A team of oxen couldn't keep her away.

"I don't think we have enough gasoline rations for me to drive, but I'll try to get there by bus," she said. "No, I take that back . . . I *will* get there by bus." Charlie took down Elaine's address and phone number and promised she would see him soon. She would walk all the way if she had to!

CHAPTER EIGHT

Oh, why couldn't he keep his mouth shut? Something was wrong, bad wrong, and he didn't know what to do about it. Who would believe him? Besides, he had secrets of his own. All this time he'd had an uneasy feeling he needed to look over his shoulder, but now it was more than a feeling, and he knew it as well as he knew his name. Somebody wanted to kill him.

The bus to Rome was a sea of khaki, and although almost every seat was taken when Charlie got on in Atlanta, at least ten servicemen rose to offer her a place. Thanking them, she declined and made her way to the middle of the bus, where she squeezed in beside a grandmotherly woman with a lapful of knitting.

"Socks," the woman told her. "Socks for the servicemen. It keeps me occupied, and I like to feel I'm doing my part for the war effort, no matter how small." Mrs. Estelle Addington was on her way back home to Lindale, Georgia, after visiting her sister in Atlanta, and within five minutes Charlie knew she had two grandsons in the army and one in the navy; her husband, Ralph, had just retired from the cotton mill; and the summer before, she had put up forty quarts of tomatoes and forty-three of green beans from her victory garden.

To save time, Jo Carr had insisted on driving her daughter to meet the bus in Atlanta. Where else would she use her gas coupons? she said. And to save money, Aunt Lou had packed a lunch of fried chicken, deviled eggs, and dainty cream cheese and olive sandwiches cut into triangles with the crusts trimmed off. Charlie's seatmate accepted a drumstick but refused more, saying she had eaten a huge breakfast and expected her daughter to have dinner ready when she got home, so Charlie shared with the two young soldiers across the aisle. They were on their way home on leave, they said: one to Acworth, and the other would get off in Cartersville. The bus stopped at every little crossroad along the way, and where some passengers disembarked, others took their places. Some of them slept, most looked tired, and all were young. After polishing off his third deviled egg, the private who would get off the bus in Cartersville said he planned to catch a ride home from there, and Charlie assured him he wouldn't have a long wait. Most people made a point to offer a ride to anyone in uniform, and it was considered unpatriotic to pass one by.

Today, Charlie decided, she would put the puzzle of the missing shotgun, the gruesome discovery of the skeleton, and Phoebe Chadwick's peculiar behavior from her mind and concentrate on the long-awaited reunion with Will. How refreshing it would be to pretend—even for a little while—that it was all a bad dream! She had boarded the bus early in the day, but it seemed to take forever to reach its destination.

In the small city of Marietta, rows and rows of tiny apartments, shaded by pines, lined the road to provide living quarters for the thousands of men and women who had come there to work at the Bell Bomber Plant, where they labored steadily to produce the fighter planes Will and his fellow pilots might one day fly. She knew that Miss Dimple's brother, Henry, lived nearby and was involved in the development of a special project there.

The bus was sweltering, and Estelle and her lapful of yarn took up more than her share of the seat. Somebody behind them was eating a banana, and the smell of it was almost overpowering. One of the young men who had shared her lunch insisted on treating her to a Coke when they stopped at tiny Kennesaw, and Charlie drained the bottle gratefully. From the bus window she could see the still-green slopes of Kennesaw Mountain, the site of a major battle during the War Between the States, with the village scattered below.

Charlie was glad Aunt Lou had thought to provide lunch as the stops were frequent and tiresome, and morning wore slowly into afternoon. By the time they reached Emerson, her clothing was sticking to her back, and she took advantage of a restroom break to dash cooling water on her face.

The blond pageboy she had taken so much trouble rolling on socks the night before now hung in damp, limp strands about her face, and her dress looked as if she'd slept in it. As much as she looked forward to seeing Will, Charlie hoped she would have time to freshen up and change when she reached the college, and since Shorter was located several miles from the bus station, she would have to take a taxi to get there.

Her friend across the aisle waved good-bye to her as he left the bus in Cartersville, and a few miles down the road, her seatmate squeezed past her to reunite with her waiting husband in Lindale. Charlie smiled as she watched the older couple's shy embrace, which amounted to a brief "half hug" and a kiss on the cheek. Would she and Will be like that when they grew old? And how would he greet her now?

Charlie scooted next to the window to make room for a young mother with a sleeping baby in her arms. The baby—a girl, the mother said—was not quite three months old. Her father, an ensign in the navy, was on duty somewhere in the Pacific, and they were on their way to Rome for an extended visit with her parents.

Charlie told her about her sister, Delia, and how much joy little Tommy had brought into their lives. "I'm getting to be an old hand at changing diapers and mixing formula," she said.

The young mother smiled, but she seemed tired, and Charlie offered to hold the baby so she could rest. In a very few minutes, her seatmate fell into an exhausted sleep with her head nodding on her chest.

The baby was hot against her breast, and Charlie shifted her onto her shoulder. She smelled of sour milk and sweet baby sweat, and her hair curled in fair damp ringlets above her tiny ears. Although Charlie spent a lot of time taking care of her nephew, the main responsibility of his care belonged to Delia. How would she cope if she were in the same situation? Charlie wondered. Would she still be able to teach? And how awful it must be to be separated from your child's father, not knowing if he would ever be coming home. She knew this was probably why her sister grasped each opportunity to take part in the social activities of the community, why she spent so much time with the new coach's wife. Fun things. It kept her from thinking of all the horrid disasters that might take place.

It was hard enough to be apart from Will knowing of the dangerous training he was undergoing and that soon he would be in combat. But still, she longed for more—to be a part of him and to share his life

Soon . . . soon. The outskirts of Rome raced by the window. Soon she would see his face, feel his arms around her.

"Don phoned from Gadsden, and they should be here before too long," Elaine said on greeting her. "They want to take us to the General Forrest for dinner, and my aunt Pat has invited us over for

dessert. She and my uncle don't live far from here, so we'll be able to spend some time there before we have to be back in the dorm." Because she was a senior, Elaine said, she was allowed to stay out until eleven on weekends. The curfew was familiar to Charlie, who had graduated from Brenau College less than two years before.

Charlie did the best she could with her hair and changed into a dark skirt and the apple green blouse she'd bought for the occasion from Emmaline's daughter, Arden, at Brumlow's Dry Goods. Because most of the nylon was now being used in the manufacture of parachutes, women had to rely on cheap rayon stockings, which were prone to tear and run. Some had even resorted to "painting" a seam on the back of their legs with an eyebrow pencil.

Charlie smoothed her rayons on carefully and hoped they would be presentable for at least this one night. Her three-year-old pumps, shined and resoled, and her mother's pearls completed her attire.

Plain! I look so plain! Charlie made a face at herself in the mirror. Well, it was too late now. She would just have to wear what she'd brought. The General Forrest, Elaine told her, was a nice hotel and the food was good, but you didn't have to dress to the nines. Charlie added a dab of lipstick and pinched her cheeks for color. She was glad to see Elaine in a modest sweater and skirt.

The young men, they were told, were waiting for them in the lobby, and Charlie's heart thundered so on the way downstairs, she was sure Will must have heard it. He sat in a wing chair by the fireplace with his hat on his knee, and of course he stood when they entered. Charlie held her breath. She just wanted to stand there and look at him.

"Just let me look at you," Will said, and Charlie laughed. How did he know she was thinking the same thing? He didn't touch her except to take her hand because the housemother was sitting by the window with needlework in her lap, but they all knew her eyes weren't on the needlework. Elaine took care of introductions all around; the housemother told them she hoped they would enjoy their dinner at the General Forrest, the two women signed out in the little book beside the door, and they were free!

Will and Charlie climbed into the backseat, and he waited until they were a good way down the drive before he pulled her into his arms and kissed her. "I've been thinking about this for months," he whispered. So had she. Charlie kissed him again. His uniform was different, his hat was different, even the insignia was different, but his kisses were the same, and it would have suited her just fine to spend the rest of the night right there in his arms.

The dark interior of the General Forrest Hotel felt cool after the heat of a September afternoon, and the two couples were seated at a table in the corner. A bowl of pink roses sat in the center of the table that was covered in a spotless white cloth. Spreading starched white napkins on their laps, they gave their orders to a white-coated waiter.

Elaine recommended the fried chicken, so Charlie and Will ordered that, and then Charlie was sorry because she made such a mess while eating it. Will dipped a corner of his napkin in his water glass and wiped her chin, and although she would have been embarrassed or even humiliated if anyone else had done that, because it was Will, Charlie found it a tender gesture. The chicken was as good as Elaine claimed, as were the homemade rolls and rice and gravy, but Charlie had left her appetite in Elderberry.

Don, who shared a room with Will at the base in Courtland, said that he and Elaine had both grown up in Chattanooga and had been dating since high school. They seemed to have a friendly, easygoing relationship, and Charlie found it relaxing to be in their company.

It wasn't relaxing, however, to hear the two men talk of some of the dangers involved in their training. One of the men in their class had been killed during their first nighttime cross-country flight. It had been pitch-black dark, Don said, with no moon and no lights, and they had to rely strictly on their instruments. The pilot went into a spiral and was flying too low to correct it in time.

"You didn't tell me about that," Charlie said, catching Will's eye.

"And what good would that have done?" he said. "It shouldn't have happened, but it did, and it took a toll on everybody. It's one of those things we have to deal with."

The tone of his voice let her know he didn't want to discuss the subject further, so she asked them about conditions at the base.

"Hey, not as bad as you might think!" Don said. "We have a new PX with a theater—"

"And new runways, too," Will added. "The housing's okay, too, except when it rains, there's a lot of red mud."

Charlie laughed and reminded them that, being from Georgia, she was accustomed to red mud.

"Have you found any more bodies back in Elderberry?" Will wanted to know.

Don looked up from buttering his roll. "Will told me all about that. Did they ever learn who it was?"

Charlie had written Will about Annie's finding the skeleton on the banks of a flooded creek the day they picked cotton, so they took turns explaining the situation to Elaine.

"I'd be more interested in who put it there," Elaine said, and Charlie agreed. She didn't tell them about Buddy Oglesby's peculiar comment at rehearsal that had led people to believe he knew more than he wanted to admit.

On the drive to her relatives' home for dessert, Elaine pointed out where the statue of the fabled characters Romulus and Remus once stood in the center of the city.

"What happened to it?" Will asked.

"It was a gift from Italy, from the city of Rome," she explained. "Like Rome, Italy, you may have noticed, this is a city of hills, and that's where the town got its name, but when we went to war with

Italy, they took the statue down." She shrugged. "Kind of a shame, really. It was a nice statue, and I miss it."

Elaine's uncle and aunt lived in a spacious residential section of the town and, true to her description, the terrain rose in a series of curves and hills. As a guest, Charlie was in no position to object to the plans for the evening, but she didn't look forward to spending her remaining hours with Will making polite conversation with Elaine's aunt and uncle.

She was soon relieved to find that wasn't to be the case. After joining them for coffee and a delicious peach cobbler made, Aunt Pat said, with their own peaches she had canned earlier in the summer, the older couple excused themselves, suggesting that the four young people might enjoy the comfort of the wraparound porch or the privacy of a walk in the garden.

Charlie resisted the impulse to throw her arms around them and kiss them—first of all for the gift of this special time together, but also for the cobbler with a hint of almond and a generous dollop of real whipped cream on top. She would never admit it to Odessa, but she thought she had probably found her match.

"You should've brought your guitar," Charlie said to Will as they stepped out on the porch with its wicker swing and comfortable rocking chairs. He didn't like to admit it, but Will Sinclair had a better than average singing voice and could remember the words to more songs than anyone she knew.

"I can think of better things to do," he said, taking in the surroundings. "Would somebody please pinch me? I think I must've died and gone to heaven!" Will stood on the steps of the welcoming porch and held out his arms to the scene before them. Sandy paths led over a wide green lawn to an arbor heavy with fragrant yellow roses. More roses of every color bordered a walkway that meandered along a stream overhung with weeping willows.

"The roses are almost gone now," Elaine said, "but some of them will last until the first frost."

Charlie took a deep breath to inhale the scent. If the garden were more beautiful than it was now, she didn't think she would be able to handle it. "People can peaches," she whispered to Will. "They can vegetables, and even meat. I wish we could can this garden—this night."

For an answer, Will tipped up her chin and kissed her. "And the essence of you," he said, holding her close.

As dusk descended, lamplight illuminated the edges of the lawn, offering just enough light to see and, without a word, Will led her to a bench beside the stream, where the silence of the evening was broken only by the soothing sound of water. Don and Elaine, Charlie noticed, had strolled back to the porch, leaving the two of them alone in the deepening twilight. Soon it would be dark.

Charlie talked some of school and the entertainment they planned for the rally, and of the adorable baby called Pooh who had become an important part of their lives, and Will told her of his training and how they had thrown everybody into the shower—clothes and all—after they soloed for the first time.

They kept track of the time . . . seven thirty . . . eight o'clock . . . two and a half hours to spend together in this peaceful place, as it would take them a half hour to drive back to the college.

Elaine had a friend in her dormitory whose parents were driving up from Atlanta and would take her that far on her return trip the next day, Charlie told him. "But the bus ride here wasn't that bad. It just seemed to take forever." She told him about sharing her lunch with the soldiers and of holding the baby on the last leg of the trip. "I don't know how that young mother manages," she admitted. "It must be an ordeal for her just to listen to the news on the radio."

Will nuzzled her ear. "Have you ever thought that one of these days we might have a baby of our own?"

Charlie smiled. She had thought of little else. She reached up to touch his face, ran her fingers along his clean jawline, traced the outline of his lips.

Will caught her hand in his and kissed her fingers, one at a time. "It might be a good idea if we married first," he said.

Charlie laughed. "I can imagine what Froggie Faulkenberry would think if we didn't!

"We could have the wedding right here in this garden," she continued, taking his suggestion lightly. "And serve some of that great peach cobbler at the reception. I'm sure Elaine's aunt and uncle wouldn't mind."

Somewhere nearby a cricket chirped, water lapped against the banks of the stream. Will spoke in a quiet voice. "I wasn't joking, Charlie."

"You weren't? You mean . . . is this a proposal?"

He drew her close and kissed her ear. "That's exactly what it is. Will you marry me, Charlie Carr?"

"I will! Of course I will. Yes, yes!" She threw her arms around his neck and buried her face in his shoulder, the uniform rough against her cheek. If only he could hold her like this forever.

"It won't be for a while, you know, but I'll sure feel better knowing you're waiting in the wings. And I don't have a ring yet, but I'll get one—just tell me what you want."

Charlie thought of all the years she had dreamed of being engaged and wearing a diamond ring, but now the ring didn't matter at all. "I want you," she told him. "I don't care about a ring."

Will laughed and pulled her to her feet. "Well, that's too bad because you're going to get one. Now, let's go back and tell the others."

Arm in arm they strolled back through the garden, the scent of roses all around them. "I'll never see a rose," Will said, "that won't remind me of you."

Charlie walked a little faster. She not only wanted to share their news with Don and Elaine. She wanted to tell the world.

CHAPTER NINE

$\mathcal{E}$very seat was taken in the Good Shepherd Sunday School classroom at the First Baptist Church. Miss Dimple Kilpatrick nodded pleasantly to young Mrs. Sullivan, who waited her turn at the end of the row and responded to greetings from those on either side of her: the new coach, Jordan McGregor, on her left, and Angie Webber, one of her former students, on her right.

"It won't hurt much, will it, Miss Dimple?" Angie said. "I've never given blood before."

"It's a bit uncomfortable at first, but after that it usually goes quickly." Miss Dimple smiled, and patted the girl's arm. "And just think of the life you might save."

Coach McGregor leaned across her to reassure the young woman. "Now, don't you worry another minute about it. When I donated back in the summer, I was through in less than fifteen minutes. It'll be over before you know it."

Angie looked as if she wasn't too sure about that, and her face turned even paler when they saw sturdy Reynolds Murphy being escorted to a cot by two nurses when he nearly passed out after donating.

"I was nervous about giving my first time, too," Miss Dimple said.

"I don't think it's one bit unusual to feel that way." And most of the people around them agreed. Today, she thought, the worst thing about donating was having to wait your turn, as those who were able to give blood usually tried to do their part when the Red Cross came to town, and because this was a Saturday, the turnout was even greater.

She was almost through filling her pint of type O negative when Sebastian Weaver came in to register and acknowledged her with a wave of his hand.

"We don't need no German blood!" somebody muttered behind her. Miss Dimple couldn't see who had said it, and fortunately Sebastian was too far away to hear, but it hurt her far worse than the needle in her arm. There was just no accounting for ignorance!

Later, Miss Dimple took her time walking back to Phoebe's that afternoon. A disturbing little moth of doubt had begun to flutter in her mind. Something wasn't right! It wasn't right at all. Miss Dimple took a deep breath and picked up her pace, but she just couldn't shake it.

❧

Will and Don left to drive to Gadsden immediately after seeing Charlie and Elaine back to the college, where they reluctantly kissed good-bye under the glaring lights of Cooper Hall. After spending the rest of the night with Don's uncle in Gadsden, the two cadets would leave early Sunday to hitchhike back to the base.

Charlie had breakfast with Elaine in the school cafeteria the next morning and accompanied her and several others to church afterward. It was a Presbyterian church, she thought, because the congregation said "debts" instead of "trespasses" in reciting the Lord's Prayer, and the sanctuary was a beautiful stone building with burgundy carpeting and stained glass windows. The choir sounded lovely and the minister had a soothing voice, but she couldn't remember a word he said. Recalling a joke her father used to tell, she supposed he preached about sin and was "agin" it, but her mind and her heart were at Courtland Airfield with Will Sinclair. The fact was, she wasn't too sure about anything that happened after Will took her face in his hands and whispered, "I love you," before leaving her on the steps at Shorter College the night before.

After church, Charlie insisted on treating Elaine to lunch at a small restaurant near the college that specialized in hamburgers, and as soon as she stepped inside and inhaled the onion perfume, her appetite came back with a vengeance.

"Your aren't going to tell me, are you?" Elaine asked after they found seats in a booth in the back and ordered burgers with everything on them and large glasses of Coke.

Charlie shrugged. "Tell you what?" she asked, although she could guess what she meant.

Elaine blew the paper off the straw and laughed when it sailed into Charlie's lap. "Have you and Will set the date for your wedding yet, and, if so, *when?*"

"We didn't get that far, but from the way he talks, I think he wants to wait until things are more settled."

"You mean *until after the war?*"

"I'd marry him tomorrow if we could, but you know as well as I do we can't plan anything until he's completed his training. After this they'll go to Craig Field in Selma for advanced flight training, and after that . . ."

Elaine reached across the table and grasped her hand. "After that they'll get their wings and be commissioned. They'll go where they're sent."

They'll go where they're sent. Those words occupied her thoughts all the way back to Atlanta. Mr. and Mrs. Martin were a pleasant couple and kind enough to offer her a ride, so Charlie tried to keep up with the conversation. In addition to their daughter in college, the Martins had a son who was in his last year of high school and eager to enlist in the military.

"He's only seventeen," his mother said, "and I'm not giving my permission for him to take that step just yet. I'm hoping the war will be over soon and he'll be able to go on to college."

Her husband, Charlie noticed, reached over and patted his wife's hand. Charlie knew that he knew this war wasn't going to be over anytime soon.

❧

The week ahead was a whirlwind of planning for the approaching War Bond Rally and rehearsing for the entertainment afterward, but it didn't take long for the news of Charlie's engagement to spread like sunrise over the little town.

"I knew it! I just *knew* it!" Annie said when Charlie telephoned her Sunday night. After sharing her news with her family, Charlie couldn't wait until the next day to tell her friend about the most glorious night of her life.

"You aren't going to get married and leave us, are you?"

"You should know better than that! Your own brother's an air cadet. Is *Joel* getting married anytime soon?"

Annie laughed. "Joel Gardner won't even settle on a steady girl-friend. But you and Will . . ."

"What about Will and me?" Charlie asked.

"I wasn't sure if you two would be able to wait that long," Annie teased.

"Who says you have to wait?"

"Charlie, you *didn't?*" *Annie's words came in gasps.* "Oh, my gosh, you *did*, didn't you?"

"For heaven's sake, of course we didn't. It would have been kind of awkward with another couple along—but it's not that I didn't think of it," Charlie admitted.

Annie giggled. "I'll bet Will thought of it, too."

"If he didn't, there must be something wrong with him, and I'm pretty sure there's not. Damn it, Annie, this war just isn't convenient at all!"

When Miss Dimple arrived at the library early the day of the rally to sell tickets for the evening's entertainment they were calling *Home Front Follies*, the whole town of Elderberry was a corridor of red, white, and blue. Flags lined the main streets of town, and posters were plastered in every store window. Reynolds Murphy displayed a mannequin in an army uniform outside the five-and-ten. A sign on the box of small American flags on a table beside him read, *Wave one for me!* and were to be given to the children who came to watch the parade later that day.

At the library, Virginia was in such a frenzy, poor Cattus had taken refuge under a boxwood behind the chimney and refused to come back inside. "I can't begin to tell you how glad I am to see you, Dimple!" she began. "People have been coming in to buy tickets for the follies since I opened the door this morning, the children are due soon for story hour, and then there are those who want to check out books."

"I'll gather the children on the porch for story time. Thank goodness the weather's nice and we can set up a table out there for ticket sales," Miss Dimple assured her. "Isn't Buddy supposed to be helping with that?"

"Called earlier and said he was giving them a hand restringing the banner across Court Street as it had blown down during the night," Virginia said. "He'll be here later if you don't mind filling in until then." She stamped a copy of *Miss Minerva and William Green Hill* for Willie Elrod, who was already dressed in his Scout uniform for the parade that afternoon. "This is about the third time you've read this, isn't it, Willie? Wouldn't you like to try something else?"

But Willie shook his head stubbornly. "I'm not tired of this one yet."

"I've always liked that book, too, but I think I know of another one you'll enjoy as well." Miss Dimple quickly scanned a shelf in the children's section and pulled out a copy of *Treasure Island.* "Let me know what you think when you finish reading it," she said, giving the book to Virginia to stamp.

Willie looked doubtful. "I dunno . . . what's it about?"

"Oh, things like pirates, and treasure, and a boy not much older than you," Miss Dimple said.

"Really?" Willie shoved the two books under his arm and hurried out the door, but she noticed he got only as far as the front steps before he sat down to leaf through it.

She settled the smaller children at the far end of the rustic front porch shaded by wisteria vines from the morning sun and read to them about Goldilocks and Snow White, as well as several of her favorite selections from *A Child's Garden of Verses.* By the time the last little person had been collected, a line of people had assembled to purchase tickets for *Home Front Follies.*

"Coach McGregor tells me he's to be one of the bridesmaids," Louise Willingham said as she bought a ticket for the show. She laughed. "Thank goodness Ed doesn't have to wear a dress as father of the bride. Pastels wouldn't flatter him at all."

"Did Ed ever find his missing shotgun?" Miss Dimple asked, tossing Lou's fifty cents into a metal box.

Lou shook her head. "No, and I can't imagine what could've happened to it. Jesse Dean says he saw it last on the prop table and they've searched every inch of the backstage area. Reynolds Murphy gave him a BB gun from the dime store to use as a substitute, but that shotgun was special to Ed. It was a gift from his father."

Miss Dimple said she certainly hoped they would find it and began to tear off tickets for the next in line. The cast of the womanless wedding as well as the other characters scheduled for tonight's performance were a diversified assortment. She was sure the entertainment of the evening would be well worth the price of the ticket and was looking forward to a few hours of sheer frivolity, but yet . . . *that annoying sense that things were not as they should be still nagged at her, and she just couldn't put her finger on it.*

Phoebe Chadwick stood with others from her rooming house with the crowd of people lining the streets to watch the parade. The afternoon was hot and the sun showed no mercy, but she was glad that at least it hadn't rained. Across the street, her cook, Odessa Kirby, waited with her husband, Bob Robert, under the shelter of an awning in front of the hardware store, and Phoebe wished she had thought to stand on the shady side of the street. Bob Robert's niece, Violet, would be marching in the parade with the band from the colored high school, and they had been looking forward to this all week. It was a given that they could outplay, outmarch, and outstrut their white counterparts at Elderberry High, and the group received cheers of applause whenever they appeared.

A few minutes later Lou Willingham and her sister, Jo, pushing her little grandson in a carriage, made their way through the crowd to a spot beside the Kirbys and acknowledged Phoebe with a wave. Lou's husband, Ed, would be in the parade with the cast of the womanless wedding, and Charlie and her sister, Delia, along with Annie and several others, planned to ride on a float promoting the follies.

Beside her Lily Moss dabbed her face with a pink-embroidered hankie. "I do hope this isn't going to last long! I wouldn't be surprised if somebody didn't have a heatstroke in this sun."

"For heaven's sake, Lily! I told you not to wear that sweater. It must be close to eighty out here." Velma Anderson, who shared a room with Lily, dug in her purse and brought out a folded bulletin from the Methodist church, which she passed along for her roommate to use as a fan. Although flushed, Velma looked comfortable enough in her trim gingham dress, and Phoebe herself was glad she had thought to wear light summer clothing.

Much against her wishes, Dimple had been assigned a seat on a platform in front of the courthouse with the mayor and several other dignitaries, as that was where the rally was to take place. Phoebe looked around for Sebastian and found him conversing with Bessie Jenkins beside Murphy's Five and Ten.

Flags waved, and excited children wove through the crowd of people who milled about, calling and waving to one another. A shout went up as they heard in the distance the measured beat of a drum, and onlookers pressed forward to get a glimpse of the soldiers in the Georgia Home Guard who would lead the parade. The uniformed volunteer group was made up of those who were either too young or too old for military service and would be responsible for defending the town if the need arose.

So many familiar faces. Phoebe Chadwick looked about. *Was it one of them? Someone she knew, had known most of her life? Which of these innocent-seeming bystanders was sending the malicious reminders that were making her life miserable?*

CHAPTER TEN

*I*t was there! Just as expected. Inside the old Prince Albert *tobacco tin concealed behind a loose brick in the corner of the wall were three tightly folded ten-dollar bills and a note that read:* Who are you and why are you doing this? Please leave me alone! I can't give you any more.

But there was more where that came from, so why shouldn't it be shared? The empty tin went back into its hiding place to wait for the next collection. And what a convenient find this place was! The wall surrounded an abandoned house on a backstreet of the town where few people ever went. There were no neighbors to pry; children were afraid of the deserted old place because they thought it was haunted; and today just about everybody would be at the parade.

In a few days, just when Phoebe Chadwick would begin to think it was all behind her, she would receive another reminder.

❧

"Annie, what's wrong? Is Emmaline on the warpath again?" Charlie hurried to find her place on the float near the front of the parade route. As Goldilocks she wore a white apron borrowed from the high-school home-economics department over a baby blue dress Bessie had quickly stitched together and a huge ribbon in her hair. She looked as ridiculous as she felt, but Annie didn't smile.

"Frazier's being shipped out." Annie made room for her next to Delia, who dangled her legs from the flatbed truck and was wearing a red and white striped nightshirt with matching cap and fuzzy slippers for her part as Sleeping Beauty.

"Oh, Annie, I'm sorry! Where? When? Will you be able to see him before he leaves?" Still intoxicated with joy from her brief time with Will, Charlie felt her friend's disappointment even more sharply.

"I don't know. He doesn't know—or at least he's not telling. He's supposed to call me soon, so maybe I'll know more then." Annie made a face and groaned. "Double, double, toil and trouble . . ."

"Uh-oh, don't look now, but here comes your friend the deputy," Delia whispered.

H. G. Dobbins hurried to the float in front of theirs while tugging a lilac ruffled dress over his head, and stopped to speak to Annie. "Guess I'll see you tonight," he said. "Maybe we can go somewhere for a Coke or something afterward."

Annie's face tightened. "I don't think so," she began. "I'm sorry, I have . . ."

But giving a hasty wave, Deputy Dobbins lifted his skirts, climbed on the float ahead, and found his place just as the truck jerked to a start.

※

Miss Dimple was relieved to find her seat was at the rear of the platform between Buddy Oglesby and Alma Owens, who was slated to sing "America the Beautiful," which happened to be one of Dimple's favorite songs. She hoped that just this once, Alma would stay on key. Virginia had confided that when Alma learned she was to be in charge of the rally, Alma had pestered her until she finally agreed to let her take part in the program.

Virginia shared the front row with the mayor, who had somehow managed to find a stovepipe hat in patriotic colors; the Baptist minister who would give the invocation; and a minor representative from the War Finance Committee, looking most uncomfortable in suit and tie. Behind them, Emmaline Brumlow, as chairman of the evening's entertainment, sat next to the proud color guard from Elderberry's Boy Scout Troop 39. Virginia, who disliked speaking in public, had confessed to her friend earlier that she had fortified herself with a generous glass of homemade muscadine wine in advance of the formalities. Dimple hoped the Baptist minister wouldn't notice.

Dimple shifted her chair a few inches to take advantage of the shade provided by a redbud tree on the courthouse lawn, noticing that the ladies of the Cherokee Rose Garden Club had planted the area around it with vibrant yellow chrysanthemums. Beside her, Buddy held on his lap the satchel that held change for today's sale of bonds and stamps. Miss Dimple kept a hand on her yarn-garnished handbag containing the change she would need for those who wanted tickets for *Home Front Follies* she intended to sell at the end of the ceremonies that afternoon.

She could hardly help noticing Buddy's glancing constantly from right to left as if he expected to be ambushed at any second. He was a tall, gangling man whose spasmodic foot tapping and nervous habit of cracking his knuckles were beginning to be most annoying. Tempted to reach over and give the poor fellow a reassuring pat, Dimple was relieved when the Home Guard, followed by the high school band, turned the corner into Court Street with all instruments blaring "The Stars and Stripes Forever." This was followed by a float carrying the cast of the womanless wedding dressed in all their finery and a decorated truck filled with several others who would take part in the show, including many of the high school dancers.

Shouts, cheers, laughter, and whistles greeted the marchers, and Miss Dimple waved at members of the green-clad Girl Scouts, most of whom she had taught as first graders, and at Willie, who, in his blue and gold uniform, marched proudly at the head of the troop of younger Scouts holding the American flag.

The cheering grew even louder as the band from Westside, the Negro high school, pranced by, and everyone laughed when the flower-covered float from the First Baptist Church proclaiming *God is love* was immediately followed by one decorated by local students from the University of Georgia with a banner reading, *To hell with Tech!*

The mayor, Miss Dimple thought, took longer than necessary to welcome those assembled and to remind the good people of Elderberry that neighboring towns of Covington, Griffin, and Eatonton were working not only to reach their quotas but also to exceed them. This created quite a stir among the members of the population, many of who could be seen muttering to one another about outselling the competition, which, of course, is exactly what the mayor had in mind. Also, he added, everyone who purchased a twenty-five-dollar bond or larger would be treated to a short film at the Jewel featuring actor Walter Pidgeon and a real-life "Rosie the Riveter."

Miss Dimple attributed the minister's brief prayer to the heat of the afternoon, and was grateful for it. After the color guard led everyone in the Pledge of Allegiance, Alma, accompanied by a trio from the reed section of the high school band, gave her rendition of "America the Beautiful." Thanks to the three young musicians, the soloist stayed more or less on key, and the few times she strayed, they managed to drown her out.

Dimple found she had been clenching her fists for the duration of the song, but had actually flinched only once. It had been less than a year, she recalled, since President Roosevelt had the salute to the flag changed from holding the right hand out toward the banner to placing it over one's heart because the former resembled the heinous tribute to Adolph Hitler.

Virginia spoke briefly, reminding everyone that some types of bonds would pay nearly three percent a year, were backed by the U.S. Treasury, and should be a welcome asset someday to help buy a home or pay for an education.

"I'm sure most of you know Buddy Oglesby, who will be assisting me at the booth just behind us on the courthouse lawn for those who would like to purchase bonds or stamps. There will be a bond booth as well in the lobby of the high school auditorium for anyone attending tonight's performance of our own *Home Front Follies* and, believe me, you don't want to miss that as I understand Delby O'Donnell will take your breath away in his—er—*her* wedding finery! My good friend, Miss Dimple Kilpatrick, will have tickets for that available after today's ceremony at the table to the right of the platform."

The fellow from the War Finance Committee who followed Virginia had now removed his tie and loosened the collar of his shirt. He thanked the town, bragged on the Scouts, the bands, and even the soloist, reminding everyone of the importance of supporting their country in this all-important effort to bring the war to a victorious end, and sat down, mopping his face with a monogrammed handkerchief.

Members of the Home Guard took charge of holding back the surging crowd, forming orderly lines for the many who wanted to invest in war bonds and stamps. In the hour that followed, the Elderberry Woman's Club made thirty-five dollars selling lemonade at five cents a glass, and Miss Dimple Kilpatrick ran out of tickets for the *Home Front Follies*. Tonight they would play to a packed house.

Charlie's stomach growled as she waited backstage for their skit to begin. She and Delia had rushed home after the parade to gulp down a bowl of canned soup and a few soda crackers before they were due at the auditorium. Their mother would follow after she fed Tommy and dressed him for bed before the sitter arrived for the evening. Delia had asked Odessa's niece, Violet, to help them out and was relieved when she agreed. The teenaged girl was wonderful with children and therefore popular with many of the town's young mothers.

"I'm glad we're early on the program so we can relax and enjoy the rest of the show," Delia whispered. "I don't want to miss Uncle Ed giving the bride away."

Millie McGregor, as Red Riding Hood, fanned herself with her cape. "It's sweltering back here. Wish I'd thought to play a character who doesn't wear so many clothes!"

"Better get ready. You're on next," Buddy Oglesby whispered behind them. He had been commandeered by his aunt to assisting backstage and looked as if he'd rather be anywhere else.

Charlie jumped at the sound and stifled a cry. "Good Lord, Buddy, you nearly scared me to death! I didn't see you back there."

Buddy made a face. "That's because Aunt Emmaline made me wear black so the audience wouldn't notice me. I've been burning up in this shirt all night, and during intermission I have to go back out to the lobby and give Virginia a hand with the bonds sales."

Charlie noticed that Jesse Dean, who was helping with props, wore dark clothing as well. From the wings on the other side of the stage, Annie watched, smiling broadly, as the fifth- and sixth-grade girls under her instruction finished their song and dance to a roar of audience applause. "How are we supposed to follow *that*?" Millie muttered under her breath. Then the stage went dark, and they hurried to take their places.

After the excitement and energy that went into the parade and rally that afternoon, everyone seemed to be in a mood to relax and enjoy the show, and the audience responded with laughter to the fairy-tale skit and another that followed. Charlie and some of the others rushed to change backstage before joining the audience for the rest of the evening. The high school dancers seemed actually to enjoy their time onstage, and a quartet from the school chorus charmed everyone with several selections, including "Any Bonds Today?" a special song by Irving Berlin.

Spying Miss Dimple sitting with Virginia in the back of the auditorium, Charlie and Annie slipped into seats beside them. "Have you sold many tonight?" Annie asked Virginia, who held on her lap the satchel containing bonds and receipts from earlier sales.

She nodded. "Quite a few, and frankly I'll be glad when all this is out of my hands. Thank goodness I was able to turn over to the bank the money we took in at the rally this afternoon."

"Isn't Buddy going to give you a hand during intermission?" Charlie asked.

"Yes, thank goodness! It's going to take both of us to handle this crowd," Virginia said. "Bobby Tinsley promised to send somebody over from the police department to give us a little security, but I haven't seen a sign of him yet."

"Perhaps we should call," Miss Dimple suggested. "I can't imagine what's holding him up."

"Where would we do that? Except for the gas station across the street, which is probably closed, the only telephone around is in the school office, and that's locked," Virginia said.

"I'll see if I can find the principal," Charlie offered. "I'm sure he's around here somewhere, and I saw Velma sitting down front. Maybe she knows who has a key."

"I think you should hurry," Annie advised. "Buddy's getting ready to award the prize for the best poster, and after that it's intermission. Everyone who wants to buy bonds will start moving to the lobby."

"Then I suppose I'd better be ready for them." Clutching the satchel, Virginia rose to her feet.

"I'll go with you," Miss Dimple said, following her. "I can fill in until Buddy gets there."

Charlie and Annie went in two directions: Annie to find Velma Anderson, who taught secretarial science at the high school, and Charlie to locate Elias Jackson, the principal.

Making her way through the crowd was like swimming upstream, but Charlie finally wove her way to a side aisle to get a better view and spied the principal in animated conversation with Phil Lewellyn, the pharmacist who had been partner to her father.

"Well, of course you can use the phone in the office," the principal said when Charlie explained the situation. "I'll certainly feel better myself with someone from law enforcement around. I don't understand what could be keeping them."

Charlie followed him down the familiar side hall and waited in the office while he made the call.

"Well, that explains that," he told her, frowning as he hung up the phone. "Warren Nelson says the chief was called out a while ago when somebody reported a break-in over on the north end of town, and Warren's the only one left on duty, so he can't leave."

Then I guess we'll just have to deal with it on our own, Charlie thought. She didn't suggest requesting the help of Deputy Dobbins because she didn't think anyone would take him too seriously in his lilac ruffled gown.

The houselights were blinking when Charlie hurried back to her seat after spending most of the intermission dodging Linda Ann Orr's mother, who just couldn't understand why her daughter hadn't won first prize in the poster contest. Annie, already seated next to Miss Dimple, admitted that she had taken refuge backstage for the same reason. "Oh, well," she said, "according to my friend the Bard, 'asses are made to bear . . .'"

Virginia collapsed into her seat as the lights went down and let out an audible sigh. "Thank goodness that's behind me! Never again!"

"Did you make your quota?" Annie asked.

Virginia beamed at the idea of outselling the neighboring competition. "That and more—much more! Chief Tinsley finally got here—thank goodness—said it must've been a false alarm, and Buddy's turning the money over to him. He'll keep it in the safe over at the jail until the bank opens Monday."

Somewhere behind the footlights, Sebastian began playing a jazzed-up version of "I Love You Truly" and, from the back of the auditorium, a tuxedo-clad "groomsman" ushered a weeping Bo Albright, in flowered hat and garish gown, to a seat in the front row; the soloist warbled "At Last" while the "minister" in an ancient frock-coat stopped up his ears in mock—or not-so-mock—horror. The wedding had begun.

The bridesmaids jogged, loped, and plodded down the aisle in a most undignified fashion while scratching themselves and tripping over the hems of their gowns. Two, who seemed to be in a race to finish first, even pummeled one another with their bouquets.

It would have been difficult to tell whether the audience laughed more when one of the grapefruit in Coach McGregor's brassiere bounced onto the stage and rolled away, or when the "pregnant" bride waddled down the aisle with a huge pillow under his/her dress. In fact, after the show ended, everyone was still laughing so hard it took most of them a minute or so to react to the gunshot backstage.

CHAPTER ELEVEN

*E*d Willingham tossed aside the tight cummerbund, loosened his tie, and fumbled in his pocket for a handkerchief. Those stage lights were hot as blazes and his old tuxedo was a size too small. At least he didn't have to wear a long dress or one of those ridiculous wigs like some of the other men. He had to admit he had fun as the shotgun-totin' father of the bride, but Ed was glad it was over. He'd rather stand on his feet all day long poking about in somebody's mouth than be under those stage lights in that dad-blasted tuxedo for another five minutes!

After bows, the "wedding party" (minus the bride's pregnant padding, at Emmaline's insistence) had assembled onstage for Bo Albright's assistant to take pictures for next week's Eagle, and Ed had made his way backstage as quickly as possible. The first one to reach the small dressing room, he hurried to shed his jacket and stiff, confining shirt and was buttoning a comfortable one he'd brought from home when everything suddenly went dark.

Stumbling into the hallway, he crashed into someone with an enormous pillowlike bosom trailing what seemed like an acre of lace.

Delby O'Donnell swore under his breath "Will you get off my foot?

I can't see a damn thing back here and if I don't get outa this outfit, I'm gonna pass out from a heatstroke!"

"Sorry." Ed backed away and stepped on somebody else. "Who's messing with the lights back here?" he shouted, and had started to return to the dressing room to avoid further confusion when the deafening sound of gunfire stopped him in his tracks. Ed froze, crushed against the wall by Delby's lace-shrouded bulk, as from the opposite side of the stage, someone shouted out in pain.

From her seat in the back of the auditorium, Charlie was horrified to see many in the audience flood the aisles in a rush to get to the door. Others, like her, were apparently too stunned to react right away. When the houselights came up she saw her mother and aunt Louise with determined looks on their faces bulldozing their way to one of the side doors that led to the backstage area.

"My uncle Ed's back there!" Charlie yelled, jumping to her feet, but Miss Dimple put a hand on her arm.

"Wait! You'll get crushed in all this crowd, and that won't do your uncle or anyone else any good. I expect someone was playing with one of the props back there."

What Miss Dimple said made sense, and Charlie restrained herself until she realized her uncle hadn't brought along any ammunition for the BB gun he'd borrowed from Reynolds Murphy, and she couldn't imagine why anyone else would need a firearm for the follies. When a cry went up from the backstage area, Charlie climbed over the seat in front of her and threaded her way down a side aisle with Annie close behind her.

"What happened? What happened? Is anyone hurt?" she asked several people as they clamored to find out what had taken place.

"I heard somebody's been shot!" It was obvious that Oscar "Froggie" Faulkenberry was attempting to control the tremble in his voice. He held a picture hat of purple lace with a bedraggled pink flower drooping from its brim like a shield in front of him. "I was just coming offstage when it happened and have no idea what's going on—but I intend to find out."

"Is Doc Morrison still here?" somebody asked, and Charlie had to look twice to recognize her sister, who had changed from her Sleeping Beauty costume but still wore pink circles of makeup on her cheeks.

Elias Jackson, the high school principal, grabbed the mike and asked for order. "There has been an accident, but it's nothing to be alarmed about," he announced. "Please proceed calmly to an exit. If there's a doctor in the audience, you're needed backstage immediately."

Charlie knew Doc Morrison was in attendance as she'd seen him earlier. The other local doctor had been about to retire when the war broke out and was called upon only in emergencies.

"Here he is!" she shouted, noticing the doctor making his way toward the stage. "Everybody make room and let him pass."

"Back here!" Charlie's uncle Ed, white-faced and grim, met the doctor onstage. "I've tried to stem the bleeding, but we have to get him to the hospital." He grabbed the principal's arm. "We need an ambulance *now!*"

Stepping aside to let the doctor pass, Charlie asked who had been hurt.

"It's Jesse Dean," her uncle said. "Took a bullet in the shoulder. Whoever fired that rifle seemed to be aiming at the area around the props table. It's a miracle he's still alive!"

Charlie, exchanging looks with Annie, rushed after them. Not only was Jesse Dean Greeson a good friend, but the three of them had survived a dangerous situation together the year before. Why would anyone want to harm kind, meek-mannered Jesse Dean? she wondered. In addition to clerking in Harris Cooper's grocery, he was diligent in his volunteer position as air-raid warden and always seemed glad to lend a hand wherever needed. Certainly it couldn't be that someone resented the fact that he wasn't serving in the military, as almost everyone knew the young man had done his best to enlist but was rejected because of poor eyesight.

Jesse Dean lay on the floor where he fell, with Harris Cooper kneeling by his side, holding a cloth in place to try to stop the bleeding. The grocer looked up in obvious relief as the doctor stooped beside him. The wounded man's face was pale and wet with perspiration, and Charlie resisted an impulse to blot it with the hem of her skirt, which was just as well because Doc Morrison barked at them all to get back and give him room.

His eyes were closed, but Jesse Dean moaned when the doctor checked his wound, and although he was able to answer the doctor's questions, Doc Morrison had to bend down to hear him. "There doesn't seem to be an exit wound," Doc said, more to himself than to anyone else. "I'll have to get you to the hospital to get a closer look, but you're doing fine, son. You just stay with us, and we'll have you back bullying all those folks on your route in no time."

Jesse Dean managed a weak smile, and Charlie found herself smiling, too. Their street was on his route during air-raid drills, and everyone on it knew you didn't dare show a sliver of light. Jesse Dean took his job seriously.

"Well, where's that blamed ambulance?" Doc demanded, rising to his knees. "We could get him there faster in a pack saddle!"

"Should be here any minute," Delia told him. "Mr. Jackson said Emmett Riley was on the way."

Hardly a minute passed before they heard the siren of the approaching vehicle, although everyone knew it wasn't an ambulance but a hearse, as Emmett was one of the town's two undertakers along with Harvey Thompson. Charlie's aunt Lou loved telling her long-standing joke about the obvious competition between the two men, who always turned on the siren when passing the other's establishment. "Well, I see Emmett's on his way to the grocery store again," she'd say, and much of the time it was true.

"The weapon could still be around here somewhere," H. G. Dobbins reminded them after Jesse Dean and the doctor were on their way to the hospital. A worried Harris Cooper, still in makeup, followed in his own car. "Has anybody thought to look?" H.G. asked.

Elderberry's police chief, Bobby Tinsley, had left the auditorium earlier to put the proceeds from the evening's rally sales in a safe at the jail for safekeeping, so the deputy stepped in until he could be reached.

Nobody had thought about the weapon, of course, because their attention was on Jesse Dean.

"It sure sounded like a rifle shot to me," Ed Willingham said, "and it had to have come from the opposite side of the stage. The curtains were closed right after the photographer from the *Eagle* finished taking pictures, so anybody could've stood back here waiting and no one would've paid any attention."

His wife frowned. "Waiting? Waiting for what? For Jesse Dean?"

"He was the one who usually helped with the props," Millie said. "Except for the last few rehearsals . . ."

". . . when Buddy stepped in to give a hand," Annie finished. "There are two props tables, one at stage left and the other at stage right, and Jesse Dean was having trouble keeping track of things on both sides until Buddy's aunt Emmaline suggested he help out."

"Where is Buddy?" A quiet voice spoke up from the fringes of the group and Charlie recognized it as Miss Dimple's. "I hope he hasn't been injured as well."

"He was backstage just awhile ago, but I don't see him around now," Froggie Faulkenberry said, looking about, and no one else had seen him, either.

"Well, there's no rifle backstage—at least that we can find." Evan Mitchell, the Presbyterian minister, still in pink organdy, and Sebastian Weaver had searched the dressing areas they said, but the two classrooms used for chorus and drama were locked. "If there's a weapon back here, I don't know where it could be," Sebastian added.

"It's certainly not on the prop table over here," Charlie told them, "but this must be where somebody stood to fire the shot."

"But *Jesse Dean* . . ." Annie shook her head. "I just don't understand why anyone would do this to him."

"Quite possibly Jesse Dean wasn't meant to be the victim," Miss Dimple suggested. "If you'll remember, both men were wearing black—"

"And they're about the same height and build." Lou Willingham spoke up. "Do you think somebody might have shot Jesse Dean by mistake?"

Virginia Balliew stepped forward from where she had been standing with Miss Dimple. "Then don't you think we'd better warn Buddy? If he was the intended target, he could be in danger."

"We'll have to find him first," Coach McGregor reminded them. "I just hope we're not too late."

"Maybe he left with his aunt." Reynolds Murphy, who had managed to unbutton the top of his gold taffeta gown, fanned himself with the billowing skirt. "I saw Emmaline leaving while they were taking pictures."

Coach McGregor turned to go. "Then they should be at home by now. I'll see if I can find them."

"Whoa! Not so fast!" H.G. held up a hand. "It'll be quicker if we call." He nodded to the principal, who nodded in return and ran to use the telephone in his office. He looked, Charlie thought, as if he'd been up all night, and the last time she'd checked the time it was only a few minutes before eleven.

"I think it would be a good idea for all of us to stay together until Chief Tinsley gets here," the deputy continued. "I'm sure he'll want to ask questions of anyone who was backstage at the time we heard the shot."

"Buddy seems to have disappeared," Reynolds Murphy said. "And Harris followed the ambulance to the hospital." Frowning, he looked about. "But I think the rest of us are here."

"Golly!" Delia whispered to Charlie. "I feel like we're in the middle of a real whodunit."

"Yeah. I'll bet Jesse Dean feels that way, too," Charlie said. "I hope he's going to be all right."

"Harris Cooper said he'd try and let us know as soon as he learned anything," her mother said, "but since your aunt Lou and I weren't backstage when all this happened, we're going to head on home."

"Oh, my gosh! I guess Violet's wondering where on earth I am," Delia gasped. "I'll go with you."

H.G. rose on his toes and exhaled so that all could hear. "I'm sorry to have to inconvenience anyone, but it would be an advantage, I think, to have a few of you remain who might have observed something from the audience." He looked right at Annie. "I hope you don't mind. Of course I'll see that you get home safely."

"Certainly," Annie said with a sidelong glance at Charlie. "Charlie will stay and help me, won't you?"

Charlie nodded. "Sure. And please don't worry about getting us home. Uncle Ed can give us a ride," she said with a meaningful look at her uncle.

"If you learn anything, please wake me when you get home," Jo whispered to Charlie on the way out, and Charlie promised that she would.

Miss Dimple and her friend Virginia left at the same time, and the rest of them were sitting in the first few rows as H.G. had instructed when Elias Jackson dashed in to tell them in a breathless voice that Buddy Oglesby had not left with his aunt and that Emmaline didn't know where he was.

Charlie noticed that the deputy frequently focused his gaze on Annie as he spoke, and apparently Annie noticed it, too, as she fidgeted in her seat and seemed intent on looking at the floor. Fortunately, Chief Tinsley and another officer arrived shortly and, after thanking the deputy, politely requested that he join the others.

"First of all," he told them when everyone was settled, "Harris called from the hospital to let us know that Jesse Dean's doing all right. Doc removed a bullet from his left shoulder and patched him up just fine. He's sleeping right now, and from what Doc says, I doubt he could tell us much anyway, but I sent Warren over there to keep an eye on things."

Ed spoke out from the second row. "To tell you the truth, we're concerned about Buddy. Nobody's seen him since before this all happened, and he was working that side of the stage earlier, so we're not so sure he wasn't the one who was meant to take that bullet."

The policeman frowned. "Did you check with Emmaline?"

Ed nodded. "She hasn't seen him, either, but said he sometimes stays out late. I think he plays poker with some of the men from the Home Guard on Saturdays."

"Do you know who they are?" the chief asked, and Ed gave him a couple of names.

Bobby Tinsley looked at his watch and said something to Fulton Padgett, the policeman who had accompanied him, who nodded and left immediately.

He turned again to Ed. "Didn't you report a missing rifle a week or so back?"

"That's right. Did you find it?"

"Not yet," the chief said, "but I think we found one of the bullets. Doc took it out of Jesse Dean's shoulder. Doesn't your rifle shoot a 22 LR?"

Ed Willingham's face turned stormy. "You mean some tomfool idjit used *my* rifle to shoot Jesse Dean Greeson? Well, that just gripes my middle kidney!"

It was as close to cursing as he would come.

CHAPTER TWELVE

*W*here was he to go? And what was he to do? Who would've thought it would come to this, especially in an auditorium packed with people, but that had been the perfect cover, hadn't it? The sudden darkness, the pandemonium that followed the gunfire. And the board that controlled the stage lights was right beside the props table on that side of the stage. How convenient was that?

Buddy drove to the pinewoods on the edge of town and parked his car to think about what to do next.

From their seats in the third row of the auditorium, Charlie and Annie wrote down the names of all those they remembered seeing near the stage close to the time they heard the shot. At Chief Tinsley's request, others were doing the same.

"Most of those who were in the earlier skits left as soon as the womanless wedding was over," Annie told him. "The fifth- and sixth-grade girls went home with their parents, and I heard the high school kids in the dance number talking about going somewhere for Cokes."

Charlie sighed. "As far as I know, except for Sebastian, the men in the wedding were the only ones back there."

"What about Millie?"

Annie looked about. "I remember seeing her backstage *after* we heard the shot. Before that she was sitting somewhere near the front with Delia, wasn't she?"

"Right." Charlie frowned. "But where is she now?"

"Nervous stomach," Coach McGregor explained of his wife. "Gets all torn up in emergencies. Been like this since I've known her, but she'll be fine," he added, seeing their concern. "Just needs to get home and rest. Said she'd catch a ride with the Baptist minister and his wife. They live just across the street, so I expect she's probably asleep by now."

"Before you heard the shot," the chief said, continuing, "did you notice anyone going backstage who was *not* involved in the wedding?"

Charlie shook her head, as did Annie. Neither had observed anything unusual.

"What about afterward?" he asked the two of them. "Did you see anybody *leaving* that area?"

"I just remember people scrambling to get out while we were trying to wade through them in the opposite direction," Charlie told him. "The only ones I saw backstage, in addition to those who were in the wedding, were friends and relatives frantically trying to find out what happened."

"And it was black as pitch back there until somebody finally managed to turn on the lights." Geneva's husband, Sam Odom, spoke up. "Why, Adolph Hitler himself could've been standing right next to me and I wouldn't have known it."

Bobby Tinsley sat on the edge of the stage and seemed to study his feet. "All right then," he said finally. "Can any of you give me an idea when you last saw Buddy Oglesby?"

"He was at the props table on the right side of the stage just before we took our bows," Reynolds Murphy volunteered. "I noticed him when I left my flowers there."

Charlie held back a smile as she remembered the hideous mismatched bouquets of artificial flowers the bridesmaids had carried.

"And I got rid of my fan there, too," Delby said. A couple of others added that they, too, had happily shed some of their wedding accessories at Buddy's table. Others had exited on the other side, where Jesse Dean collected their props.

Chief Tinsley looked from one to the other. "So what made Jesse Dean switch to the other side?"

"I think I know." Ed Willingham spoke up. "I'm afraid that might be my fault. I borrowed some of my costume from Mrs. Brumlow, and she made good and sure we all knew she wanted everything kept together. But I dropped one of the gloves during the wedding, and somebody picked it up and threw it backstage to Jesse Dean's table on the left. As soon as the show was over—but before we took our bows—I left the other glove, along with the top hat and ascot, on the other side with Buddy because that's where I always exited. Jesse Dean must have noticed the glove was in the wrong place—you know how conscientious he is—and everybody knew Emmaline would've had a fit if she didn't get all of her stuff back, so it looks like he made a point to return it to the table with the other things."

"And which side was he on before the lights went out . . . before you heard the shot?"

This was met with silence as the men looked at one another in an effort to remember.

"He was still on the left!" Sam Odom, who had played the minister, exclaimed. "I remember him looking kind of shocked when I threw down the book I was using for a Bible. It was actually an outdated textbook I had back in college."

"So he must have gone over to return the glove while the rest of you were taking bows," Bobby said. "I guess that's when Buddy left since none of you seems to have seen him since . . ." The police chief took a pencil from his pocket and threaded it through his fingers. "That is, *if* he left. Did any of you notice anything out of the ordinary about Buddy tonight?" Bobby asked.

"I doubt if any of us had time to notice much with all that's been going on," Reynolds told him, "but . . . well, maybe it was just me, but I thought Buddy had seemed on edge the last few days. I just assumed it was because of all his responsibilities for the rally."

Several others admitted that they had noticed it as well. "And don't forget how he reacted at rehearsal the other night when somebody mentioned that skeleton they found," Sam added. "I thought he was going to hit somebody."

Chief Tinsley frowned. "But, think now . . . let's be sure . . . none of you has seen him since the incident with the rifle tonight?"

Everyone jumped as the front doors of the building slammed abruptly and Officer Padgett hurried down the aisle to speak in an undertone to the chief.

Bobby Tinsley stood with a sigh. "I might as well tell you we haven't had any luck locating Buddy Oglesby with any of his poker buddies, and his aunt says he *still* hasn't shown up there . . ." He shook his head as he reached in his pocket for a handkerchief to mop his glistening forehead. "I don't mind telling you, it isn't looking good."

"Do you think it will be all right if we leave now?" Reynolds asked, half-rising from his seat. "It's really late, and I have to check on things at the store before I can go home."

The chief held up a hand. "Now, just hang on a minute there! How many of you who were in the wedding drove here tonight?"

The high school was located several blocks from the main residential area, and every one of the men raised a hand.

"We still haven't located the weapon that was used, and I've asked a couple of my men to search the classrooms that were locked, as well as the cars," Chief Tinsley said. "After that, you're free to go. Sorry for the inconvenience, but it looks like we have a dangerous person running loose, and that rifle might still have prints."

The two young women, he added, were free to leave, but because they were riding with Charlie's uncle Ed, they would be forced to remain as well.

"I'm glad to stay if you think it will do any good, but that rifle is probably at the bottom of the river by now," Jordan McGregor said, yawning.

"I think you're right," Sebastian Weaver agreed. "Whoever used that weapon tonight wouldn't put it back in his own car. It just doesn't make sense."

"None of this makes any sense to me!" Sam Odom muttered.

"Well, then, let's hurry and get on with it," Uncle Ed said. "It was past my bedtime an hour ago."

"You can search the whole town for all I care, but I'm getting out of this blasted dress!" Reynolds Murphy announced, tugging at his gold taffeta gown.

❧

He had changed into a lightweight shirt and comfortable trousers a few minutes later when one of the older policemen returned with a weapon held over his head like a trophy.

"Is that my rifle?" Ed asked, rising.

"You tell me," Bobby Tinsley said, holding the gun at a distance.

"Sure looks like it," Ed said, trying to get a closer look. "Where'd you find it?"

The large room grew silent as Chief Tinsley looked about before answering. "Under a blanket in the trunk of your Plymouth, Reynolds. Mind telling us what it was doing there?"

The merchant's face grew red as he glared at him in apparent confusion. "How am I supposed to know that since I sure as hell didn't put it there? Is this some kind of joke?"

"If it is, it isn't funny," Coach McGregor said. "Anybody could've put that gun in there."

"That's right," Ed Willingham echoed, stepping up to stand with Reynolds. "I don't see how you could even think that of Reynolds, Bobby. Why, you've known him all your life."

"Right," Delby added. "Besides, when do you think he would've had time to do it?"

Chief Tinsley pretended to study about that for a minute. "Well . . . being as most of your vehicles were parked just behind the auditorium, it would've taken only a short time for somebody to dash out one of the back exits, shove the gun in the trunk, and be back inside before any of you noticed he was gone. With all the confusion when the lights went out and after the shot was fired, how many of you can vouch for Reynolds—or anybody else—during that time?"

"Huh! I can damn well vouch for Ed!" Delby claimed. "He stepped on my foot, and I'm almost sure he tore my train."

This brought laughter in spite of the seriousness of the situation, except for Reynolds, who continued to frown.

"And I can do the same for Delby," Ed said. "I honestly don't see how he could have run outside and back in that getup with all those pillows in his bosom. Besides, he was standing next to me when we heard the shot."

"What about the rest of you?" the chief asked. "Any of you re-member who was near you at that time?"

Sebastian said he had just passed Sam Odom and Evan Mitchell in the passageway behind stage right and had heard both men shouting questions after the shot was fired. H. G. Dobbins, on his way to the dressing room, claimed to have heard them as well.

"For what it's worth, I was on my way backstage to get out of that long-tailed dress when the lights went out," Reynolds volun-teered.

"Any idea who might've been near you?" Bobby Tinsley asked.

Reynolds shook his head. "No, but all hell broke loose after we heard that shot, and then Jesse Dean hollered, except we didn't know yet it was Jesse Dean. Somebody bumped into me as I was fumbling around, trying to find my way in the dark, but I couldn't tell who it was." He looked about at the others. "You all *do* believe me, don't you?"

A chorus of positive endorsements followed, and Charlie found herself agreeing with the rest of them. She had always liked Reynolds Murphy and while in high school had spent a couple of weeks during Christmas vacation working in his store for spending money. Murphy's Five and Ten was a favorite place for many of the local children as well because Reynolds let them browse freely through the comic book selection.

The local police chief, she noticed, maintained a stoic expression. "Oh, go on home, all of you!" he said finally. "But, Reynolds, don't plan to take any trips before we get to the bottom of this."

Charlie found Jo and Delia waiting up for her when she got home that night. Her mother had sacrificed precious sugar to make hot chocolate, and the three sat sipping it at the kitchen table. She was certain her aunt Lou had stayed up to greet her uncle as well.

"Poor Reynolds!" her mother said. "Why in the world would he want to shoot Jesse Dean?"

"Everybody seems to think Buddy was meant to be the victim," Charlie told her.

"Well, why would he want to shoot Buddy, either?" her mother huffed. "That's just plain ridiculous! Somebody must've planted that rifle there."

"Wonder why they chose that particular car," Delia said.

"I don't know. Maybe it was the closest one," Charlie said, yawning. She wished she had a marshmallow to melt in her drink. She missed marshmallows, which were in short supply, along with most everything else. Charlie drank her chocolate slowly, relishing the rich, dark sweetness. Thank goodness she didn't have to go to school tomorrow! She felt she could sleep for a year.

"Poor Reynolds!" her mother sighed again. "Well, at least they didn't arrest him."

But soon they would hear otherwise.

CHAPTER THIRTEEN

Oh, this was just too good! What luck! If one played one's cards right, there was no telling how much this could be worth. Of course there was danger involved, but it would be worth it, wouldn't it? Actually, the thought was stimulating. Not that the other little scheme wasn't proving profitable. Not by a long shot, but that was easy money. This would require caution—extreme caution—in addition to some long-term planning, and, of course, a good bit of luck.

But that was what made it fun.

Miss Dimple Kilpatrick sat in her usual pew in the fourth row from the back on the left-hand side of Elderberry First Methodist Church and fingered the tiny gold bar pin at her throat. The pin had belonged to her mother, gone so long now Dimple could barely recall her face, but touching the simple jewelry somehow brought her closer, as well as bringing a brief respite of peace.

With all the war going on in the world, peace would be most welcome here in her little town, but that was not to be. Even here in this sacred place the talk before the service was of nothing but the shocking news of the night before.

The morning was warm, and even with the windows open, people in the congregation stirred the air with cardboard fans showing Jesus blessing the children on one side and an advertisement for Riley's Funeral Home on the other. It came to her attention that someone nearby was wearing Evening in Paris cologne, and the scent was overpowering. Miss Dimple reached for a fan.

The minister chose to speak that day about pathways and the choices thereof, using as a reference Robert Frost's "The Road Not Taken," a favorite poem of hers. Miss Dimple wondered what pathway Buddy Oglesby might have taken since he seemed to be missing. There had even been speculation earlier that perhaps he was fleeing from Reynolds Murphy or whoever shot poor Jesse Dean. And now Reynolds was being questioned, not only on suspicion of shooting Jesse but of killing his own wife!

For now the pathetic remains in the water-soaked grave had a name: *Cynthia Murphy*. Everyone thought she had run off with a traveling salesman when she'd disappeared several years before, and no one, it seemed, had been shocked, or even surprised. Cynthia Murphy was a well-known flirt, and most people considered her absence good riddance, except for Reynolds, who had never stopped looking for his wife or expecting her to return. Finally, feeling inadequate to raise his young son alone, he had enrolled the boy in an expensive military school. Everyone knew Reynolds Murphy was an expert marksman and even instructed the men of the Home Guard in riflery, but was he capable of committing murder? She fervently hoped not, yet *someone* had buried Cynthia Murphy in the Hutchinsons' river-bottom field, and the fact that the woman's dental records matched the teeth on the skeletal remains had recently come to the attention of the authorities.

She had been pleased when, at the beginning of the service, the minister had announced that Jesse Dean was improving and requested the congregation pray for his recovery. Miss Dimple planned not only to do that but to visit her friend as well. Perhaps Phoebe's cook, Odessa, also a friend of the young man, would bake him some of her special gingerbread cookies.

Across the aisle Louise Willingham plucked at the neckline of her dress as she fanned. Being rather generously endowed, Lou seemed to suffer more in the heat than her slender sister Jo, who sat beside her. Ed Willingham had not accompanied his wife to church today, she noted, probably because he wanted to avoid talk of all the dreadful happenings of the night before.

Louise, on the other hand, had seemed to relish the attention before church that morning as she attempted to answer questions right and left. As fond as she was of Lou Willingham, Dimple Kilpatrick knew without a shadow of a doubt that every story the woman told would grow like Jack's beanstalk as the day wore on.

"Well, for all we know, poor Buddy Oglesby could be lying dead out there somewhere," Alma Owens said after church that day as people gathered in hushed clusters on the lawn. "I heard nobody's laid eyes on him since that happened to Jesse Dean. And is it true they found the rifle in Reynolds Murphy's car? It's hard to believe he would do such a thing!"

Bessie Jenkins, who happened to overhear, stepped up, eyes snapping. "You can hardly blame Reynolds for whatever happened to Buddy, Alma, since he was right there in the auditorium the whole time."

Alma sniffed. "He managed to get away long enough to hide that gun in his trunk, didn't he?"

"Miss Bessie's right," Charlie said, slipping an arm around her neighbor. "We don't know who put that rifle in Reynolds's car." In fact, she thought, they were a long way from knowing much of anything.

She had been saddened and shocked when they learned the identity of the remains that morning, although even back in high school Charlie had heard rumors about Cynthia Murphy, who was, according to whispers, "no better than she should be" and "too fast for her own good." Apparently, Charlie thought, the latter had been true. "This must be horrible for Reynolds," she said. "He never gave up hoping Cynthia would come back—even had the kitchen remodeled with new cabinets and everything. Said she'd always hated the ones they had."

"Looks like she was 'one that loved not wisely but too well,'" Annie said as they walked home.

Charlie smiled at her friend's choice of quote. "Doesn't seem like she loved too well, either. Somebody must not have thought so."

Annie shook her head. "But you know how nice Reynolds is! I just can't believe he'd do a thing like that."

Charlie frowned. "I remember when she disappeared. Reynolds had been on a buying trip to Atlanta and came home to find her gone. Ross, their son, was on some kind of outing with the Scouts, and nobody was at home. They say he was frantic not knowing where she was."

"Who could blame him?" Annie said. "Didn't they have any idea what might've happened?"

"A waitress at some dive in the next county said she'd seen her with a man not long before they discovered her missing." She paused. "The man wasn't Reynolds. Maybe we'll know more after they check the gun for prints," Charlie added. "It won't tell us who killed Cynthia, but they might be able to know if Reynolds handled the gun last night."

"Even I would know better than to shoot somebody and not wipe my fingerprints from the weapon," Annie said.

"Or put it in my car where anybody could find it," Charlie added. "A little too convenient if you ask me!"

"You think somebody planted it there on purpose? Who?"

Charlie shrugged. "I don't know, but I think it'll be a long time before anybody in Elderberry puts on a womanless wedding."

"At least it brought in a lot of money for the rally. In addition to the ticket sales, Virginia told me last night they sold several thousand dollars in War Bonds."

"I know she's glad this is over," Charlie said. "All the responsibility of being in charge of the rally must've been stressful. What happened to Jesse Dean last night had nothing to do with her, so I think we should congratulate her on a job well done."

"I didn't see Virginia at church this morning," Annie said. "I hope she's all right, but I guess she's just exhausted after all this."

Charlie nodded. "Probably still asleep." She walked a little faster. "We're having hot dogs and baked beans for lunch. Wanna join us?"

"I thought you'd never ask!"

"Virginia?" Dimple Kilpatrick stood at the door of the small bungalow on Myrtle Street and peered in the narrow side window. She really hadn't expected to see her friend at church that morning after the exhausting activities of the day before, but Odessa had baked date-nut bread earlier and Virginia was fond of having it with cream cheese for supper.

"Virginia?" Again Miss Dimple called and twisted the old-fashioned bell in the center of the green-painted door. The Sunday issue of the *Atlanta Constitution* had been tossed into the boxwoods by the steps, and she retrieved it, clamping it under one arm while holding the bread wrapped in wax paper in the other. Now she was beginning to be concerned. Virginia Balliew was never too tired to read her morning paper.

The interior of the house appeared dark. On the table by the window she saw the back of a photograph she knew was of Virginia's late husband, Albert, beside a stack of books her friend planned to read. Across the room on the mantel, yellow and orange bittersweet berries cascaded from a brown earthenware pot.

Miss Dimple pressed her face against the window glass to see if anyone moved inside. Perhaps Virginia had fallen or was too ill to get out of bed. She was startled when suddenly a light came on in the hallway and someone—could that possibly be Virginia—crept slowly into view.

Her friend never locked her door, but she fumbled so in trying to open it that Dimple wished she could do it for her. Stepping inside, she took the woman's arm and led her to a chair. "You're not well. Let me get you some water. Have you spoken with the doctor?" She felt her friend's forehead and found it relatively cool. "You don't seem to have a fever. Is it something you ate?"

Virginia moaned and shook her head. "It's not something I ate, Dimple. It's something I did—or didn't do! A horrible thing has happened, and I'm absolutely sick with worry!"

Dimple quickly filled a glass of water from the sink and brought it back to her. "I hope you're not referring to what happened to Jesse Dean last night. You are *not* responsible for what took place after the rally, and you should be proud of the fine work you did for the War Bond effort, Virginia."

She reached out to touch Virginia's shoulder but found herself rebuffed. "No! No!" Virginia shook her head and Dimple found herself wondering if perhaps her friend was having a nervous breakdown. She knew that sometimes happened to people but had never experienced one herself and wasn't quite sure how to handle the situation. "I'll make tea," she announced, and shoved the hassock under her friend's feet. "Whatever the trouble is, it can just wait."

But Virginia was having none of it. She pushed the hassock aside and stood. "You don't understand, Dimple. The trouble is already here! Part of the money is missing, the money I was responsible for last night."

"You mean *the War Bond money?*" Dimple put a steadying hand on the back of Virginia's chair. Now *she* needed to sit down. "What on earth happened?"

"If I knew that, it wouldn't be missing," Virginia said. "Oh, I'm sorry, Dimple! I know I'm being snippy, but I'm just beside myself. Now everyone will think I took it. I should've been more careful . . . I know I should've, but Emmaline insisted on having Buddy Oglesby help, and now he's gone and so are a lot of the proceeds we took in last night. I honestly don't know what we're going to do."

Dimple Kilpatrick headed wordlessly to the kitchen, filled the kettle with water, and set it on the stove to boil. First of all she would make tea.

"Now," she said a few minutes later as they sat at the kitchen table with a pot of ginger-mint tea and a plate of date-nut bread spread with cream cheese between them, "are you sure the money was taken? Isn't it possible it was mislaid?"

"You don't *mislay* over two thousand dollars, Dimple." Virginia took a sip of her tea and sighed. "Bobby Tinsley took two canvas bags to the safe at the police station last night for safekeeping until Hubert Chadwick could put it in the vault at the bank this morning." Her hand trembled as she replaced the cup in its saucer. "One of those bags was filled with folded programs from last night's entertainment!"

"What about the money you took in from the bond sales during the parade yesterday afternoon?"

"That was turned in earlier, thank heavens! I gave it to Hubert personally as soon as we closed down the booth, and he immediately took it to the bank," Virginia said. "The missing money was from last night's sales."

"And Buddy Oglesby hasn't been seen since." Miss Dimple examined the Linoleum at her feet: green squares with cream-colored flowers in the center. "I wonder why he didn't take both bags."

"Because the other was filled with checks." Virginia shrugged. "Looks like he only deals in cash."

"How large were those canvas bags?" Dimple asked.

"Oh, I don't know . . . about the size of your purse, I suppose, but rectangular with a zipper."

"Then someone could've hidden it inside a coat or a handbag or some other kind of container," Dimple said. "With people going back and forth with costumes it's possible someone might have taken it backstage until they could manage to leave. Do you remember when Buddy left?"

"According to the police it was either just before or right after the bows, but he wasn't wearing a— Wait a minute!" Virginia interrupted herself. "He was wearing a black shirt. I remember him complaining because he said it made him hot, but Emmaline wanted him to help with props, and he was less noticeable backstage in black. He might've brought extra clothing to wear home."

Miss Dimple frowned. "It seems odd that he would stay as long as he did after switching the money. He was certainly taking a chance that Bobby Tinsley wouldn't check the contents of the bags."

Virginia nibbled a corner of her bread and broke off another. "You know, I was becoming rather fond of Buddy. He outdid himself with the publicity, and seemed to be making a serious attempt to be responsible. Now . . . well, I hesitate to say this, Dimple, but I'm wondering if Buddy might have been the one who shot Jesse Dean, although I can't imagine why he'd do such a thing."

When Dimple didn't answer right away, Virginia suspected her friend wasn't telling her everything. "What is it? What's wrong?"

"I'd forgotten you weren't at church this morning, so you probably haven't heard . . . Last night they found the rifle that was used under a blanket in the trunk of Reynolds Murphy's car," Dimple said.

"They think *Reynolds* shot Jesse Dean? Why, anybody could've put that gun in there. Surely they haven't arrested him on such superficial evidence."

Dimple poured her friend another cup of tea. "Not yet, but they're questioning him about a murder as well. It seems the remains that turned up on the Hutchinsons' farm were those of Reynolds's wife, Cynthia."

CHAPTER FOURTEEN

All that money! Not enough yet, but it was a beginning. Travel . . . adventure . . . exotic places . . . things dreams were made of. But then there was the war—the rotten war! Well, plans would have to wait. It wasn't time yet, but how long? How long? Did anyone suspect? One couldn't be sure. They couldn't be allowed to get too close. That wouldn't do. It wouldn't do at all.

❧

Charlie gave her aunt's grocery list to Harris Cooper. "What do you hear from Jesse Dean, Mr. Cooper? It sure seems strange not seeing him in here."

"Don't know how I ever got along without him, but he's making good headway. Jesse Dean's tougher than he looks. He's home now, you know. A neighbor's looking in on him, and he tells me the folks at Jesse's church have brought enough food for ten people! Doc says he'll probably be able to come back in a week or so if he doesn't do any heavy lifting for a while."

Charlie noticed that Harris Cooper carefully avoided the subject of Reynolds Murphy. By noon Sunday the grim news of Cynthia Murphy's body being identified was all over town, but there seemed to be a loyalty of sorts among many of Elderberry's men, and they were reluctant to discuss it. "As far as I'm concerned, the man's not guilty of anything except a poor choice of a wife," Uncle Ed had declared over supper the night before. "Anybody could tell you that woman was as fast as greased lightning and ran around with anything in pants. Why, there's no telling who might've put her there."

Now the grocer frowned as he studied Lou Willingham's hastily scrawled list. "What's all this? Hazelnuts, swiss cheese, maraschino cherries, *fresh crabmeat*! What does Lou think I'm running here, a gourmet shop? There *is* a war on, you know."

Charlie nodded. "I know." It was impossible to miss the notice on the wall behind him:

Buy wisely—Cook carefully—Store carefully—Use leftovers!
Where our men are fighting, our food is fighting!

Every time she saw it Charlie pictured a couple of loaves of bread and a bunch of carrots going at each other with bayonets. She looked away so the grocer wouldn't see her smile. "Aunt Lou said canned crabmeat would be fine if you don't have the fresh. She needs it for some kind of dip . . . you know, for that party she's giving for the new coach and his wife."

"Right. Nice fellow, Jordan. His wife told me about his war injury and all. Angela and I are sure looking forward to that, but I reckon Lou's gonna have to change her menu. I can put in an order for the cherries, and that cheese is gonna cost her dearly in ration stamps, but she'll to have to settle for canned tuna instead of crab—or even salmon if she's lucky."

"Thanks. I'll tell her." Charlie dreaded having to deliver the bad news. Once her aunt got something in her head, she was bound and determined to carry it through, but this time Uncle Sam had other ideas.

"Be sure and tell your little friend we all thought she did a great job with the womanless wedding," he said.

Charlie frowned. *Little friend?* Then she smiled. He must mean Annie, of course, who at barely five-two made Charlie look like a giant. "I'll tell her," she said. "It *was* a lot of fun, wasn't it? But I hated what happened to Jesse Dean. The next time you see him, please tell him we miss him and I'm going to make some of those spice cookies he likes as soon as I get home from school tomorrow."

Harris Cooper took a rag from his back pocket and polished the top of the glass counter. "I'd sure like to get my hands on whoever did it! A lot of meanness going on around here lately." He shook his head, "A *lot* of meanness!

"Your friend, now," he added, looking up, "seems to me she's kinda taken with that fella of hers. Hope she doesn't do anything silly like letting him talk her into getting married," he called after her. "There'll be plenty of time for that once this war is over."

Charlie found herself singing snatches of "Night and Day" as she walked home that afternoon. Annie was so excited about the prospect of spending time with Frazier she might as well have been wearing a billboard around her neck, but Charlie didn't think there was any danger of the two getting married. Not because they wouldn't want to, but because there wasn't enough time to complete all the required regulations.

She did know that if Will Sinclair wanted to marry her right away, she wouldn't hesitate to say yes. In his last letter Will had said it didn't seem likely that he could get a pass before they finished their training at Courtland, but if he could figure out a way to see her even for an hour, he meant to put a ring on her finger—and she could bet on that! He had made it clear, however, that the wedding would have to wait.

Although it was out of her way, Charlie decided to cut through the park instead of taking her usual route home. The afternoon sun dappled the pathway with splashes of light, and the soothing trickle of the fountain where goldfish circled offered a brief respite from war and violence. Charlie strolled over the stone bridge and through the cooling shade of the magnolias. Usually she would stop at the library, chat with Virginia, and find out if she had anything new to read, but today she had to hurry home and start supper. She would wait until tonight to telephone her aunt with the bad news about her party menu. She wasn't looking forward to the prospect.

Charlie heard her sister crying as soon as she stepped in the door and hurried inside, feeling the same horrible sensation of having a rock in her chest she'd experienced on receiving the fateful telegram about Fain. She found Delia in the rocking chair in their mother's bedroom with her baby clutched to her chest and a letter in her hand. Wishing with all her might that her mother were home from the ordnance plant, Charlie dropped to her knees beside her.

"Delia, what happened? Honey, tell me! Is it Ned? Has something happened to Ned?" *Oh, please, God! Let him be all right!*

Her sister stood, shoving little Tommy into her arms, and embraced the two of them. "Oh, Charlie! Ned's *alive*! He's all right! I hadn't heard from him in so long, and I've been so worried. I just knew something awful had happened." She kissed the tissue-thin letter and held it to her chest. "Ned says there's hardly any time to write and not much time to sleep, either, so they have to do it in snatches whenever they can."

Tommy, not understanding what was going on, began to cry, and Charlie walked about with him to soothe him while Delia sat down to read the letter again. "I'll bet your grandmama Jo has a box of graham crackers hidden away somewhere," she said, kissing the baby's soft cheek. "Let's go see if we can find them." She knew Delia wanted to be alone for a few minutes to reread her letter from Ned, and she was feeling weak with relief herself at hearing the good news. She knew that Delia was aware, as she was, that Ned's letter was several days old. *He had been alive then, but was he now?* Charlie put her nephew in his high chair, tied a bib around his neck, and gave him a cracker as a treat. One could go crazy dwelling on things like that, she thought. It was a good thing her aunt Lou would need help planning her party next weekend. They would be too busy to have much time to think.

Dimple Kilpatrick helped herself to the tuna salad and a small serving of Odessa's refreshing congealed salad of pineapple, nuts, and grapefruit sections. Like most of the people in Elderberry, Phoebe Chadwick's roomers enjoyed their main meal in the middle of the day and ate sparingly at supper. Miss Dimple sipped her iced tea and nibbled on a cracker. She hadn't had much of an appetite since her conversation with Virginia the day before, and of course much of the town was in an uproar over the news about Jesse Dean as well. She was relieved that at least the authorities had so far managed to keep the information from the public about the stolen War Bond money, but she was much afraid her friend Virginia was going to make herself sick with worry about it.

"I don't know when I'll ever feel right about trading with Murphy's Five and Ten," Lily Moss said, helping herself to the bread-and-butter pickles. "Who would've thought such a thing of Reynolds Murphy of all people!"

"We don't know Reynolds had anything to do with that, Lily," Phoebe said. "At least he didn't run away. I, for one, am curious to know what happened to Buddy Oglesby."

Velma Anderson spoke up. "Now Buddy. He always was a bit peculiar. I remember him back in high school."

"Did Buddy take secretarial science?" Annie asked. "Somehow he just doesn't seem the type."

"No, but I had him in study hall, and then he was on the annual staff when I was their faculty advisor." She frowned, remembering. "Not that he misbehaved or anything like that, and he seemed to enjoy working on the annual, but he was shy—kinda kept to himself. I don't remember him having many close friends."

"Do you still have any of those yearbooks?" Miss Dimple asked.

"I think so." Velma concentrated on spreading tuna salad on a soda cracker. "I don't keep them all, of course, but I think I did manage to hold on to a few during the years I was advisor."

Miss Dimple squeezed lemon into her tea and took another sip. Ah, that was much better. "Would you mind if I looked through them?" she asked Velma.

"Not at all, if I can remember where I put them, but I can't imagine what you hope to find in there."

Dimple wasn't sure, either, but she knew it was going to haunt her if she didn't look.

After supper, Velma obligingly stood on a chair to search her closet shelves with no success. "I can't imagine . . . oh, wait! I remember now. I stored them in a box in the basement."

"I'm sure you don't want to bother with that right now," Miss Dimple said reluctantly, although that is exactly what she *did* want her to do.

"It is rather dark down there, but if Sebastian would kindly go with me," Velma volunteered. "I think I know where I put them, but they'll be heavy, you know." Velma gave Miss Dimple a quizzical look. "Mind telling me why you want to see them?"

Dimple Kilpatrick smiled. "It's simply a hunch, that's all, and will probably come to nothing. It can wait if you'd rather not—"

"No, no! Now I'm curious, too." And enlisting Sebastian's help, the three made their way down the dim basement stairs to the box filled with high school annuals that had been stored in a corner along with an ancient badminton set, a broken rocking chair, and enough flower vases to furnish a florist.

They agreed that it would be easier for each of the three to carry several books than to try to lift the heavy box, and although Dimple didn't mind sharing the load, she was glad when they had left the damp basement behind them. The dank, musty smell stirred unpleasant memories of a dreadful experience of the year before, and it would be well with Dimple Kilpatrick if she never stepped into another basement again.

The dining room table had already been set for breakfast, so Dimple took the yearbooks into the front parlor and stacked them on the floor by the sofa. There she could spread them out, one at a time, on the low marble-topped table in front of her. Velma and Sebastian joined Annie and Lily for a few hands of bridge at a table by the window, leaving her to her quest, and although they had shown interest at first, eventually the others abandoned her and went up to bed.

The annuals covered a period from twenty-five to thirty-five years before, when Velma was a handsome young woman not long out of college, and Dimple only a few years older. It had been a short time after that that both women had come to live at Phoebe's while her husband, Monroe, was serving in what was supposed to have been "the war to end all wars," only, of course, it hadn't. Before that time, Dimple had lived with a grandmotherly lady who rented a room in her small cottage only a few blocks from town. When her landlady died, the house was torn down to make room for the Baptist manse, and Dimple had been made welcome by Phoebe Chadwick, who had since become a close friend.

She smiled as she recognized the familiar young faces of those she had taught as children. Some were grandparents now, and many had sons in the military. Even without the name, Dimple would have recognized Buddy Oglesby's face when she first found it among the junior class. He wore his hair slicked back, as did most of the boys in that day, and sported a wide tie with a high-collared shirt. The following year, she noticed, Buddy had become more casual in an open-necked shirt and pullover sweater.

Stopping for a cup of tea, she continued to pour over names and faces of the other students, and had almost given up on learning anything of interest when she came to the page featuring the senior class dance.

Buddy Oglesby, wearing a dark suit and a wide grin, stood under a flower-covered archway with a pretty dark-haired girl who reminded Dimple of Clara Bow in the old silent movies.

Underneath the photograph, the cutline read: *Buddy and Cynthia—Still waters run deep!*

Had Reynolds Murphy's wife, Cynthia, attended Elderberry High School? Certainly she didn't remember teaching her in the first grade, so she must have enrolled later. Dimple thumbed back to the beginning of the annual from that same year, which would have been the year Buddy graduated. And there, in the freshman class, already looking older and more knowledgeable than her classmates, was Cynthia Ann Noland, who would later marry Reynolds Murphy and end up in a lonely, waterlogged grave beside a cotton field.

CHAPTER FIFTEEN

Annie attached postage to letters for Frazier and her brother Joel, pressing them down with her fingers to be sure the glue held, and slipped them through the slot in the post office lobby. If she moved fast enough, maybe she could make it to Brumlow's Dry Goods before they closed for the day. She had been eyeing a certain pullover sweater on display there for several weeks and was hoping Emmaline would finally put it on sale. The sweater was a deep burgundy, the color of ripe mulberries or sweet gum leaves in the fall, and it would look perfect with her gray pleated skirt. Frazier liked her in vivid colors, and it had been a long time since she'd bought something new. Annie smiled to herself. Soon she would be meeting him in Atlanta for their last time together before he left for overseas, and she was counting the days.

She was disappointed, but not surprised, to find the price of the sweater the same. Annie didn't see Emmaline in the front of the store, but her daughter Arden, who was waiting for Bessie Jenkins to decide on a pair of gloves, smiled at her as she came in.

"I've been wanting to congratulate both of you for the fine job you did with the follies Saturday," Arden said, including Bessie as well. "The costumes were great, and you did a fantastic job with the entertainment, Annie."

Annie thanked her, as did Bessie, but neither seemed to know what to say next since Arden's cousin Buddy seemed to have disappeared, and there was still some doubt as to whether he'd had something to do with what happened to Jesse Dean. It had even been rumored that the federal government was sending somebody to investigate.

Annie wandered about the store pretending interest in a display of jewelry under the glass case until she noticed the fine lace-trimmed underwear at the lingerie counter, and her face grew warm as she thought of what it might be like to feel the delicate peach-colored panties next to her skin. What if she and Frazier . . .

"Can I help you with something, Annie?" Arden asked, and Annie quickly moved away from the counter. Bessie had obviously made her purchase and left, and Annie returned her attention to the sweater.

"I don't suppose there's any chance of this going on sale anytime soon?" she asked, fingering the garment.

Arden smiled and shook her head, then glanced toward the back of the store, where Annie supposed her mother lurked. "We overstocked on this particular item, so I can give you a few dollars off," she said in a low voice. "But please don't spread the word."

Annie knew she probably meant for her not to say anything about her discount to Emmaline and kept a watchful eye on the back as Arden rang up the sale. She wouldn't blame Arden Brumlow if she did it just for spite, as everyone knew Emmaline discouraged her daughter's marriage to her ensign fiancé to keep from having to hire extra help in the store.

At any rate, the sweater was hers, and she could hardly wait to wear it when she met Frazier in Atlanta. Annie left the store with her purchase in the familiar green-and-white bag, eager to show off the new addition to her wardrobe to her friends at Phoebe Chadwick's.

She was waiting to cross Court Street when someone blew a horn and a familiar truck pulled up beside her.

H. G. Dobbins reached across and opened the door on the passenger side. "Hop in! I'll give you a ride."

"Thanks, but I have another stop to make," Annie lied. Oh, well, she could always use a bottle of hand lotion from Murphy's.

"Then how about supper tonight? Pick you up at six?"

"I'm sorry, H.G., Miss Phoebe's planning on me for supper there, but thank you anyway." Annie glanced at the traffic light. Drat! It had changed to green, forcing her to continue standing there.

"I hear there's a pretty good movie, *The Desperadoes*, I think it's called, playing over in Milledgeville. What say we try for tomorrow, maybe grab some supper on the way?"

A few cars were beginning to line up behind him, and although most were too polite to blow their horns, Annie could tell they were getting impatient. Well, so was she, and it embarrassed her to be put in such a position. Why couldn't the man take a hint?

Stepping up to the truck, she put a hand on the passenger door and spoke as directly as possible. "I'm seeing someone, H.G., so I won't be able to go out with you . . . and I believe we're holding up traffic." She noticed that he still wore the cowboy boots. Maybe he slept in them.

The deputy frowned, omitted a loud "Huh!" and roared away. Clutching her package, Annie hurried homeward. Surely the persistent man had finally gotten the message!

❧

Charlie's aunt Lou frowned as she shoved the thick yellow dough through her cookie press. "I've never made cheese straws with margarine in my life, but it'll just have to do. Maybe they'll taste all right."

131

Charlie sat at her aunt's kitchen table cracking pecans for the miniature tarts Lou would make with dark corn syrup and heavy cream for her upcoming party. "Everything you bake tastes good, Aunt Lou, and if people don't know about rationing, they must've been living on the moon."

"All this business with Reynolds Murphy's wife turning up dead like that has sure put a damper on things, and now the police are questioning him about her murder," Lou said as she lined up dainty pastries on a baking sheet. "Why, Reynolds was crazy about that woman—gave her anything she wanted. I just don't know what to think anymore."

Charlie said she guessed Cynthia Murphy would rather not have turned up dead, either, if she'd had a choice in the matter.

"Oh, you know very well what I mean, Charlie Carr!" Her aunt Lou made a face at her as she slid the cheese straws into the oven. "And now it looks like Buddy Oglesby's disappeared with all that money from the bond sales, and poor Virginia's about to have a nervous breakdown. You can't tell me this didn't all start when what was left of that woman turned up on the Hutchinsons' farm."

Her aunt had a point, Charlie thought as she picked out the last of the nut meats and scooped the shells into a newspaper. It did seem that many of their recent problems had begun there.

"I hear Jesse Dean's home from the hospital," Aunt Lou continued. "Bless his heart, I think I'll take him some vegetable soup and cornbread. Do you think he'll be able to eat things like that?"

Charlie laughed. "He didn't seem to have a problem with the cookies I brought him, and he's able to walk a little now. He's still weak, of course, but raring to go. I wouldn't be surprised to see him back at the store before too long."

Her aunt frowned. "Does he seem uneasy about . . . well, you know . . . somebody coming back to finish the job? Poor Jesse Dean! I'd be looking behind me every minute."

"I know. He did seem a little jumpy, but I suppose that's natural after what he's gone through. From what I've heard, the police aren't sure that bullet was meant for Jesse Dean."

"Then who?" Aunt Lou asked.

"Could've been Buddy," Charlie said. "He was usually on that side of the stage, and both were wearing dark clothing."

Aunt Lou put her empty mixing bowl in the sink and filled it with water. A damp spot from leaning against the sink spread across her red striped apron, but she didn't seem to notice. "But they haven't been able to locate Buddy, so how do they know somebody didn't shoot him, too?"

"He's been acting peculiar lately—all nervous and jittery. Several people have noticed it. I don't like to believe it's true, but have you considered that Buddy might've been the one who did the shooting?" Charlie reasoned. "After all, both the War Bond money and Buddy Oglesby disappeared about the same time Jesse Dean was shot."

"If he really did take that money, he'd better steer clear of Virginia Balliew," her aunt said. "He'd have a better chance with Bobby Tinsley and his crew."

Charlie agreed, but if Buddy wasn't the one who fired the rifle, the evidence pointed to Reynolds Murphy, the genial merchant who always tossed in extra candy for children who shopped at his store. No. It had to have been somebody else.

Charlie helped herself to a glass of iced tea from the white stoneware pitcher her aunt always kept in the refrigerator. She wasn't going to think about it anymore—for a while, at least. "Who's coming to your party Saturday? Anybody I know?"

Her aunt laughed. Of course her niece knew them all. "The list is out in the hall by the telephone, and just about everybody's coming. Except for Jesse Dean, who's not able, and a couple of people who plan to be out of town."

"Of course you're going, Virginia!" Dimple Kilpatrick stood in front of the open door of her friend's closet, reached in, and chose two dresses, a blue-and-white georgette and a green tailored shirt-waist with wide lapels. "There's nothing wrong with either of these."

Virginia groaned. "The blue one's too summery. It is October, you know."

Dimple nodded. "And still warm as springtime outside, but green's more your color anyway."

Virginia pushed it away. "I never have liked that dress. Really, Dimple, I'd rather not go."

Miss Dimple hung the garments back in the closet and sat on the side of the bed. "This has nothing to do with dresses, does it?" When her friend didn't answer, she continued. "No one in his right mind thinks you had anything to do with the missing bond money, but if you keep to yourself and act like you're ashamed, they might begin to wonder."

"I just don't think I can do it. I have to *make* myself open the library every day and sit there pretending as if nothing's happened, but I know what people are thinking."

"Then perhaps you might want to consider a mind-reading booth at the Halloween carnival this year. I wasn't aware you had that gift."

Dimple was pleased when Virginia smiled. "Oh, I don't know, Dimple . . . all those people! Everybody in town will be there."

Miss Dimple touched her friend's shoulder. "And every one's a friend. Now, what about this gray one with the turquoise trim?"

Sighing, Virginia waved her hand. "If only the police had arrived sooner Saturday night, all this might have been avoided."

Dimple paused, gray dress in hand. "What do you mean?"

"Don't you remember? There was some kind of false alarm that sent Bobby Tinsley way out to the edge of town, so he was late getting to the auditorium to collect the money."

"Of course! I remember Charlie going to look for a telephone, but I didn't think anything of it at the time. I know you didn't let that satchel out of your sight during the first part of the follies."

"Buddy helped with sales during intermission and turned the money over to Bobby as soon as he arrived."

"But as it turned out, it wasn't *all* the money," Dimple said. "Someone had to switch what was in that other satchel just before the entertainment began after intermission."

"Dimple, I counted every penny of that money and put it in the satchel myself," Virginia insisted.

"And then what?"

"Well, I knew the police were on the way, so I left it with Buddy and went back to my seat in the auditorium . . ." Pausing, Virginia grasped the closet door for support. "Oh, Dimple, that must've been when he did it. He took the money out of the satchel and crammed it full of leftover follies programs before turning the satchel over to the police."

"How long do you think you were gone before the police came to collect it?"

Virginia frowned. "Not long. Probably about five or ten minutes. The lobby was empty because it was almost time for the woman-less wedding to begin."

"And Buddy was there the whole time you were gone?"

"He *said* he was, but you know as well as I do that Buddy Oglesby's word is worth about as much as last year's ration book. Dimple, what in the world am I going to do?"

Dimple Kilpatrick draped her friend's gray dress across the foot of the bed. "Well, first of all, I think you should tell Bobby Tinsley exactly what you've just told me, and tomorrow you should wear this dress and those lovely aquamarine earrings your Albert gave you and go to the Willinghams' party."

CHAPTER SIXTEEN

What a fool the woman had been! She had actually believed him when he told her they would run away together. Everybody knew she slept with any man who took her fancy. Well, he'd taken her fancy and he'd enjoyed it, but that was the end of it. And now, after all this time, she turned up like a bad penny! Still, there had been times when he'd remember her laugh, the intoxicating scent of her, and the way she could tease a man to distraction. Two years was a long time, but not long enough.

Lou Willingham passed around a silver tray of dainty sandwiches cut in a variety of shapes. The tray had belonged to her grandmother on her father's side, and she had made the sandwiches after she got home from the ordnance plant the day before. "Please have a sandwich, Marjorie, and how about another cup of Russian tea?"

Marjorie Mote smiled and selected a sandwich shaped like a pumpkin. (Lou had put her Halloween cookie cutters to good use.) "I just can't resist olives and cream cheese, and your cheese straws are always a treat, Lou. What a nice idea this was."

"I'm afraid we get so busy we don't make time to visit anymore, so this gives me an excuse and an opportunity to introduce everyone to Jordan and Millie." Lou moved along with her tray and glanced back to see Marjorie chatting with Bessie Jenkins. It was good to see her neighbor enjoying herself once again after losing a son during the first year of the war. The Motes' remaining son was now stationed with the army somewhere in Europe, and the gold star in their window had been joined by a blue one.

Phoebe Chadwick sat quietly in a corner with a plate on her lap and an expression on her face that clearly read "keep out." Earlier Lou had seen her sister, Jo, go over and speak to her, as had several others, but apparently their conversations had been brief.

Well, this would never do! Lou quickly replenished her supply of sandwiches and went over to sit beside Phoebe. "A penny for your thoughts?" she said.

"What?" Phoebe blinked and looked about. "I'm sorry, Lou. My mind's a million miles away."

Lou smiled. "With your nephew, I'll bet. How is he?"

"Harrison's doing all right, or at least he says he is. It's a shame, though, how they drill these poor boys until they're completely exhausted."

Lou set her tray aside and took the woman's hand. "They're turning them into men, Phoebe. God bless 'em. Now, let me refresh your punch. Have you tried one of my tarts?"

Phoebe thanked her and declined, sinking back into her reverie, and Lou made her way across the room, where Alma Owens had poor Harris Cooper backed into a space between two overstuffed chairs.

"And to think we've been trading with Reynolds Murphy all this time after he did such an unspeakable thing!" Alma said. "But you know, I always did think his eyes were too close together."

"It hasn't been proved yet that he did anything, Alma. They're only holding him for questioning," Harris said while signaling "help me" to Lou with his eyes.

"Well, it certainly took them long enough, and I don't know about you, Harris, but I hope they won't release him anytime soon. Why, I won't feel safe walking our streets. After all, how do we know we won't be next?"

"Well, now, I don't know about . . . that is, we just can't . . ." Harris looked frantically about for a route of escape, and Lou obligingly stepped up to the rescue. "I think someone's looking for you in the dining room," she said to Harris, nodding her head in that direction. "Another sandwich, Alma?" she asked, blocking the woman with her tray.

Catching Miss Dimple's eye across the room, Lou made her way through the gathering to inquire in what she considered hushed tones about Phoebe's strange behavior. "What on earth's gotten into Phoebe Chadwick?" she asked. "She looks like death warmed over, and I can't get two words out of her."

Unfortunately, Lou had never learned to whisper, and Dimple hastily drew her into a private corner, but she was sure those standing nearby caught every word. "Yes, I'm worried about her, too," she said, speaking softly. "I know she's been concerned about Kathleen's boy being drafted, but it's more than that, and I intend to get to the bottom of it."

Lou shook her head. "If you could just get her to tell you what's troubling her, maybe . . ."

Miss Dimple glanced at her friend still sitting gray and droopy with an empty punch cup in her lap and saw misery etched on her face. She took a deep breath. "Well, whatever it is, I plan to do my best to put a stop to it. You can count on that."

It was unlike Dimple Kilpatrick to let emotions get the better of her, but she found it difficult to disguise the anger in her voice. She was almost certain her friend had been receiving threatening messages, and *someone* was responsible, possibly someone in this very room. Noticing Lou's concerned expression, she quickly helped herself to a ghost-shaped sandwich, commented on the lovely refreshments, and moved on.

Earlier, Lou had made a point of introducing Jordan and his wife, Millie, to all the guests, and after politely weaving her way through the gathering, Millie had now established herself in the adjoining sitting room, where some of the younger people congregated. Hearing their laughter, Lou saw her niece, Delia, among them and was glad she seemed to have found a friend in the coach's wife. Delia had been kind of like a lost lamb when she and her baby came home to Elderberry after her young husband was shipped out, and although Millie was a good bit older, she seemed to enjoy Delia's company.

In the dining room, Jo was relating an apparently funny tale to Virginia Balliew and Velma Anderson, and Lou was glad to see Virginia smile as she knew she'd almost made herself sick worrying about that missing bond money. And didn't she look pretty in those aquamarine earrings?

As she watched, her sister moved to the table and helped herself to a couple of tarts and some cheese straws, and Lou Willingham shook her head in envy. Jo could eat her weight in sweets and starches and never gain an ounce, while Lou seemed to put on pounds just from the smell of chocolate. But then Jo never did like to cook, while Lou enjoyed even the challenge of coming up with appetizing menus in spite of wartime shortages. And wasn't Ed—bless his heart—always bragging about what a good cook she was?

Lou started back to the kitchen to replenish the miniature tea muffins when she heard voices in the hallway, where she found Dimple Kilpatrick in earnest conversation with Jordan McGregor.

"The heat and humidity must be unbearable in a tropical climate like that, but I understand it's much cooler in the mountainous areas. And what is the name of that river that flows through the western part of New Guinea? I remember learning about that country in geography, but unfortunately my memory's not as good as it once was."

"I can't imagine your memory being less than perfect," the coach said, smiling. "Why, just about everybody I've met here sings your praises."

Miss Dimple frowned. "It's not the Sepik, that's on the eastern side . . . no, it begins with a C . . . Car . . . something. Oh, well, I suppose it will come to me later." Miss Dimple paused for a sip of punch. "Tell me, do the natives really build their homes on platforms? I read once they do that for protection."

Coach McGregor nodded. "Well, I really—"

"And I imagine malaria must be prevalent there. A great uncle on my father's side suffered so from that. Lived in coastal Mississippi, you know, with all those pesky mosquitoes. The fever would come back on him now and again for the rest of his life. I hope you won't have that problem, Mr. McGregor."

Lou hesitated, tray in hand. Neither of them seemed to have noticed her approach—and what was all this chatter about New Guinea and malaria? She had never heard Dimple Kilpatrick speak in such a rude manner without giving the poor man an opportunity to reply. And why was she pretending ignorance when everyone knew her mind was as sharp as a bayonet? "Memory's not as good as it once was"—humbug!

"Is that a new dress, Miss Dimple?" she asked. "That color is perfect with your complexion." It was purple, of course, as was most of her attire.

"Why, thank you, Lou, but no. Bessie made this for me several years ago. I'm sure you must've seen it. I wore it to church just last Sunday." Miss Dimple made no attempt to hide her annoyance at the interruption.

"Well, you should wear it more often," Lou said, taking her tenant by the arm. "Jordan," she began "it's really a shame we never get a chance to visit, even with the two of you living right here behind us. Why don't you come to the kitchen and talk with me while I get a fresh supply of muffins?"

"Only if you'll let me help," Jordan answered, taking the tray from his hostess. Of course this left Dimple with no choice but to return to the rest of the guests in the other part of the house. Sometimes Louise Willingham could be too bossy for her own good, but at least she'd learned one thing from her one-sided conversation with the new coach. Jordan McGregor had never been in New Guinea.

Ed Willingham found Reynolds Murphy stretched out in a rocking chair in his tiny cell in the Elderberry City Jail with a pillow at his back and a plate of apple pie in his lap.

"Well," Ed said as the jailer let him inside, "I brought you some of the refreshments from yesterday's shindig, but I see you're doing all right for yourself. They taking good care of you here?"

Reynolds jumped to his feet and shook Ed's hand. "Oh, God, Ed, how'd this happen to me? Folks have been mighty good bringing me cakes and pies and all to make me comfortable, but I'm about to go crazy in here!"

Ed looked around for somewhere to sit and settled on a shelflike bunk. "I hear you've got some fancy lawyer from Atlanta representing you. I expect he'll have you out of here before too long."

"Can't be soon enough for me. I thought I'd hear from him today, or tomorrow at the latest. You know my prints weren't even on that rifle they found in my car. I know good and well somebody planted it there. Now, I ask you, why would I want to shoot Jesse Dean Greeson?"

Ed shrugged. "Why would anybody? I reckon they think Buddy was supposed to have been the target."

"And now they're saying I killed my own wife—my Cynthia . . ." Reynolds buried his face in his hands. " . . . and that I buried her in that godforsaken place! How could anybody even *think* such a thing?"

"They won't be able to hold you for long," Ed said. "After all, what evidence do they have?"

Reynolds shook his head. "None, Ed. They don't have a damn thing—because I didn't do it!

"Sounds to me like Buddy Oglesby's run off with that bond money. How do they know he didn't fire that gun? I'd sure as hell like to know where he is!"

"So would Chief Tinsley," Ed said. "Turned out to be some night, didn't it? With Cowboy Dobbins in the cast, you'd think anybody'd be afraid to do something like that."

Reynolds frowned. "Cowboy?"

"You know, H.G., the deputy who played a bridesmaid. Always wears those cowboy boots. I'll swear, Reynolds, I thought he was going to wear them down the aisle."

Reynolds didn't answer. He had noticed the boots, but he really hadn't thought much about it. Until now.

"What are we going to do about Phoebe?" Velma Anderson greeted Dimple Kilpatrick in the hallway as soon as she stepped in the front door the following Monday after school, and Miss Dimple was so surprised by the question it took her a minute to think of a reply.

"I wish I knew," she said finally, leading the way into the empty parlor so no one would overhear. "Right now, I believe the best thing we can do is to let her know we care."

Velma nodded. "I don't know what's worrying her so, but it might help if we could just get her mind on something else . . . I've heard the vines are loaded with muscadines over there beyond Peach Orchard Hill, and you know how fond she is of muscadine preserves. Do you think she might let us talk her into going to gather some? I didn't use nearly all my sugar rations, and I'll be glad to let her have what's left."

Miss Dimple said she would willingly contribute hers as well and agreed that the outing was a good idea as long as they weren't in danger of being arrested for trespassing. "I'd prefer it if we had permission, but I have no idea who owns that land."

"Well, I do." Velma hurried to the phone. "It's been in the Kimbrough family for as long as I can remember, and their granddaughter just happens to be in my typing class this year."

Minutes later she returned, smiling. "Mamie Kimbrough said we're welcome to all we can collect, but she wouldn't say no to a jar of those preserves."

It didn't take long after a whispered conference in the kitchen to enlist Odessa's help, and the three of them finally convinced Phoebe she would be letting everyone down if she didn't lend a hand with the grape harvest.

"Just think how good them preserves gonna taste on a hot biscuit," Odessa wheedled. "Mmm! I can just smell 'em now."

Velma agreed that nothing would appeal to her more, and although Miss Dimple rarely indulged in sweets, she had to admit a weakness for the heady flavor of the fruit.

Miss Dimple felt perfectly capable of walking the three or more miles to the woodsy area where the muscadines grew, but the other two women were unaccustomed to covering long distances on foot, and it would be close to four by the time they arrived. They would have to work fast to fill their pails before dark.

The afternoon was pleasantly warm, and the three only took time to slip into sweaters, collect a couple of buckets, and climb into Velma's cherished 1932 Ford V-8 before winding their way around Cemetery Hill and along the serpentine road through the orchards where sweet Elberta and Georgia Belle peaches grew in the summertime.

The oaks were tinged with scarlet, and sumac along the sides of the road had turned a vivid red. Now and then hickories flaunted their finery of burnished gold, and from her seat behind the driver, Miss Dimple longed to take pleasure in the palate of her favorite season, but the feeling wouldn't leave her that something wasn't quite right. However, the road behind them seemed clear, and she didn't see anything threatening ahead. Her brother, Henry, had accused her of worrying unnecessarily, but begrudgingly agreed it was usually for a reason. Perhaps this time, she thought, Henry would be right, and hoped it was so.

"It should be just around this next curve," Velma said, beginning to slow. "Mamie told me we'd see an abandoned barn on the left and should be able to park there . . . and here it is." She pulled off into a grassy area that had once been a road, and Dimple and Phoebe hurried to take buckets from the trunk. With Velma, they waded through knee-high grass to the wooded area beyond.

Phoebe paused at the edge of the woods. "Where now?"

"Just look up, I suppose," Velma said. "The vines grow in trees, and I was told this place is thick with them."

Dimple Kilpatrick threw back her head and took a deep breath. "I can smell them already," she said, inhaling the pungent aroma. "And, look, there're vines just ahead—why, the ground's just covered in muscadines!"

For the next half hour she put her apprehension behind her and concentrated on the task at hand. No one spoke, except to say "Pass the bucket" or "Oh, look here—there's more than we'll ever need," and Dimple noticed that Phoebe seemed more like her old self again—for a time at least.

"Do watch out for yellow jackets," Miss Dimple advised them as the small bees swarmed around the fallen muscadines on the ground, but the women concentrated on the dark, thick-skinned grapes that hung in clusters from vines overhead. The musky scent of the fruit was almost intoxicating in the dense enclosure of the surrounding trees, and when her pail was full, Dimple stretched, picked up the brimming bucket, and began to make her way back to where they had parked the car. "It's getting late," she told the others, glancing at the sky, and again the foreboding feeling pushed its way forward, prompting her to hurry. "We'd better start back before dark."

"Just a few more minutes," Velma called. "This bucket's almost full . . . uh-oh!" She held out a hand. "Is that a raindrop?"

It was, and as the others hurried after her, it began pelting them in earnest. "Your umbrella would've come in handy about now, Dimple," Velma called out as they made their way back to the road. "Let's hurry before we get stuck in the mud."

The others had the same concern, and Phoebe and Dimple hoisted the heavy buckets into the trunk while Velma jumped in to start the car. It wasn't until she started to open the rear door that Dimple noticed the left front tire was flatter than a paper doll.

"I'm afraid we have a problem," she said, explaining what had happened.

"Ye gods and little fishes!" Velma muttered under her breath. "Those synthetic rubber tires aren't worth a plugged nickel. And it's already been patched so much it looks like a quilt. Well, at least I have a spare, but I'm afraid we're going to get wet."

"I'll get the jack," Miss Dimple offered, wishing more than ever that she'd brought along her umbrella.

"I noticed some newspapers in the trunk," Phoebe said, stepping out into the rain. "Maybe they'll keep off the worst of it. At least they'll be better than nothing." Frowning, she stooped to examine the right front tire. "I don't suppose you have *two* spares, do you?"

"*What?* How in the world did this happen?" Velma, wrapped in a soaking-wet sweater, huddled in the rain to inspect first one flat tire, and then the other. "You know how careful I am to avoid sharp stones or anything that might cause a puncture. It's most unusual for this to happen to both front tires at the same time."

Miss Dimple, having found a flashlight in the trunk, knelt to get a closer look. The alarming feeling that something was wrong now screamed like a siren.

"What is it?" Phoebe asked, shivering, as Dimple held the light on one particular area and ran her fingers along the tire.

"I'm not sure," Dimple said, and she didn't speak again until she had examined the other tire in the same manner. It wouldn't do to frighten her friends, but she didn't believe they would be safe to remain with the car. It looked as if both tires had been deliberately slashed.

"Do the Kimbroughs live very far from here?" she asked Velma, trying to maintain an unruffled demeanor.

Velma frowned as she looked about. I've only been there once, back when old Mr. Kimbrough died, but if I remember right, it's just over this next hill."

Phoebe had already slid back into the passenger seat. "How far over the hill?" she asked from the open window.

"Oh, I don't know. Less than a mile, I guess, but surely someone will drive by and see us here before too long." With an exasperated sigh, Velma climbed into the driver's seat beside her. "At least we can keep dry here . . . Dimple, aren't you coming? Hurry or you'll catch your death!"

Dimple hesitated. She was already wet, what difference would a little more rain make? Would they be safer walking the distance to Mamie Kimbrough's or waiting like sitting ducks in the car? Darkness was already settling about them, and chances are passersby wouldn't notice them from the road—*except the person who already knew they were there.*

"If we leave now, we could get to the Kimbroughs' place before it gets too dark to see, and the flashlight will help," Dimple said, waving the light about. "I really don't think it's a good idea to stay here."

"I don't see why not. I'd rather wait here than risk being run over. Besides, I've been on my feet all day, and these bunions are killing me!" Velma crossed her arms, and Dimple could see she wasn't going to budge.

"Very well. I'll walk on over to Mamie Kimbrough's and use her telephone to call for help, but I do wish you'd come with me." If she warned them, it would only frighten them, and Dimple wasn't sure Phoebe would be able to walk the distance in her weakened state. She took time to take some of the folded newspapers from the trunk as protection from the rain and, telling the other two she would be back as soon as possible, set out for Mamie Kimbrough's.

"For goodness sake, Dimple, I do wish you'd stay here with us!" Phoebe called after her. "You're going to be soaking wet, and you don't know who might be out on the road this time of . . ."

Dimple gave her friends a farewell wave and let Phoebe's mournful warning dissipate on the wind. Using the flashlight, she kept as much as possible to the areas beyond the shoulder of the road. Walking was difficult because ankle-high weeds and brambles slowed her, but Dimple Kilpatrick wasn't taking any chances on being struck down by a car, and whenever she saw headlights approaching, quickly switched off the flashlight.

Rounding the curve at the top of the hill, she was grateful to see the lights of a farmhouse in the distance and hurried toward the welcome warmth. She was getting ready to cross the road and make her way to what she hoped was the Kimbrough home when pale yellow beams cut through the rain-washed night from the opposite direction, and the driver was moving slowly, as if he might be looking for someone on the road. Dimple Kilpatrick darted behind the bushy security of a dripping cedar and waited until the car had passed. Maybe, she hoped, whoever was driving wouldn't notice anyone waiting in Velma's disabled vehicle, or would choose not to inflict any more damage.

She was fortunate that Mamie Kimbrough's son, who had stopped by to drop off his mother's prescription from Lewellyn's, was gracious enough to collect the other two and drive them all back to

Phoebe's. Of course, Velma protested about having to leave her car behind, but Asa Weatherby at the Gulf Station promised he'd take care of the cherished Ford and have it ready in two shakes of a cat's tail.

And for now, the fact that someone had deliberately slashed the tires would be a secret between Chief Bobby Tinsley and Dimple Kilpatrick.

CHAPTER SEVENTEEN

*J*esse Dean Greeson finished the last of the chicken and dumplings Angela Cooper had brought him, rinsed the bowl, and put it in the sink. It bothered him to leave unwashed dishes there, but he had promised Madge Malone, who lived next door, he wouldn't lift a finger doing anything that wasn't absolutely necessary. "The girls and I will take care of those dishes in no time," Madge had promised. "Now, you just look after yourself and get some rest!"

Jesse Dean yawned. He was tired of resting, although he had to admit he enjoyed all the attention as well as the good food his friends had heaped upon him. He couldn't make up his mind which was better, Odessa Kirby's bread-crumb pudding or Louise Willingham's applesauce cake, and if he didn't watch out, he just might get fat. Jesse Dean smiled at the thought. He had been tall and lean since he'd reached his full height, and hadn't slumped once since he'd taken that job of air-raid warden, but proudly drew himself up to the measurement by his kitchen door, which was six feet, one and three-quarter inches.

Doc Morrison seemed to think he would be able to get back to his old routine in a few more weeks, and although his shoulder still hurt some, he felt a lot stronger than he had when he first got home a few days ago.

Jesse Dean wrapped himself in his old flannel robe to check the locks on the doors. Before this he had never even thought to lock his doors at night, and even though everybody seemed to think he'd been shot by mistake, the bullet had been real, and he wasn't taking any chances. When he first came home he'd been as jittery as a sinner at the Pearly Gates every time he heard footsteps on the porch or somebody passing by his window, but now he'd almost convinced himself he just happened to be in the wrong place at the wrong time.

Polishing his glasses on the sleeve of his robe, Jesse Dean turned on the lamp beside his chair and picked up the copy of A Tale of Two Cities Miss Virginia had brought him from the library. He was well into the second chapter when he thought he heard someone in the shrubbery outside his bedroom window.

Maybe he should telephone Chief Tinsley, but he had called him once before when he'd thought someone was trying to break in, and it had turned out to be a raccoon feasting on the contents of his trash can. Jesse Dean turned on the front porch light in time to see a neighbor's gray-striped cat jump from the railing and dart into the shadows by the walk. Shaking his head in relief, he turned off the porch light, laid his book aside, and climbed into bed. He must've been more tired than he thought as he could hardly keep his eyes open, and soon fell asleep.

Was it the smell of smoke or the pounding that woke him? Jesse Dean bolted upright in bed and reached for his glasses. Something was burning. Had he left a pan on the stove? And then he remembered that Mrs. Cooper had brought his dinner hot from her own oven, and he hadn't even had to heat up a thing.

Not bothering to find his slippers, Jesse Dean threw aside the covers and made his way to the window, where he could see a glimmer of brilliant orange from beneath the window shade. At the same time someone began shouting near his window, while voices and urgent pounding came from the front of the house. Jesse Dean recognized one of the voices as belonging to Reynolds Murphy.

Jesse Dean! For God's sake, wake up, man! You have to get out of there now! Now someone was beating on his window, and Jesse Dean threw open the shade to see a flame of fire shoot up from the corner of his house to the roof above. Two figures were silhouetted against the blaze as they struggled to wrestle the burning barrel away from the house. Jesse Dean recognized one of his neighbors standing below his window urging him to go to the front door.

"Thank God!" Reynolds shouted as he opened the door and yanked him unceremoniously into the frosty night air.

"Ouch!" Jesse Dean grabbed his sore shoulder as Reynolds threw a heavy coat about him.

"Sorry!" Reynolds patted his other shoulder. "I was just in a hurry to get you out of there. Are you all right?"

Jesse Dean coughed and nodded numbly. "I think so. What's going on?"

"What's going on is that it looks like somebody tried to burn down your house," Chief Tinsley said. "If Reynolds here hadn't been passing by and alerted your neighbor, it might be a lot worse than it is."

"And how bad is it?" Jesse Dean found that he had trouble standing and sank into the familiar old porch rocker where his granny used to sit to shell peas.

"Looks like the side of the house is scorched and a few shingles on the roof are charred, but nothing serious," his neighbor said. "Somebody shoved a barrel of trash up close to your house and set fire to it."

Jesse Dean shook his head and waited for that to sink in while the fire truck arrived, siren sounding, and woke the rest of the neighborhood. It took less than five minutes to extinguish the fire.

"I don't know what brought you over into our neck of the woods," Jesse Dean said to Reynolds after the commotion had died down, "but I sure am glad you were here!" He had learned earlier that Reynolds Murphy had been released on bail, and if what he heard was true, bail was set for more money than he could ever imagine.

"I reckon you can thank my sweet tooth for that," Reynolds told him. "I was working late at the store trying to catch up on my books *after being a guest of the city*," he said, with a nod to Bobby Tinsley. "Now, I don't mean to complain about the food or anything like that, but ice cream just wasn't on their menu, and along about nine o'clock or so I decided I had to have some. The Super Service over there is the only place around here that stays open that late."

The house was free of what little smoke had drifted inside by then and the group had moved into the living room. Jesse Dean was familiar with the Super Service a few blocks on the other side of the hill from where he lived and knew it was a favorite with children, who for a nickel could buy ice cream in small cardboard containers with the picture of a movie star on the lid, as well as candy and soft drinks.

"Well, Mr. Murphy," Jesse Dean said, "when I get back to work, I sure hope you'll drop by the store because I'd like to treat you to all the ice cream you can eat!"

Everyone laughed at that, and one by one the neighbors began to drift away, leaving only Reynolds, Bobby Tinsley, and Madge Malone, who had dashed out with her late husband's old overcoat over her flannel nightgown. Jesse Dean flushed as he noticed a flutter of pink eyelet ruffle when she walked.

"I don't like to think of you staying here alone after what happened tonight," Madge said, taking a determined stance. "You just come on home with me, Jesse Dean, and we'll set up a cot in the dining room. It's not safe for you to stay on here."

Oh, my! Jesse Dean felt his face getting as hot as a kettle. Madge Malone was old enough to be his mother, and in fact her two daughters were not much younger than he was, but he just wouldn't feel right spending the night in a houseful of women.

Madge noticed his hesitancy. "At least for tonight," she insisted. *"What if whoever started that fire comes back?"*

"In that case, they won't find you at home. Get your belongings together, Jesse Dean. You're coming home with me." Harris Cooper stood in the doorway, unnoticed until now. Jesse Dean wasn't aware when he arrived, but he sure was glad to see him. One of the neighbors had called him, Harris said, acknowledging that this was a hell of a thing to have happened and that Jesse Dean was welcome to their spare room for as long as he wanted.

"Should've thought of this in the first place!" Harris muttered later as he carried Jesse's bag to the car. Jesse Dean leaned back against the fuzzy upholstery and closed his eyes, feeling his energy drain from him, along with the newly found hope that his injury had been an accident. He was thankful for the safe retreat with the Coopers, but resented the fact that he couldn't recuperate in his own home. *What had he ever done to provoke someone to want to kill him?*

The conversation at Phoebe Chadwick's dinner table the next day centered on Jesse Dean's close encounter with possible death.

"I still don't understand why anyone would want to hurt Jesse Dean," Velma said. "And to try to set fire to his home—why, it's just unbelievable!"

"Thank goodness the fire was discovered in time," Geneva said. "I understand he's now staying with the Coopers."

Lily Moss set down her cup with a clatter. "There are some dreadful things going on in this town. Dreadful! And now they've let Reynolds Murphy out on bail. Do you suppose he really had something to do with his wife's death?"

"It does seem the spouse is usually the most logical person to suspect," Geneva said. "He must've known she was running around on him; still, it's hard to believe he would go to that extreme."

"Who knows what someone would do in the heat of the moment," Velma added. "And Reynolds does have a temper. Remember when the Starnes boy threw a rock and shattered that big plateglass window in the front of the store? Did it on purpose, too, because Reynolds lectured him for stealing candy. He not only made the boy clean up the mess, but he had to sweep out the store every Saturday for a month. Of course the boy had it coming, but I was there shopping when it happened, and I've never seen Reynolds so upset."

Lily sighed. "Well, I don't even know what to think anymore."

Dimple was inclined to agree with her as she watched Phoebe quietly excuse herself from the table. At her suggestion, Bobby Tinsley had inspected Velma's tires at Asa Weatherby's Gulf Station and admitted that the tire slashes seemed deliberate. As for Reynolds Murphy's guilt, well, she wasn't so sure about that. Yet.

"Do you have any idea who might have a reason to do such a thing?" he'd asked, and she hadn't been able to give him an answer.

"What about your friend—Miss Anderson? Could it have been one of her students? It seems a vindictive act—maybe by someone who received a failing grade?"

But when Dimple finally confided in Velma, her friend couldn't think of anyone in her class who would do such a thing and didn't remember the last time she had given a failing grade to a student in her secretarial science classes. "I suppose it was just some sorry somebody who had nothing better to do," Velma decided, "and it won't do us any good to worry about it now."

Now Miss Dimple listened to the conversation around her without commenting. The fire at Jesse Dean Greeson's house made no sense to her at all, but she was beginning to believe the slashed tires on Velma's car might have been meant as a warning.

"Have you noticed anything unusual in the way Phoebe's been act-ing lately?" Charlie asked Annie as they crossed over into the school grounds that afternoon.

"You mean because she stirred milk into her iced tea today at dinner? And she always looks like she's been crying? I think Miss Dimple's been trying to help her, but I doubt if she's had any luck, and Odessa's worried, too. She asked me this morning if I thought Phoebe had some kind of terrible illness."

"Do you think she has?" Charlie walked faster as the first bell rang. "She looks terribly thin and hardly eats a thing."

Annie shrugged. "If Miss Dimple can't get to the bottom of it, I don't know who can."

⟡

It had to be someone in Elderberry, possibly even someone they knew. Miss Dimple had seen Phoebe's name printed in block letters on one of Phoebe's earlier messages, and from the way her friend was acting, she suspected she had recently received another.

Dimple Kilpatrick was in a dilemma, and the next morning, as she set out on her customary walk before breakfast, she battled with a decision. Phoebe Chadwick not only had opened her home to her years before but also had become a trusted friend. When Dimple thought of home, she thought of the rambling frame house on Ivy Street only a block from the school with its familiar over-stuffed furniture, worn over the years into comfortable lumps and mounds to fit the various forms of those who shaped it. Dimple's favorite was a faded chintz-covered armchair by the window where one could catch the last of the afternoon light before evening shad-ows claimed the room. In winter she often watched the reflection of the fire on the dented brass fender and found comfort in the patterns on the rug that had once been a rich burgundy and gold but had worn into soft shades of rose and a delicate blending of yellow, reminding her of the primroses she'd once seen on a visit to New England.

Dimple adored her brother, Henry, and looked forward to their time spent together during holidays at his rustic mountain home, but she was less fond of Henry's wife, Hazel, and her ditto of a sister, who seemed forever about. It was always pleasant to look forward to returning to the place she called home. But most of all, she cared about the people there: Odessa Kirby, surely one of God's finest creations; her fellow teachers, who, although different in many ways, were dedicated one and all to their profession and to the students in their care; and especially Phoebe herself.

Miss Dimple crossed Katherine Street, sidestepping a puddle from last night's rain. The sun had begun to paint the dusky streets in a soft gray light, and the air smelled as new as dawn. Oak trees that had been planted when the town was young made a canopy of mottled colors of gold and red against a lingering green. Dimple took a deep breath and turned toward town, walking briskly past the sleeping storefronts. What a shame about all the troublesome business with Reynolds Murphy, she thought as she passed the five-and-ten, and now kindly Jesse Dean, but her concern today was for Phoebe.

Dimple remembered Phoebe's husband, Monroe. It had been difficult to like Monroe Chadwick. Unfortunately, she had never managed to do so, however hard she tried, and she had never understood just why someone as warm and caring as her friend could cast her lot with his. However, as her grandmother used to say, there was no accounting for tastes.

Pausing to spear a piece of litter with the point of her umbrella, Dimple dropped it into a bag she carried for that purpose and moved on. Past Lewellyn's Drug Store she walked, past Brumlow's Dry Goods and Cooper's Store, and with each step she became more determined. She had tried every way she could to be helpful in a tactful manner, but her friend was on the verge of a breakdown—or worse, and someone had to step in.

Dimple Kilpatrick walked faster. She knew what she had to do.

"Have any of you seen the picture showing at the Jewel?" Dimple asked innocently during their noon meal the next day. "A comedy, I believe. I'm thinking of seeing it with Virginia tomorrow if I can convince her to go. We can all use a little laughter in our lives, don't you think?"

"That's the one with Don Ameche, isn't it?" Annie asked. "He's always good, and I heard it was funny."

"I thought about going this afternoon," Miss Dimple said, "but Virginia just got in a shipment of new books, so I guess we'll wait until tomorrow. It should be a nice day to see a picture with the weather turning so chilly and damp."

Phoebe, she noticed, took that opportunity to take the empty tea pitcher into the kitchen.

Charlie helped herself to just one more green-tomato pickle. Nobody made them like Odessa, crunchy and tart with just enough spice. She had never heard Miss Dimple object to being out in harsh weather before. In fact, she usually seemed to favor the cold.

Now Odessa, putting away freshly ironed table napkins, shut the buffet drawer with her ample hip. "You all talking 'bout that picture show 'bout heaven what's on downtown? Bob Robert and I went to see that last night, and I don't know when I've laughed so hard."

Miss Dimple smiled. She had bought tickets for the couple the day before, and Odessa had promised not to mention where she got them. "Right. *Heaven Can Wait.* I believe it's only going to be here for another day or so," she added.

Charlie turned to Annie. "Why don't we go after school today? Anybody want to join us?"

Lily Moss pursued the last bite of baked apple on her plate. "Well . . . I shouldn't with all those papers to grade, but I don't want to miss it."

"My afternoon should be fairly free," Miss Dimple said. "I can give you a hand if you like, Lily."

"Good! Then that's settled." Velma laid down her fork. "I'll go along, too. We can stop at the drugstore and have a Co-Cola—make it a real party."

Geneva said she'd love to join them but knew her husband wanted to see it, and Sebastian had to rehearse the high school chorus after school.

Dimple smiled her thanks at Odessa, who pretended not to notice. Geneva lived at home and took only her noon meals with Phoebe, and the rest of the boarders would be away that afternoon for two hours or more. That should give her a clear field.

※

Phoebe sat at the kitchen table polishing silver and hardly looked up when Dimple came in and sat beside her. The house was quiet and empty as the others had left for the picture show, and earlier Odessa had made a stew of today's leftovers and put it in the refrigerator for supper before leaving for home.

Dimple picked up a sterling fork in the familiar Forget-Me-Not pattern, dipped a rag into the polish, and began to work in earnest. She didn't speak.

After a few minutes of silence, Phoebe Chadwick sighed and tossed a polished spoon into the center pile with a clatter. "Well, you might as well tell me what it is," she said.

Miss Dimple eyed her fork and started on another. "What *what* is?"

"Oh, Dimple, you know very well *what*. I know you're up to something. Just tell me what you want."

"Very well, I'll tell you." Dimple pushed back her chair in order to look more closely into Phoebe's pale face. "I want to know what is the matter with you, Phoebe, and don't even think of saying it's nothing because I know better. For over a month now we've watched you become almost a shadow of yourself. You don't eat, and I doubt if you sleep because I've heard you down here walking around in the middle of the night. You jump at the slightest noise, and your eyes are constantly red from crying. You are my dear friend, and I'm worried about you. We all are."

"So that's why everyone conveniently decided to go to the picture show," Phoebe mumbled; her head sank onto her chest.

Miss Dimple spoke up brightly. "Virginia and I plan to see it tomorrow. You should come, too."

"I have circle meeting tomorrow," Phoebe said dully.

"Oh, blast circle meeting!" Dimple Kilpatrick surprised herself. Why, she sounded just like her brother!

"Why, Dimple! I've never heard you talk like that."

"And I've never seen you act like this. What's going on with you, Phoebe? Are you ill? Is something wrong with your niece, with Harrison? We all care about you, you know, and Odessa's just about beside herself with worry. What can we do to help?"

"Nothing. There's nothing anyone can do." And Phoebe laid her head in her arms and cried.

"It's the messages, isn't it?" Dimple asked after the crying finally subsided, and Phoebe nodded silently, searching in her pocket for a handkerchief.

Dimple supplied her with a clean one with delicate purple tatting on the edges. As she suspected, her friend was being blackmailed. "Do you have any idea who's sending them?" she asked, filling the kettle with water for tea.

Phoebe shook her head. "It's every week or so now. They want money, Dimple. More and more money, and I don't have it to give."

"And you certainly shouldn't have to! Have you spoken with the police?"

She took Phoebe's silence as a negative. "And why not?" she persisted.

"I'll show you why not. Wait here. I'll get them." When Phoebe Chadwick left the room she moved like someone twenty years older, and Dimple found it difficult not to rise to her assistance. While her friend was gone she scalded the teapot with boiling water and brewed some of her special ginger-mint tea. At this point, a cup would benefit both of them.

There were four of the messages, all printed in block letters on cheap dime-store notepaper, all but one mailed from the local post office. Phoebe lined them up on the table, then put her hand on top of them. "Before you read these, there's something I must tell you," she said, speaking quietly. "Kathleen is not my niece, but my daughter. Her father and I were engaged to be married before he went off to fight in the Spanish American War. Ellis and I were very much in love, and of course we expected to be married as soon as he came home." Phoebe held her teacup in her hands but did not drink. "He didn't come home, and he never knew about the baby. He was killed only a month or so into his service, and no one here ever knew I was . . . in the family way."

Dimple reached for her friend's hand. "How dreadful for you. Phoebe, I'm so sorry. What did you do?"

"My parents sent me to stay with an aunt in Tennessee. She was kind, and I had good care, but we all knew I wouldn't be able to keep the baby. When Kathleen was born, my older sister and her husband adopted her and raised her as their own. Dorothy and her husband were never able to have children, and as far as I know no one ever suspected."

Phoebe took a sip of tea, and it seemed to revive her. "It nearly broke my heart, of course, but I was able to see her grow up and to be a part of her life—and later of Harrison's."

Dimple frowned. "Are you sure no one here knew about Kathleen?"

"I can't imagine who it would be. My parents told everyone I was in college there, and no one questioned it when I came home. I don't understand why anyone would wait this long to bring it up. Kathleen was born forty-four years ago, Dimple. Why now?"

Dimple looked at the messages. The first one consisted of three sentences:

> I know Kathleen is your daughter. If you want me to keep quiet, leave 20 dollars in the tin box behind a loose stone in the wall in front of the empty house on Legion Street. Keep quiet and come alone or everyone will know.

Phoebe's hand trembled as she set the cup back in its saucer. "I left the twenty dollars as instructed, but the next time it was twenty-five, then thirty, and now they want fifty! I don't know what I'm going to do!"

Miss Dimple poured both of them another cup of tea, pausing to give her friend's shoulder a reassuring touch as she did so. "Did Monroe know about Kathleen?" she asked, resuming her seat.

"Monroe? Oh, dear! Oh, my goodness, no!" Phoebe sighed. "You must know how straitlaced the Chadwicks are, Dimple. He would never understand."

And Dimple did understand. Monroe and his family were unbending in their everyday struggles to achieve and maintain their roles of leadership at both the city and state levels.

"I married Monroe three years after Kathleen was born hoping we might have children of our own, but it was not to be," Phoebe said. "Frankly, I don't believe he wanted them, and I've always felt an emptiness there."

Dimple nodded. She had filled her own emptiness by loving other people's children. How sad it would be if she couldn't! "What about Kathleen? Did you or your sister ever tell her the truth?"

"Dorothy didn't want to, so of course I never brought it up, but after my sister died, I did think about it. Sometimes I believe Kathleen must have suspected, but she's never said anything."

"But Phoebe, Monroe's been dead for several years now. Would it be so terrible if people knew the truth?"

Phoebe stood and took their empty cups to the sink. "I doubt if they'd brand me with a scarlet letter, but you know how people are, Dimple. I really wouldn't care if all the Chadwicks shunned me, but there would be talk, and Elderberry's a small town. I don't want to go through that, and I don't want Kathleen to have to, either. No, I'll just have to find out who's behind it. This can't go on."

Dimple Kilpatrick agreed that it couldn't, and if she had her way, it wouldn't. This poor excuse for a human being had to be stopped— and soon.

CHAPTER EIGHTEEN

Somebody had been asking far too many questions. That old schoolteacher with the umbrella was just too nosy for her own good! Well, those flat tires oughta warn her! Oughta warn all of them! One had to keep an eye on that one or she'd ruin the whole thing, and if she didn't watch out, she was going to be sorry!

❧

Perhaps she should ask Velma, but after what had happened the day they picked muscadines, maybe that wouldn't be such a good idea. It had to be somebody with a car, and of course she would pay for the gas, but then Lily would want to know where they were going, and Lily was afraid of her shadow. Chances are her constant worrying would give them away. No, she would have to ask somebody else.

Light was just beginning to break as Miss Dimple walked past the abandoned house where Phoebe had been told to leave money behind a loose stone in the wall. Of course she didn't hesitate there as, for all she knew, the blackmailer might be watching, and it would seem obvious if she made a habit of walking past, yet there must be some way to find out who was reaping ill-gotten gains at her friend's expense. Dimple risked a brief backward glance when she reached the corner and made note of a tangle of overgrown shrubbery among the saplings that had taken root in the vacant lot next door. The old house had burned and was torn down years before, but what was left of a driveway was still discernable through the underbrush that covered the lot. Dimple Kilpatrick stopped to spear a bit of litter and added it to her collection. She was almost certain no one would notice a car parked there from the street. And her friend Virginia had a car.

◈

"Oh, I don't know, Dimple," Virginia said as the two walked home from the picture show that evening. It was almost time for supper, and Virginia had invited her friend to share her meal. "Does Phoebe know you plan to do this? And how are you going to know when this person will show up? What would we do if he saw us?"

Dimple sighed. She had expected this. As a rule, Virginia relished a bit of adventure, but the loss of that bond money had left her listless and depressed. Why, even the comedy they had just seen had failed to elicit a laugh. No, Dimple thought, what Virginia needed was to get her mind on someone besides herself, and by the time they had walked the distance to her friend's front door, she thought she had her convinced.

Phoebe not only knew of her plan to watch the house but had volunteered to come with her. She was finally persuaded, however, that whoever was doing this would become suspicious if they happened to see her there.

"It has to be either very early in the morning or after dark," Phoebe had told her. "That area of town is practically deserted, but there are a few houses down the street, and I wouldn't think they'd take a chance on being noticed."

Dimple didn't believe it would be a bad idea to ask these

164

neighbors if they had seen anyone there who didn't live nearby, but Phoebe didn't want to risk anyone questioning the reason behind it.

The next morning, supplied with a Thermos of coffee, date-nut bread for Virginia, and a couple of Dimple's fiber-filled Victory Muffins and ginger-mint tea for herself, they began their vigil. It had taken a few minutes of reasoning on Dimple's part to convince Virginia that no one would notice her gray Chevrolet in its cover of underbrush and vines in the early morning mist. Fortunately, they were in a position to have an unobscured view of the portion of the wall with the loose stone.

Unfortunately, the only living creature that approached it was a dog relieving himself on the crumbling column. That evening they had no better luck, although they maintained their watch for several hours and passed the time with word games and conversation. It would've been nice to have something to read, Dimple thought, but they dared not use a light for fear of being seen.

They were seen, however, but neither was aware of it. Louise Willingham happened to be driving past that night on her way to take Ida Ellerby home after choir practice at the Methodist church when she noticed Virginia's car backing out of the empty lot where that old house had burned. Now, some people in Elderberry might have dismissed it as a couple of teenagers who'd been up to things they had no business doing, but Lou recognized Virginia's car, and in the headlights of a passing vehicle caught a brief glimpse of the person in the passenger seat.

Now, what in the world were Dimple Kilpatrick and Virginia Balliew doing back there in that old overgrown lot? She decided not to mention it to Ida for everyone knew how Ida Ellerby blew everything way out of proportion, and maybe Virginia was just using the area to turn around. Still . . .

"I tell you it was Dimple Kilpatrick and Virginia Balliew," Lou said to her sister, Jo, the next morning as they rode the bus to their work at the munitions plant in Milledgeville. "I wonder what they were doing there. Something's going on, and I'm dying to find out what they know about it."

"They were probably just turning around. I'll bet there's broken glass and who knows what else in that old lot. I can't imagine why else they'd be there."

Lou sat up a little straighter and pulled off her gloves, then wished she hadn't. Her fingers were still stained from picking out all those pecan meats for the party. "Well, I'm going to drive by there again tonight just to see what I can see. I wonder if they're looking for the stolen War Bond money."

"I heard it turned out those weren't Reynolds Murphy's fingerprints on that gun after all. Whoever used it had wiped it clean," Jo said, eager to change the subject. She knew how easy it was to get hijacked into one of her sister's wild schemes.

"I knew all along he had nothing to do with that," Lou said as they left Elderberry behind them.

"But there's still some question about what happened to his wife," Jo added. "He's only out on bail, Louise."

"I just don't see how anybody in this town could believe he had anything to do with that. Why, everybody knows Cynthia Murphy was wild as a haint. There's no telling who she ran off with—and look what happened to her! I think it's just awful that somebody would hide that shotgun in his car so people would think he had something to do with what happened to poor Jesse Dean!"

Jo agreed and called her sister's attention to the deep red color of the sumac on the side of the road, pleased that she had guided her safely past her curiosity about Dimple and Virginia.

"It wouldn't take long," Lou said after a few minutes of silence.

"What wouldn't take long?"

"Just to ride past there a few times—about the same time I saw them, you know. If we see them there tonight we'll know something's up for sure."

"You can forget the *we* part," Jo told her. "I don't want anything to do with it."

Louise sighed. "Very well, Josephine. I'll go without you, but if I *do* see them there again, then will you believe me?"

"Oh, all right!" Jo Carr smiled to herself. She knew she was safe.

⟡

"I don't think anyone's going to show up," Virginia said that night after two more unsuccessful surveillances.

"They will if they think Phoebe's going to leave fifty dollars there," Dimple said. "I expect they're just giving her time to get the money."

"What makes them so sure she's going to do it? I wouldn't."

"You have nothing to hide, and of course she's not going to do it, but they don't know that yet. She's frightened, Virginia. Whoever is doing this has done an appalling thing to Phoebe. I just hope we can find out who it is before it goes any further."

Virginia yawned. "Well, they're not going to show up tonight, and my feet are freezing. I hope no one has seen us here. They'll think we're both crazy. A car drove past last night just as we were leaving, and I'm sure they could see who we were."

"I wonder if it might've been the person we've been waiting for," Dimple said. "Perhaps we should stay a bit longer tomorrow night."

"Then you'll have to do it on your own," Virginia said. "Saturday's always a busy day at the library, and tomorrow night I plan to have an early supper and relax in a warm bath."

And tomorrow would probably be the night someone showed up, Miss Dimple thought, but it couldn't be helped. She couldn't keep an eye on the place every minute unless she camped out on the lawn, and that hard, cold ground didn't look one bit inviting.

⟡

Saturday morning turned out clear and bright with a crisp feeling of fall in the air, and Annie took advantage of it by curling up in

Phoebe's front porch swing to write a long letter to Frazier. Soon Miss Dimple and Velma Anderson followed suit and made themselves comfortable in two of the rocking chairs—Dimple with an Agatha Christie mystery, and Velma with a guest towel she was embroidering for her niece's birthday.

"I've been meaning to ask if you ever found what you were looking for in those old annuals we brought up from the basement the other night," Velma said to Dimple.

"As a matter of fact, I did." Dimple closed her book, marking her place with a scrap of paper. "And I've been wondering if it's of any importance. I'm reluctant to make an issue of something that might be irrelevant, yet . . ."

Velma set aside her needlework and Annie her letter. "Yet what?" they asked, speaking together.

"You might not remember this, Velma, but Reynolds Murphy's wife, Cynthia, was a student here during her freshman year in high school, and perhaps even after that. Her maiden name was Noland."

Velma shook her head and frowned. "Name's not familiar. Of course I don't remember all of them."

"Is that what you were looking for?" Annie asked.

"To tell you the truth, I wasn't sure," Miss Dimple said. "I knew Buddy Oglesby had gone to high school here but wasn't certain of the dates until I looked through Velma's annuals. Virginia told me how he reacted when someone in the follies cast suggested the remains that were uncovered probably belonged to a tramp passing through. Of course we didn't know it was Cynthia at the time, but later it made me wonder if he might have known the woman earlier or if there was a connection somehow."

"And was there?" Annie asked.

Miss Dimple nodded. "They went to the school dance together. It was during Buddy's junior year when Cynthia was only a freshman."

Annie heard herself gasp before realizing she'd done it. From what she'd heard of Cynthia Murphy, she didn't seem the type to be interested in Buddy. Of course at that time he might have appealed to her as an "older man." And to object so strongly to her being described as a tramp, he obviously still felt something for her. "But he didn't even know—" she began. The thought was so horrible, she couldn't bring herself to finish.

"How did he know who was buried there unless he put her there himself?" Velma pointed out. She had no such qualms.

Miss Dimple remembered how Buddy had reacted when they discovered the sad remains beside the cotton field. How silent and pale he had become, and she had worried that he might not be composed enough to drive the bus.

"That was so long ago. They were practically children," Dimple said, "and I don't know how long after that their relationship continued. Still, I suppose I should mention it to Bobby Tinsley."

Velma jabbed the needle through the linen in her embroidery hoop, where a circle of morning glories was slowly emerging. "Somebody has to be behind all this devilment going on around here. How do we know it isn't Buddy Oglesby?"

"Do you think he might still be around?" Annie asked. "If he took that money, I'd think he'd be as far away from Elderberry as he could get."

Miss Dimple laid her book aside. "I wonder . . ." she said.

CHAPTER NINETEEN

Eyes burning from the fumes, Buddy Oglesby turned the handle of the old metal food grinder as a potent mélange of onions, cabbage, peppers, and green tomatoes oozed from the blades, mounding in the large bowl beneath. Already, gleaming jars of the finished product lined the counter behind him and still more simmered on the stove in an enormous enamel pan.

"How many more jars of this stuff do you plan to make?" he asked, wiping his eyes on his sleeve.

"As many as we can until we run out of ingredients," she said, frowning. "I gotta do something with all this stuff from the garden, and you might as well make yourself useful. You don't have anything else to do." She shrugged. "Besides, chow chow sells well over at the general store, and I can use the money."

Well, he couldn't argue with that. In fact, he couldn't argue period. After all, she'd let him stay here, hadn't she? And it sure as hell wouldn't do to upset her! He had to stay out of sight, and where else was he to go? Sighing, Buddy fed another wedge of cabbage into the grinder and thought back to the day he'd arrived.

"I need a place to stay for a while," he'd said.

Ima Jean Acree narrowed her eyes. She had put on at least fifteen pounds since he'd seen her last, and a diapered child of about two tugged at her skirts. "Buddy? Good Lord! What are you doing here? I haven't seen you since I was working up in Atlanta . . . What's it been? At least five years."

Buddy Oglesby smiled. "I know, and I'm sorry about that. It's just that I've been—well—kinda busy. You know how it is. We sure had us some good times though." He glanced behind him to make sure he hadn't been followed. Thank goodness Ima Jean still lived in her mother's old place a few miles on the other side on the little town of Winder and so far out in the sticks nobody would think to look for him there.

"Is anything wrong, Buddy? What's going on?" Ima Jean stooped to pick up the baby. The screen door remained closed between them, and she made no move to let him in.

He sighed. "There's been sort of a mix-up, Ima Jean, and I just need a place to stay." Buddy reached back to rub his neck. He'd slept in his car all night and ached in places he didn't even know he had. "It won't be long, I promise, and I have a little money. I can help you out with groceries and things."

"Well, you can't stay here. I reckon you haven't heard, but I got married a few years ago. My husband's in the army, and I don't think he'd like it a whole lot if he was to hear you were living here with me."

"Oh, no! *No!* It wouldn't be anything like that. Don't you still have that little building out back? The one your mama used for a sewing room?" Buddy glanced at the baby and tried to look interested. "Come on, Ima Jean, please! I really need somewhere to stay, and you could use a little extra money, couldn't you? I won't be any trouble, I promise."

He could see she was relenting, but she still didn't open the door. "What have you done, Buddy?"

He sighed. "Ima Jean, I reckon you know I wouldn't hurt a soul. It was all a big mistake, and I can explain . . . oughta be cleared up in no time . . . please, you gotta believe me!"

"You better not be lying!"

He raised his right hand. "I swear. Just for a few days . . . okay?"

"Heck, there's nothing out there to sleep on except that old sofa," she said, "and no bathroom, either, but I guess you could use the one Daddy had put in off the back porch."

"How are your folks?" Buddy asked. If those two were still around, they might not take too kindly to this arrangement.

"Daddy died a year ago," Ima Jean told him. "And Mama's gone to live with my sister in Americus, but just 'cause it's just me here with the baby don't mean you don't have to behave, Buddy Oglesby!"

Again Buddy raised his right hand and swore he'd be as good as gold.

❧

The day had finally come! Annie woke early and stretched, luxuriating in the double bed in the room that had been assigned her. It was definitely a boy's room. College pennants and framed photographs of sports teams lined the walls, and a snapshot of a pretty girl smiled at her from the bedside table. It was signed, *Love, Mary*, and Annie wondered if she was a special girlfriend of the sailor whose room she was using.

After catching a ride to Atlanta with one of Phoebe's neighbors, she had been welcomed the night before with a light supper by Geneva's aunt Maggie. Afterward they listened to a radio program featuring the All-Girl Orchestra with Evelyn and her Magic Violin, and Maggie shared pictures of her son, who was serving under Admiral Nimitz in the Pacific Theater. He had just begun his sophomore year at Georgia Tech, his mother said, when he enlisted with several of his friends.

When the radio program ended, they listened quietly to the news, Maggie concentrating intently on every word, and when it was over, she took a deep breath and smiled. "Well . . . no news is good news—for now."

Annie hoped it continued. She was glad her hostess understood the importance of this time with Frazier and had assured her she was not to worry about the hour she returned as the door would be unlocked.

Frazier was staying with parents of one of his old Georgia Tech fraternity buddies and would have the use of their car for the next day. Earlier, she had given him the phone number and address of Geneva's aunt, and the two women were finishing breakfast when he telephoned.

"I'm not that far away and can't wait to see you," Frazier began. "I can probably be there in fifteen minutes."

Annie glanced at her polka-dotted flannel pajamas, her feet in blue fuzzy slippers. "Could you make that twenty?" she asked.

After the fourth try with the hairbrush to tame her short dark curls, Annie gave up in disgust. She added a dab of powder, although it did little to disguise her freckles, and fastened the locket Frazier had given her for her birthday around her neck. The gold oval looked perfect against her new burgundy sweater, and she had even found a shade of lipstick that matched it.

Less than twenty minutes later, Annie watched him swing up the front walk in his easy, long-legged stride, overseas cap in one hand and a bunch of red roses in the other. As he drew nearer, she could distinguish the silver first lieutenant's bar from a recent promotion on his collar.

She was breathing too fast! *Please, God, don't let me pass out!* He was so handsome with his dark hair and eyes the warm color of chocolate that could look right into her heart. So wonderful, and

173

so *right*, Annie couldn't wait another minute. She flung open the door and threw herself into his arms.

He picked her up off her feet and kissed her right then and there while Geneva's aunt looked on discreetly from the living room and, after brief introductions, they were on their own for an entire day in Atlanta.

"I've a surprise for lunch," Frazier told her after spending the morning sharing peanuts with the elephants and monkeys at Grant Park Zoo. "I hope you don't mind my planning our day, but I thought you might enjoy seeing some of the places most people like to visit when they come here."

The October weather was sunny but cool enough for a sweater, and leaves were just beginning to turn red on dogwood and sumac. Soon sweet gum would join them with darker hues, and hickory would show off in glorious gold.

Annie didn't care what they saw as long as she was with him, and told him so. He took her hand as they walked back to the car. "I don't think you can beat the atmosphere of the place I've chosen, but we have to make a stop first," Frazier said.

Annie was surprised when, after a short drive, they pulled into the parking lot of a restaurant on Ponce de Leon Avenue. The Ship Ahoy looked like a good place to eat, but *atmosphere?* Maybe it would be different on the inside, she thought.

"Come on, I'll introduce you around," Frazier said, leading her to the door. "I worked here while I was at Tech, and I *still* like the food."

After hugs and greetings from all the staff, Hugo the cook presented Frazier with a huge picnic basket filled with good-smelling things and covered with a red-and-white-checkered cloth.

"Oh, no you don't!" Hugo insisted when Frazier tried to pay. "This is our going-away gift to you with blessings from all of us. Just come home safely," he said, clearing his throat before turning away. The waitresses all cried, and the maître d' kissed him on both cheeks and walked with them to the door.

"Wow!" Annie sighed upon reaching the car and, sniffing, swallowed a salty tear. "Now I think I'm going to cry."

"Don't you dare!" Frazier told her, but she noticed that his eyes were wet, too.

A few minutes later they spread their cloth in the shade of a large oak in Piedmont Park and enjoyed a lunch of baked ham, deviled eggs, pickles, potato salad, and crusty french bread, followed by rich, dark brownies with pecans and fudge frosting. Their friends at the restaurant had also included disposable dinnerware, cups, and a container of sweet iced tea.

"What? No wine?" Frazier peeked in the basket and feigned disappointment.

"Heavens, what would Froggie say? You want to get me fired?" Annie laughed. "Besides, I don't need spirits to lift me up today." She blew him a kiss and lay back on the cloth after they cleared away their lunch things, and Frazier stretched out beside her as they watched a group of local musicians set up for a concert in the bandstand.

"You didn't tell me there would be entertainment," Annie said as people began to gather in groups around them.

"Especially for you." Frazier leaned over for a quick kiss and laughed. "Well, to be honest, I didn't know, either."

The band could've been led by Glenn Miller, Harry James, or Benny Goodman and it would have made no difference to either of them as they sat beneath *their* tree and talked about a future together when the fighting would be over and their loved ones safely home.

"I wish we could carve our initials on this tree," Frazier said, running a finger over the rough bark, "but I doubt if park officials would approve."

"We don't need to mark it to make it ours," Annie reminded him.

"One of these days we'll bring our children here." Frazier pulled her to her feet and, to the delight of onlookers, lifted her face for a kiss. "That is, if you'll have me."

And Annie Gardner threw her arms around his neck and cried all over his uniform.

Stroking her hair, Frazier laughed softly. "Uh-oh! Is the very thought of marrying me that terrible? I didn't mean to scare you."

Annie took his hand and kissed it. "What scares me is having to let you go, but I'll be right here when you come back, and don't think for one minute I'm going to let you forget your offer."

"I'm counting on it," Frazier said, "and, just to be sure, maybe this will help you to remember." And while the band played "When Johnny Comes Marching Home," he slipped a ring on her finger.

"I meant to give you the ring tonight, but I just couldn't wait," Frazier said later as they strolled the meandering pathways of the park.

"I'm glad you didn't. I'll probably never have another chance for a standing ovation." Annie's face was still burning from the applause they'd received from the surrounding crowd, many of who had offered congratulations and hearty good wishes for a happy life together.

The gathering grew thin as evening shadows crept across the grass, and the group on the bandstand packed up their instruments and left. Soon the park would close, and still Annie clung to Frazier's hand, taking comfort in his nearness. This time tomorrow he would be on his way back to Fort Benning to join his company, and all he could tell her was that they would be serving in the European Theater. When would she see him again? *Would* she see him again?

This won't do at all! He is not going to remember me as dreary and weeping on our last day together before he ships out. "I guess we'd better head back to the car before we get locked in the park for tonight," Annie said in what she hoped was a spirited tone.

"Would that be such a terrible thing?" he whispered in her ear.

"But you're right. If we're going to make it to the Place to Be, we'd better get a move on or we might not get back before midnight."

"The Place to Be? What in the world is that?"

"Only where you'll find the best barbecue in the world. It's a little place between here and Athens where I'm taking you for dinner. Don't worry. It's less than an hour away."

"Frazier Duncan, how can you even think of eating again after all that food we put away at lunch?"

"But that was hours ago, and I'm a growing boy," he said as he stowed the empty picnic basket in the trunk of the car. "As my always-ailing aunt Hortense used to say, 'I believe I might be able to sit up and take some light nourishment.'"

"And I *believe* I'd better learn how to cook," Annie said with determination.

It was soon after they drove through the small village of Winder that she saw him. "Frazier! Turn around—we have to go back!"

"Why? What's wrong? Are you sick?" Frazier slowed the car and looked for a place to turn around. "Annie, what is it?"

"It's *him*—Buddy Oglesby! The man who disappeared with the War Bond money. Remember? I told you all about it."

"Where? Are you sure?"

"I saw him go into that little store back there. I know it's him, Frazier. Nobody is as tall and lanky as Buddy. Hurry! I have to find out for sure."

But in the five minutes it took to turn around and go back to the store where she'd seen him, Buddy Oglesby—or the man who looked like Buddy Oglesby—was no longer there.

CHAPTER TWENTY

If he hadn't had a hankering for a fried bologna sandwich, she never would've seen him—and chances were, she hadn't. But how could he be sure? Ima Jean had on occasion been good to share what she'd had with him, but a fellow can eat just so many pinto beans, and lately he'd been remembering how his grandmamma used to fry up sliced bologna with onions until he could pretty near smell it. The general store down the road stayed open pretty late, and if he walked fast, he could get there before it closed. He could almost taste that bologna.

And now look where it had gotten him! He had paid for his purchases and was getting ready to leave the store when he saw her getting out of the car only a few yards away. Buddy slipped behind a shelf of canned goods and looked again. Sure enough, it was Annie, the pretty little teacher who'd helped with the follies back in Elderberry.

Frantically, he looked around. The door behind him opened into a storeroom and then to the outside. Gripping the bag of bread and bologna, Buddy Oglesby took his chances and ran.

"Are you sure it was him?" Charlie asked. "I mean, could you really tell from that far away?"

Annie nodded. "Had to be. It wasn't quite dark yet, and the storefront was lighted. He crossed the road right in front of us, and I'm sure he went into that store—but then it seemed like he just disappeared."

Charlie frowned. "Did you mention it to the store clerk when you went back?"

"He said somebody matching Buddy's description was just there, but unless he's become invisible, he didn't leave the way he came in. I think he must've seen me and slipped out the back."

"I just can't imagine what Buddy Oglesby would be doing in Winder," Charlie said.

"Hiding out, I suppose. Waiting for a chance to spend all that money he took." Annie kicked a twig from the sidewalk and took pleasure in imagining it was Buddy. "I told Chief Tinsley about it, and he said he'd look into it, but I don't think he believed me."

"Do you think Buddy might've had something to do with setting that fire at Jesse Dean's? If he was the one who shot him, he might've come back to—"

Annie stopped in mid-stride and turned to face her. "Oh, Charlie, I hope not! It's awful to think he'd be capable of something like that, but when you think about it, Winder's not that far away."

"You're right. It isn't, and if Buddy didn't do it, then who did?" It was Monday following Annie's weekend trip to Atlanta and the two were walking back to school after their noon meal at Phoebe's, where everyone had made a big production of admiring Annie's ring, although a few had seen it on her return the day before.

"If Will gave me an engagement ring I think I'd walk around with my hand out in front of me for everyone to see," Charlie said, admiring her friend's diamond as they waited to cross the street.

Annie laughed. "Just wait! It won't be long. Do you think you'll be able to see him before they move on to advanced?"

"I doubt it. You know as well as I do their time's not their own. When's the last time you saw Joel?"

"You're kidding, aren't you?" Annie said, smiling. "My brother has more important things to do than spend time with me, but he said in his last letter they expect to be moving on to advanced training the end of this month."

Charlie nodded. "And Craig Field's in Selma. That's way down in the middle of the state. Will thinks we *might* be able to meet in Columbus or even Montgomery sometime during Thanksgiving."

"Wouldn't *that* be appropriate? The two of you met a year ago on Thanksgiving. Remember?"

Just thinking of it made Charlie feel warm inside in spite of a chill wind bringing rain. How could she ever forget?

"Well, I hope Bobby Tinsley will pay attention to you and Annie now," Phoebe said when Dimple told her what she'd learned about Buddy's connection with Cynthia Murphy. "Thinks nobody knows anything but him. I never saw a man so thickheaded!"

Odessa had left early that day, and Dimple was helping her friend set the table for a light supper. "Yes, well, we had a little chat, and he seemed most interested when I told him Buddy and Cynthia were a couple back in high school. He admitted he didn't take it seriously when Annie told him she thought she'd seen Buddy in Winder, but I'm confident that he'll look into it now." She put a bowl of potato salad on the table and went to the buffet for a serving spoon. "I keep thinking of how upset Buddy was the day they found Cynthia's remains. He must have had some idea who it was even then . . . the thought disturbs me."

"Just one more good reason why Buddy Oglesby should be behind bars—and the sooner, the better!" Phoebe said. "Reynolds has been told not to leave the area, so they obviously believe he had something to do with his wife's death, but from what you're telling me, it might've been Buddy who killed her."

She pulled out a chair and sat abruptly. "Oh, Dimple, you don't suppose *he* set that fire the other night, do you?" She lowered her voice. "And could Buddy be the one who's been sending me those notes?"

Miss Dimple shook her head. "Let's hope they get to the bottom of that fire business soon, but I don't know about the notes since all but the first one were postmarked here." She paused to sit beside her. "We're going to find out who's doing this, Phoebe. When I walked past the house on Legion Street early this morning everything looked the same, but Virginia promises we can try again tomorrow night."

Phoebe ran her fingers over the starched white tablecloth, worn thin in spots and patched in others. "You can't keep on watching that place forever. Perhaps I should tell the police . . ."

"Whoever is doing this certainly waited a long time to try and take advantage of the situation," Dimple said. "*Think*, Phoebe. It must be someone new to the area, perhaps someone who lived here before and knew you in the past."

Phoebe frowned. "Buddy Oglesby was raised here and lived away for several years, but he wasn't even born when—well, when I went to stay with my aunt and had Kathleen, and I think we can rule out Sebastian, since he spent most of his life in Austria."

"What about Coach McGregor and his wife?" Miss Dimple hadn't told anyone what she suspected of the new coach, and didn't plan to until she had a chance to speak with him privately. She liked Jordan McGregor in spite of her doubts and was reluctant to pursue her suspicions without further evidence.

"I don't think so. At least I hope not. I hear he's doing wonders with the football team this season." Phoebe rose to set a stack of plates at the end of the table and added a basket of napkins. She didn't have fifty more dollars to give to the person behind this faceless threat, and if it weren't for Kathleen and Harrison, she wouldn't concern herself about it at all. But the fact that someone would circulate vicious gossip about those she loved best spread like poison through her thoughts.

❧

"They were *there*!" Lou Willingham spoke in a triumphant voice over the telephone Saturday morning.

"Who was there?" her sister asked.

"*You know*," Lou whispered. "The people we talked about on the bus yesterday." One had to be careful when using the telephone in Elderberry as you never knew when Florence McCrary, the local operator, might be listening in. "You promised to go with me tonight, remember?"

Jo sighed. "Oh, Lou, you know how you imagine things. I want to write Fain, and if I don't finish that article about the Woman's Club's Harvest Social for the *Eagle*, it won't get in next week's edition." Jo Carr took her part-time job as society editor for the local weekly seriously. "I don't have time to go riding around in the middle of the ni—"

"Shh! I tell you they were there again last night, and you *did* agree to go with me. Aren't you the least bit curious?"

Jo had to admit that she was. "But I can't stay out to all hours."

"Don't worry. I don't have that much gas," Lou said.

"What does Ed think about it?" Jo asked. Lou's husband didn't always go along with her outrageous ideas, but he seldom had a choice in the matter.

"Oh, Ed will be asleep. Conks out as soon as he listens to H. V. Kaltenborn and the news. He'll never know I've been gone."

Jo tried to think of a thousand reasons why she couldn't go along, but she knew it was no use to argue.

"I'll come by there in about an hour and we can go over our plans," Lou said, and hung up before her sister had time to answer.

182

Annie hadn't been home a day before nearly everybody in Elderberry knew that Buddy Oglesby was seen at a store in a little town not far from Atlanta. Some said he had already spent all the bond money and was driving a fancy new car (although it was a mystery where he'd gotten it as American manufacturers had begun putting all their materials into the war effort soon after Pearl Harbor and drivers had to make do with the ones they had). A few even claimed he had gone over to the other side and was spying for the Germans.

Josephine Carr dismissed all that, however. She really didn't think Buddy would go over to the enemy and wasn't even sure he had taken the money. She did wonder, though, if he might've had something to do with putting that shotgun in Reynolds Murphy's car. "I think Buddy ran away because he was frightened," she said as she and Lou discussed their nocturnal surveillance plans that afternoon.

"Frightened of who? Of what?" Lou wanted to know.

"I don't know, but Charlie, and Annie, too, said he'd been acting strangely before all this happened. They told me Buddy said something that gave them the impression he might even know who killed Cynthia Reynolds."

Louise peeled an apple and cut off a wedge. "Huh!" she said. "They must think Reynolds did it since he's only out on bail. I wonder if Buddy was referring to him."

"I guess Bobby Tinsley and his bunch must have their reasons, but if they ever do find Buddy, he'll have a lot to answer for."

"I sure do feel sorry for Reynolds's son," Lou said. "How old you reckon he is now? Twelve? Thirteen?"

"Ross? Well, he was around ten when his mama ran off—well, we *thought* she'd run off, so that would be about right," Jo said. "Reynolds sent him to that military school, remember? Said he couldn't give him the care he needed at home. I always thought that was a mistake."

"I never understood that, either, but I guess he did what he thought best at the time. I wonder if the boy knows about his daddy being arrested." Lou popped a slice of apple in her mouth.

"I hope not. At any rate, he's out of jail now, and a good thing or that fire at Jesse Dean's might've been a lot worse than it was. I hope they can get all this mess cleared up soon. Don't we have enough to worry about with this horrible war?"

Lou noticed the catch in her sister's voice and covered Jo's hand with hers. "What do you hear from Fain?"

"As you know, we don't hear often, and then he can't tell us anything, but we did get a short letter a few days ago. He sounds all right, but of course that's what he *wants* us to think. We don't know anything until we hear it on the news, but I guess that's the way it has to be."

Charlie and Delia had taken the baby out in his carriage to visit some of the neighbors, and Jo and her sister visited in the sitting room, where a small coal fire burned on the hearth.

"I think we should wait until it's good and dark before we go tonight," Lou said, tossing her apple core into the fire. "We don't want anyone to see us."

"What if Virginia and Dimple see us? They might be curious as to why on earth we're following them," Jo said. "Frankly, I'm not one bit sure they were the ones you saw, Louise. Any number of people have cars the same color as Virginia's, and what if these people are up to no good? You know, black market or something?"

But Lou brushed that aside as she stood to leave. "It was them, all right, no doubt about it. And what if they're in some kind of trouble? They might need our help, Josephine."

From what she'd heard of Miss Dimple's past adventures, Jo thought she could probably take care of herself, but her sister was already on her way out the door muttering something about fixing Ed something to eat for supper.

"Where are you going so late, Mama?" Charlie looked up from the rolltop desk in the sitting room, where she was writing letters.

Jo hesitated. Should she tell her the truth? Uh-uh! "Oh, you know your aunt Lou—she's found these old pictures in the attic, and it's driving her crazy to know who they are. She thought maybe I could help."

Charlie started to rise. "Do you want me to—?"

"No, no. I'll be all right and the walk will do me good, but I think little Tommy's fretful tonight with teething and your sister could probably use a hand." She paused before leaving. "Writing to Will?"

"Will, and Fain—and Hugh, too. I promised I would, and he likes to hear all the hometown news. I worry about Hugh, Mama. He's always going to be in the middle of some kind of terrible battle."

"That's why he trained for the Medical Corps, Charlie. It's what he wanted to do. Emmaline won't let on how she feels, but I know she worries about Hugh as much as I do about Fain."

For a while Jo thought her daughter was in love with Hugh Brumlow, and Charlie thought she was, too, but one short afternoon with Will Sinclair had changed all that. Charlie still cared for Hugh and had corresponded with him faithfully, especially after he had been assigned to a ship a couple of months before. Neither Charlie nor his mother knew exactly where he was.

Lou waited at the corner, her car parked in deepest shadow, silent and mysterious. Jo squelched a little shudder of excitement. She was *not* going to let her sister get carried away this time! Still . . . Jo remembered when, as children, she and Lou had worked up the courage to pick cherries from Jed Fletcher's tree. Known for his stinginess, the old man lived about midway between their house and school, and they had eyed those cherries daily, watching them turn a lovely dark red until they could almost taste the sweet, ripe, forbidden goodness of them. It had been Lou's idea, of course, Lou's dare, and the two had ducked under the barbed wire fence and indulged themselves shamelessly until, with an angry shout, Jed Fletcher chased them, finally giving up when they took refuge in a wooded lot across the road. There they had collapsed behind a huge sycamore tree with red-stained hands and faces and laughed at their escape as, still muttering, their pursuer gave up the chase and turned for home. What fun that had been! Jo found herself smiling at the memory.

"What's so funny?" Lou asked as her sister joined her in the car.

"Nothing, why?"

"You were smiling. What is it?"

"I wasn't smiling, Louise. I was shaking. It's freezing out here." She was *not* going to give Lou the satisfaction of knowing she *kind of* enjoyed the risk of danger. After all, they were two middle-aged (well, all right—*a little past* middle-aged) women who had no business prying into things that didn't concern them.

The car smelled of buttered popcorn and Ed Willingham's pipe tobacco and, because it had no heater, was probably a lot colder than the inside of the Carrs' Frigidaire. For comfort, Lou had brought along an ancient hand-knitted afghan and two bags of popcorn from the picture show. (Bessie Jenkins, who worked there Saturdays, would let you in to buy it if she knew you were of good conscience.)

"Have you seen them?" Jo asked, helping herself to the popcorn. If she could bottle the smell of it, Jo thought, she would make a fortune.

"Not yet. I drove around the block a couple of times. They might already be there. I can't see a thing from the road."

"Then how are we going to know?" Jo asked. "And if it turns out not to be Miss Dimple and Virginia, then what?"

"We don't have to go all the way in, Josephine—just far enough to see if there's a car back there. We'll pretend we're just turning around. Then we can park around the corner and see who comes out."

Jo sighed. Maybe this wasn't such a good idea after all. "For heaven's sake, what good will that do?"

Apparently Lou hadn't thought of that because it took her a while to answer. "Then I guess we'll follow them, Josephine, or come back in the daylight and try to find out what's going on here. Maybe they've left some kind of evidence behind." And, as if taking her sister's silence for agreement, she started the car and drove into the weed-choked driveway of the vacant lot in question.

"Oh lord, Louise, how can you see where you're going? It's pitch-black dark. Turn on the headlights!"

"In a minute. I don't want them to know we're coming," Lou said as a sapling bent and crunched under the left front tire. "Uh-oh! What's that?"

"You ran into a tree, that's what!" Jo strained to see in front of them but could see nothing. "There's no car back here, Louise. Turn on the headlights and let's get out of this place!"

"Don't yell! I'm trying." Lou switched on the headlights, but the engine stalled as she attempted to shift into reverse. "Something's caught under the car. Oh, lordy! Ed will kill me."

But that wasn't the least of their troubles at the moment, Jo realized, as a dark figure dashed in front of the yellow glow of the headlights and disappeared in the surrounding darkness, and there was something vaguely familiar about the way he moved.

CHAPTER TWENTY-ONE

*D*amn! The Prince Albert can was empty! Looks like the old girl wasn't as rich as she'd thought and probably needed more time. Well, Phoebe Chadwick had better come up with that fifty bucks—and soon—if she knew what was good for her.

But there should be even more money in this other one. And easy! Why, it had dropped into her lap like pennies from heaven—better than pennies! She giggled at the thought. Well . . . maybe not heaven. She'd been walking through the parking lot beside the auditorium the night of the follies when she saw him put the shotgun in the trunk of that car! And how lucky was that?

The message should've arrived yesterday—plenty of time to get the money and leave it in a place where nobody would ever think to look, a place out of sight from anyone passing by. And there was money to be had—lots of it. No reason she shouldn't enjoy some of it, was there? After all, think what he had done!

Making her way carefully around the tangled undergrowth in the front yard to the back of the house, she switched on her flashlight and threaded through long-neglected shrubbery to the place where she'd left the small metal box beneath sagging back steps. Straggly grass and *vines concealed it so only she and one other person would know to look for it there.*

Yes, there it was! She could see the glint of metal through the foliage.

But what was that? Something moved in the dry weeds behind her. The rustle of leaves and the faint snap of a twig sounded more frightening than cannon fire in this remote place. Someone was watching her. Waiting.

She ran, not toward the front but to the dubious safety of the vacant wooded lot behind it, where the cover of darkness and trees would protect her. It didn't.

～

Josephine Carr cringed beneath the afghan. Would it be safer to stay in the car or make a break for it and run? And didn't she swear she'd never let her sister lead her into a situation like this again? "Did you see that?" she croaked.

"I saw it. Probably some teenagers out sparking." Lou pumped the clutch and managed to bring the engine to life, but the car wouldn't budge. "Something's stuck under there. We'll have to get out and move it."

"Maybe you didn't see what I saw. There's a man—well, I think it's a man—out there, Louise, and for all I know, he might not be alone." *Where had she seen somebody run like that? She just couldn't pinpoint it.*

"Do you want to sit here all night? We're going to have to do something soon because I have to go to the bathroom."

"Well, just don't think about it," Jo said. "Sit on your foot or something."

"I think he's gone. It looked like he—she—it—whatever it was—was running away," her sister said. "You can sit there like a bump on a log if you want to, but I'm getting out."

What would be worse, Jo thought, getting out of the car to be murdered by an evil maniac or sitting safely inside while her sister was being attacked? Taking a deep breath, which she knew might be her last, she opened her door and felt her way around the car. The dim headlights did little to illuminate the ground in front of them, and she could hear Lou struggling with whatever was impeding their progress underneath the driver's side of the car.

"You hold the flashlight," Lou directed, "while I pull." And that's what they did, at least for a while, until Jo put down the light and joined in the tugging. Finally, something cracked, and they both fell to the ground with rosin on their hands and the strong smell of pine all around them.

"Hurry and get in and let's try it again," Lou said, pulling herself up with great difficulty.

Her sister needed no urging, but the stubborn car only shivered and lunged a few inches forward before digging deeper into its rut.

"It looks like we're stuck," Lou announced after the motor sputtered to a halt. "You'll have to push, Jo."

"Me? Why not you? You got us into this mess." But she was cold and tired and wanted to go home, so Jo reluctantly climbed out of the car and began to push. However, after a few tries, the wheels only created a trench in the soft dirt.

Jo deliberately refrained from glancing at the darkness that surrounded her as she attempted to move the car from behind. If anything was out there, she didn't want to know it. "I think we're going to have to find some branches to put under the wheels to get some traction," she said, hoping the imitation-rubber tires would hold up under the stress. Because of the war, rubber was in short supply, and what passed for rubber inner tubes required constant patching.

"Branches under the wheels? Isn't that what caused this in the first place?" Lou said.

"Your driving into a tree is what caused it," Jo said crossly. Her feet were cold, her hands were scratched, and *she wished Lou hadn't mentioned needing to go to the bathroom!* She looked for somewhere to wipe her sticky hands but found nothing. "Come on, you've got to get out and help me find something that will do. I'm not wandering around here in the dark by myself."

Using the headlights would drain the battery so, except for the flashlight, the two were in complete darkness. Stumbling into the undergrowth around them, Lou probed the area with the pale yellow beam, stopping now and then to break off a spray of cedar or pine, while Jo walked closely behind her, gathering what she could.

Neither of them noticed what appeared to be a fallen limb in front of them until they tripped over it and tumbled to the ground.

"Oh, lordy, what if there's a snake in here?" Jo said as they struggled to help one another to stand. "Don't they like to hide under logs?"

But just then the "log" groaned.

When she could think again, Jo wished her sister would stop that screaming, but it wasn't Louise making all the noise, it was both of them, with Jo doing more than her share. Lou had Jo's arm in a death grip and was attempting to drag her back the way they had come. "Forget the car!" she said. "We're getting out of here."

Stumbling along behind, Jo finally managed to wrench free. "Wait, Louise! We can't. There's somebody back there and they're obviously hurt. We can't just run off and leave them."

The beam of the flashlight made erratic circles in the night as her sister attempted to plow her way through a forest of brambles and vines. "We'll send help. Come on, Jo! We don't know who that is back there."

Still, Jo held back. Whoever it was didn't seem to be in a position to harm them, and she stubbornly refused to go on until they at least found out how badly the person was injured. The year before both sisters had enrolled in a Red Cross first aid class, and she was aware of the danger if someone went into shock. The night air was cold, and the ground even colder. "What if that's Miss Dimple lying back there, or Virginia?" she said.

Her sister hesitated. "Oh. I guess you're right," she said, and turned around abruptly. "Can you remember where we were?"

Jo couldn't, but feeling their way cautiously and shining the light from side to side in front of them, they made their way back to the now-silent form on the ground.

"Lou, it's a woman!" Jo said, kneeling beside her. The woman lay on her side with an arm over her face, and Lou focused the light on the back of her head. "Is she breathing? Oh, dear Lord, she's not dead, is she?"

Jo felt for a pulse in the darkness and was relieved to find one. "What happened? Can you talk?" she asked, gently turning the woman's face to the light.

"Why, Jo that looks like . . . it *is*! It's *Millie McGregor!*" Panting for breath, Lou squatted beside her sister and brushed matted hair from the woman's eyes. "Millie, who did this to you? We're bringing help, honey. It's going to be all right."

But Millie's eyes remained closed, her face, still and pale, and she was bleeding from a gash in her forehead. Jo leaned closer and found her breathing shallow. "We've got to get help, but we can't move her, Lou. She might have broken bones or something. Let's cover her with the afghan—at least she'll be warmer, and we'll flag down somebody to help."

"You go," Lou said. "You can move faster than I can. I'll stay here with Millie."

"I don't like leaving you here alone. What if—"

"Will you please go on? We don't have time to argue. I'll be fine—now hurry!"

Leaving her sister with the light, Jo picked her way to the car for the afghan and hurried back, waiting as Lou tucked it around Millie. "Go to the first house showing a light," Lou said—"and be careful!"

Now that her eyes were becoming accustomed to the darkness, Jo was able to find her way to the street without a major incident, although it seemed every limb snagged her hair and every briar, her legs, but she dared not rush. If she became injured and couldn't walk, what would happen to Lou and Millie? *And what if the person they saw running away came back to finish the job?*

Josephine Carr couldn't afford to think of that. She paused to decide which direction to turn and broke into a run. By the end of the first block, which seemed deserted, she had a stitch in her side and was almost out of breath. Surely she wasn't this out of shape! Somewhere in the distance a dog barked, and Jo hoped it was confined by a fence. The last thing she needed was an angry dog nipping at her heels.

The few houses in the second block were in darkness, and knowing it would take several minutes to bring someone to the door, Jo passed them by. Spying a yellow square of light up ahead, she ran on.

After what seemed like forever and a day, Fred Rankin came to the door with a glass of milk in one hand and a poker in the other. His wife, Mabel, her hair rolled in rags, peeked out from behind him. The poker, Jo realized, was a would-be weapon—just in case.

"Jo? Is that you?" Mabel, whose daughter Grace had gone all through school with Fain, recognized her almost immediately. "What on earth's the matter? Are you all right?"

Jo Carr didn't waste any words explaining the situation.

❧

Fred Rankin obligingly abandoned his bedtime milk to deliver Jo to the vacant lot where she had left her sister and Millie. Naturally, Mabel insisted on going along as well. She was afraid to stay by herself, she said, with a criminal on the loose in the neighborhood. Why, for all she knew, he might be watching them this very minute. A couple of phone calls from the Rankins soon brought a procession of rescuers rushing to the scene. Doc Morrison and Chief Tinsley arrived at the same time, followed soon afterward by Harvey

Thompson, who had outraced his competitor in his ambulance/ hearse.

"Are you sure you left them back here?" Fred asked as, using his flashlight, they shoved aside clutching brambles and waded through things they couldn't see that rustled and crunched underfoot in the darkness.

"What if whoever did this to that poor woman is still here somewhere?" Mabel asked, clinging to her husband's coattails.

Then that would be all the more reason to hurry, Jo thought, but considered it better not to say it aloud. Instead, she called out, hoping she was leading them in the right direction. "Lou! Louise! Where are you? Answer me!" *What if that person really had come back?* Jo ducked under a limb and pushed forward.

"I don't hear a thing," Mabel said. "And what's this up ahead? It looks like—"

"A car," Fred said, and threw out an arm to stop them.

Lou's car! "Lou, Lou! We're coming!" Jo shouted, and began running in the direction she hoped was right.

In answer, a sallow shaft of light wavered in the distance. "Here! Over here!" her sister called out. "Hurry! We have to get her out of here. She needs a doctor," Lou added.

"Doc Morrison's on the way." Jo knelt beside her sister and touched Millie's wrist. At least she still had a pulse, but for how long?

"I'll go back out to the street and flag him down," Fred volunteered, but that wasn't going to be necessary, they learned, as the sweep of headlights from an approaching car illuminated the darkness behind them.

"How long ago did you find her?" the doctor asked as they moved aside to make room for him.

Jo exchanged looks with her sister. How long *had* it been? Thirty minutes? An hour? It seemed like they had been here forever.

Lou frowned. "Does anybody know what time it is?"

Doc Morrison pulled out his pocket watch and held it in the light. "A quarter after eleven."

"Then we've been here about an hour and thirty-five minutes—or at least that's when we saw somebody running away. Ed was asleep and snoring by nine-thirty when I left home, and it took about ten minutes after that for Jo and me to get here."

Stooping beside Millie, the doctor gently felt for broken bones. "And when you found her—was she conscious?"

Jo shook her head. "We thought she was a log or something—or we did at first. Lou and I—well, we kind of stumbled over her. We were trying to find branches to put under the tires so we could get unstuck, you see."

"Tell him about the man who was running away," Lou urged.

And so Jo did. But, she added, she wasn't really sure it was a man. "That was when we decided it was time to get out of here . . . but then we couldn't."

"And what in the h— world were you two ladies doing out here at that time of night?" The voice came from behind them, and everyone turned to see Chief Tinsley hacking his way through the underbrush to reach them.

Again, Jo looked to her sister. What good would it do to bring Miss Dimple and Virginia into this when there was probably a perfectly good reason they'd been frequenting the area? She had let Lou's wild imagination get her into trouble for the last time! Well, *no more,* but she would try her best to worm her way out of this one.

"Well . . . we only meant to turn around . . . and then I saw what I thought was a lycopodium fern back in here. They're supposed to be kind of rare, you know, and I thought no one would care if I took a little tiny piece of it." Jo couldn't see her sister's face in the darkness, but she was sure she was rolling her eyes. "I've nursed the one on my porch along for several years now, but I didn't even know what it was until Beatrice Caskey gave that talk at garden clu—"

From what she could see of the look on Bobby Tinsley's face, Jo

Carr got the definite impression he thought she had the intelligence of a flea. Well, so be it.

"Fred tells me you think you saw a person running away just before you found Mrs. McGregor," he said. "Can either of you give me any kind of description?"

"It looked like a man, but it was too dark, and he was too far away to be sure," Lou told him.

"Well, whoever it was, he's long gone now," Fred Rankin muttered.

Somebody had obviously managed to get word to Jordan McGregor, who had stayed late to discuss the upcoming game with Eatonton after a meeting of the Elderberry School Board, and he arrived as Harvey Thompson and associates were transporting his wife to the ambulance.

"I'm here now, honey, it's going to be all right," he whispered repeatedly, hovering over the still figure on the stretcher, but in the transparent yellow beam of the vehicle's headlights, the man's distraught face belied his words.

Jo Carr couldn't even bring herself to feel sorry for her sister, who had to explain to her husband the next day why his car was stuck in the mud in a vacant lot on the other side of town.

Later, in bed, she said a prayer for Millie McGregor and for her husband, who would get no sleep that night or probably for the next few, either. And after all the frenzy of the evening's excitement, she finally allowed herself to say aloud the thought that had plagued her all night.

What was Millie McGregor doing in that vacant lot at that time of night?

CHAPTER TWENTY-TWO

*O*h, God! What had she done? And how many times had she
promised? If she lived through this, they would have to relo-
cate again, and they were running out of places. He would
have to come up with some kind of story to try to satisfy the police, but
this time it might be too late.

So why did he still love her?

❧

"I heard your mother was the one who found her," Geneva said to
Charlie during their noon dinner at Phoebe's the following Monday. "How lucky that she and your aunt happened to come along."

"They must've been terrified," Lily said. "What a horrible place
to get stuck in the mud!" She gave a slight shudder. "Pass the fried
apples, please, Annie."

"Well, for Millie's sake, I'm glad they did," Charlie told them,
although she had her doubts about her mother's story of "using the
vacant lot to turn around." Her mother had pretended innocence
when she challenged her tale about helping Aunt Lou identify
people in old family photographs. "Your aunt was giving me a ride

home, Charlie. Surely you didn't expect me to walk home alone at that hour."

Charlie didn't know why not as she'd certainly never thought twice about doing it before. She'd asked why they happened to be driving blocks out of the way, but her mother just pretended not to hear her.

"Poor Jordan McGregor," Miss Dimple said with a nod in Sebastian's direction. "I don't suppose he was at school this morning?"

"As a matter of fact, he was," Sebastian answered. "He said it was better than doing nothing at the hospital."

"Any change in Millie's condition?" Phoebe asked him, and Sebastian shook his head. "I'm afraid it doesn't look good," he told her. "It appears she ran into a tree limb in the dark, and her head struck a rock when she fell."

"I just wonder what in the world she was doing out there," Lily said.

"They found her car a couple of blocks away," Annie told her, "so it looks like she must've run out of gas."

Velma Anderson spoke up. "That's easy to do on the teaspoon we're allowed, but why not go to someone's house for help? I'm sure anyone would've been glad to give her a ride."

"It doesn't seem as if she had that chance," Phoebe said. "The poor woman probably ran in that vacant lot to try and get away from somebody."

"Well, I hope they hurry and find who's responsible. I don't even like to think of somebody like that on the loose here in Elderberry." Lily sighed as she ladled jam on her biscuit. "What in the world is happening in our little town?"

"Meanness, that's what!" Odessa reached from behind her to refill the bread basket. "All kinds of meanness goes on in the dark o' night. Things we won't never know about."

"I, for one, don't want to know about them," Velma said, "but I do hope they'll get to the bottom of this soon. I spoke to Jordan

McGregor this morning in the hall, and I believe he's aged ten years overnight."

"Aunt Lou said the police were all over the place yesterday when they went to get the car out of the mud," Charlie said. "She thinks they might've found the rock where Millie hit her head."

Annie fished the lemon wedge from the bottom of her glass of tea and sucked out the remaining juice. "How did they know that was the rock?" she asked, trying to ignore Miss Dimple's disapproving glance. "One rock looks pretty much like another to me."

"I guess it must've had blood on it," Charlie said, and then regretted saying it as Phoebe immediately excused herself from the table and left the room.

"Don't you want any of this bread puddin'? You didn't eat enough to keep a bird alive." Odessa started after her, but Miss Dimple shook her head. "Let's leave her be for now," she said, speaking softly. "I'll look in on her before I go back to school."

By the time school was out that afternoon the news had gotten around that Buddy Oglesby had been arrested and his aunt Emmaline had made a big scene at the police department protesting his innocence. Lily Moss said she'd heard Emmaline even threw a coffee mug at Bobby Tinsley, but Miss Dimple took most of the things Lily said with a grain of salt—well, actually, a lot more than a grain.

Virginia said she wouldn't be a bit surprised if it was true. Dimple had walked to the library that afternoon to see if *Red Is for Murder*, the new mystery by Phyllis Whitney, had come in and found her friend reshelving books in the children's section. Dimple, who disliked being idle, pitched in and gave her a hand. It was hot, dirty work, so when Willie Elrod came in a few minutes later for another Hardy Boys adventure, they gave him a quarter and sent him over to Lewellyn's Drug Store for lemonade for the three of them.

"Can I get an ice cream cone instead?" Willie asked.

"Yes, you *may*, William, but if I were you I'd eat it there as you might have trouble carrying all that back here," Miss Dimple suggested.

"Aren't you afraid it will spoil his supper?" Virginia asked after the boy left, but Miss Dimple said she'd never seen the child leave food on his plate as long as she'd known him, and she'd known him all his life.

"Mama says Buddy Oglesby hit the coach's wife over the head and left her for dead," Willie said when he returned a few minutes later with two paper cups of lemonade and a chocolate-covered face and shirt.

"As far as I know, the police don't know who attacked Mrs. McGregor," Miss Dimple said, "and I certainly can't imagine why Mr. Oglesby would have any reason to harm her."

Willie licked the chocolate from his hands one finger at a time. "But look what he did to Jesse Dean. Maybe he's just bad—you know, like some of those men in the Superman comics."

"Let's leave all that to the police," Virginia said, taking a handkerchief from her purse. "Now, if you want to take home that Hardy Boys book, I suggest you go in the restroom and wash your hands and face."

After Willie sauntered out for home, the two women sipped their lemonade in the fading light by the casement windows with Cattus stretched on the rug between them. The days were getting shorter and dusk would soon settle quietly upon the town, but Virginia sometimes kept the library open past her usual five o'clock closing time to accommodate those who liked to come in after work. Today, Bessie Jenkins dropped by after her shift at the munitions plant in Milledgeville to browse through the small collection of cookbooks. She had invited Madge Malone and her two young daughters for supper tomorrow and was looking for a recipe for spaghetti.

"I've never made it before," Bessie confessed, "but Madge says the girls are crazy about it, so I thought I'd give it a try."

"You might look at the recipe in the *Woman's Club Cookbook*," Virginia advised her. "I made it several times for the young people in the Epworth League when Albert was minister, and I never had any leftovers."

Bessie smiled. "Good! Then I'll try it. Thought I'd just have bread and a green salad. Madge is bringing dessert—probably apple cobbler as it's Joyce's favorite. Now, Jean is crazy about anything chocolate."

She had become close friends with the little family when their father was tragically killed the year before and now spoke as fondly of the girls as if they had been her grandchildren.

"Have you heard how Millie McGregor's doing?" she asked after copying the recipe on the back of an envelope. "Do the police know who's responsible yet?"

"As far as I know, she hasn't regained consciousness," Virginia told her. "If she does, maybe she'll be able to tell them who she was running from."

Bessie tucked the recipe in her purse and rose to go. "Somebody told me they'd arrested Buddy Oglesby in some little town near Athens, so maybe we'll finally get to the bottom of all this, but I don't see how he could've attacked the coach's wife if he was all the way over there."

Miss Dimple couldn't, either, although she supposed he could have driven there taking a chance no one would recognize him under cover of darkness. The whole town seemed to be in turmoil over the incident. She was especially concerned about her friend Phoebe and, after Bessie left, told Virginia how Phoebe had reacted at dinner that day when they discussed Millie's tragic injury.

Virginia took Cattus on her lap and stroked him as she listened. "What if *we* had been there that night, Dimple? We might've been witnesses."

"Or victims," Dimple answered. "I must say I'm glad you chose to stay at home and relax in the tub instead."

"Well, I suppose I'd better lock up and head for home," Virginia said finally as the two sat in silence, and Dimple gathered her books and her purple leather handbag trimmed with yarn flowers, but still seemed reluctant to leave.

Virginia waited at the door with her hand on the light switch while her friend stood at the window. "Are you going to tell me what's troubling you or not? And don't tell me nothing's wrong because I know you, Dimple Kilpatrick."

And so Dimple took a deep breath and told her what had been on her mind for the last two days. *Was Millie McGregor the person who had been blackmailing Phoebe?*

Virginia had to admit the thought had occurred to her as well. "But I thought her car had run out of gas a few blocks away."

"How do we know she didn't just park it there while she checked that place in the wall for money?" Miss Dimple followed her friend out the door and stepped into the cool evening air. "It was late when she was attacked, so what else could she be doing there at that hour?"

Virginia fell into step beside her as the two walked home together. "Can you think of a reason Millie would want to blackmail Phoebe? As far as I know, she hardly knew her."

Dimple didn't answer. Maybe she knew more about her than they thought, and tomorrow she would do her best to find out.

Millie McGregor? Phoebe Chadwick sat abruptly on the cedar chest at the end of her bed. "Do you honestly think she might be the one? How could she possibly know?"

Dimple waited until the others had gone to their rooms that night after listening to *Fibber McGee and Molly* on the radio as she wanted to be sure they weren't overheard. Now she sat across from Phoebe on the chintz-covered stool by the dressing table and told her what she suspected. The staccato sounds of typing came from Velma's room upstairs, and someone was running water for a bath.

"Think about it, Phoebe," Dimple urged her. "Is there any way you could have known her in the past?"

Phoebe shook her head and frowned. "I don't see how. Except for that brief time in Tennessee when Millie probably wasn't even born, I've never lived anywhere but here, and she's only been in Elderberry a few months. I must admit," she added, "I did wonder about that when I learned where she was attacked." She had been brushing her hair and now turned the hairbrush over in her hand. "Do you think Millie might have been the one who did that to Velma's tires the day we gathered muscadines?"

Dimple nodded solemnly. She *had* thought of that but was reluctant to believe it. She hadn't tried to hide her doubts about Jordan McGregor's service in New Guinea, and it had become obvious that Millie liked to be in charge. "I think it was meant as some sort of warning. She was uncomfortable with my questions."

"Dimple, are you sure? How could she have known where we were going?"

"There's no way I can be sure, but I believe she followed us there—probably watched us leave and saw her chance to give us a fright. I think Bobby Tinsley agrees with me, but there's no way we can prove it, or would even want to now."

"No, no, of course not," Phoebe said. What a troubled person Millie was. It was frightening to think about it.

"I believe she's about the same age as your Kathleen," Miss Dimple said. "Do you suppose they might've been friends?"

"But I'm sure I must've mentioned her to Kathleen when I wrote her about Lou's party. Wouldn't she have recognized the name?"

"Not if she knew her by her maiden name," Dimple said.

Still, Phoebe wasn't entirely convinced. "How could she learn this from Kathleen when Kathleen doesn't even know herself?"

Are you absolutely sure about that? Dimple thought. But, of course she didn't say it aloud.

❧

Virginia Balliew made herself eat at least part of her bowl of oatmeal and half a grapefruit before leaving for the library that Wednesday morning. Her stomach protested the intrusion, and nothing tasted right. Her appetite, it seemed, had fled with the War Bond money, and that had been more than two weeks ago.

The investigators had been patient and kind and she didn't think anyone would accuse her of taking the cash, but she had been responsible for that money, and the suspicion would always be there no matter how innocent she might be.

There was a hint of rain in the air, and a gust of wind sent leaves swirling as Virginia left her small cottage on Myrtle Street to walk the few blocks to her beloved log-cabin library in the park. The October morning was cool but not unpleasant, and Virginia pulled a blue beret over graying hair, still streaked with red, and started off at a brisk pace. Perhaps the walk and the air would clear her mind and help to heal her heart. Although she believed most of the people in Elderberry would never blame her for what had happened the night of the follies, she knew she would always blame herself, and every time someone came into the library or met her on the street, she couldn't help wondering if they eyed her with suspicion.

Several books, she noticed, had been dropped through the opening for that purpose to the left of the front door of the library. It had been put there for the convenience of patrons who were unable to return them during library hours, and Virginia usually attended to that after seeing to Cattus, who now wove her silken self sleekly about her feet.

"And good morning to you, too," Virginia said as she picked up the cat and stroked her soft gray fur. Cattus began to purr, and she felt comforted by her warmth and affection, although she knew it would last only until she reached for the can opener.

A flick of the light switch brought the book-lined room to life, and after putting away her wraps and seeing to the needs of Cattus, she decided to leave the heater on low and build a small wood fire to take off the chill. The officers of the Woman's Club were to meet that morning at ten and would probably be grateful for the warmth as well as the cheer.

But first she would take care of the returned books. Virginia smiled to see that Ruthie Phillips had returned the library's one frayed copy of *The Secret Garden*. It was the third time she'd read it, but probably not the last. Jesse Dean Greeson, who was currently on a Charles Dickens kick, had dropped off *A Tale of Two Cities*, and Virginia had set aside a copy of *David Copperfield* for him at his request.

And what was this? Alma Owens had *finally* brought back *Gone with the Wind* after renewing it twice, and it was still two weeks overdue. Naturally, she hadn't included the twenty-eight cents she owed in fines. Virginia shook her head. She would make a note of that.

Aside from these, she found two other books and a thick manila envelope that had slipped to the side. Virginia was puzzled when she saw her name printed on the front as any correspondence to her at the library was always delivered there by Boyce Oliver, their regular postman.

Virginia took the envelope to her desk by the window and carefully slit it open. Was this a dream? She could hardly believe what she was seeing when what appeared to be several thousand dollars in a variety of denominations tumbled onto her desk.

CHAPTER TWENTY-THREE

*I*t was almost a relief to be arrested and not have to hide anymore. Buddy Oglesby sat on the bunk in his narrow cell with his head in his hands and waited for his lawyer to come.

The place smelled of sweat and urine in spite of attempts to clean it with disinfectant, and there was no telling who had been sleeping on the flimsy mattress, but where else was he to sit? Aunt Emmaline had hired some high-priced fellow from Atlanta and promised he would soon be free, but Buddy wasn't sure he wanted to be free until they locked up the person who had tried to kill him the night of the follies. The bullet that wounded Jesse Dean had had his name on it as sure as he was born. At least he would be safe here in the Elderberry jail under the watchful eyes of the local police.

Or he could be a sitting duck.

Louise Willingham just had a feeling she should drop in on Jordan McGregor at the hospital that night. The very thought of the poor man restlessly pacing those sterile halls alone while his wife lay still and unresponsive like one of those beautiful dolls children weren't supposed to play with was more than she could bear. The morning after it happened she and Ed had gone there together with roses from that late-blooming bush by the garage, and Jordan had thanked her over and over for finding his wife. She didn't admit, of course, the real reason she and Jo had been there.

As soon as she got home from her job at the munitions plant that afternoon Lou had warmed up chicken hash and leftover green beans for supper and stepped over with some of her applesauce cake wrapped in wax paper for Jordan. He had refused her invitations for supper, and she knew he wasn't eating properly. You could tell that by looking at him. Well, grief did that to people, but at least she could keep him company.

She found, however, that others had the same idea. When she arrived, Reynolds Murphy sat on the bench in the hallway outside Millie's room talking with Elias Jackson, the high school principal, but both left soon afterward. When Jordan came out in the hall to join her for a while he said Sebastian had just left and several others from the school had come by earlier. "Everyone has been so kind, so thoughtful . . . I only wish . . ."

It was obvious that he was overcome with emotion, and Lou took his hand and sat quietly beside him. "How is she, Jordan?" she asked finally.

"Not good." He shook his head and tears began a ragged pathway down his cheeks. "Doc Morrison even called in a specialist from Augusta, but her skull was crushed from the blow." He wiped his eyes on a handkerchief. "I just hope she's not in any pain."

Lou squeezed his fingers. "I'm sure she isn't." She wasn't sure at all, but what else could she say? She would be forever grateful that Evan Mitchell, the Presbyterian minister, arrived shortly afterward and was there when a nurse summoned Jordan into Millie's room to tell him his wife had died.

❧

Virginia counted the money again. She had put the bills in stacks according to their denomination ranging from one-dollar bills up to fifties. Most were tens and twenties along with fives, ones, and a few fifties. The total came to an even twenty-four hundred. When compared with the list of people who had paid cash and the size of the bonds they bought at seventy-five percent of their value, the sum came to seventy-five dollars more than the amount missing. Frowning, Virginia checked the list again: six people paid for one-hundred-dollar bonds; eleven people bought fifty-dollar bonds, and seventy-eight purchased the twenty-five dollar bonds which should total $2,325.00. So where did the extra seventy-five dollars come from?

Virginia Balliew put the money back into the envelope, locked the library door, and marched straight to the bank, where she turned it over to Hubert Chadwick. He, in turn, promptly telephoned the representative from the War Finance Committee, as well as Bobby Tinsley, to let them know the money had been returned. Chief Tinsley showed up in Arthur's office in what was probably record time.

No, Virginia told them, she didn't know where the extra money came from, but the note that was in the envelope, and which she gave to Bobby, simply stated: *I believe this is the missing bond money. I hope it is all here.*

Frowning, Bobby blew into the empty envelope and examined it again. "And that was it?" he asked Virginia.

"We got the money back—and more. Surely you didn't expect them to sign it," she told him.

After leaving the money, Virginia walked back to the library feeling as if a ton of bricks had been lifted from her. She glanced at the town clock high above the courthouse. She had just enough time before the officers from the Woman's Club arrived to drop by Lewellyn's Drug Store for a cup of coffee to celebrate. And from now on, she would gladly scrub floors, dig ditches, or even carry a rifle and drill with the Home Guard rather than be in charge of another bond rally.

Leaving Lewellyn's with coffee in hand, Virginia almost collided with Lou Willingham, who told her of Millie McGregor's death. Lou was on her way to Cooper's grocery to see if she had enough ration coupons for a small ham to serve after the funeral service on Saturday.

"They don't seem to have any family," she said, "so I've invited some of the faculty and Evan Mitchell, of course, as he's to conduct the service. I don't know how many to count on, but I have plenty of sweet potatoes and a good mess of green beans, so I guess they can fill up on that."

"I've never known of anyone going hungry at your table," Virginia assured her, and offered to contribute a congealed fruit salad. She hoped she still had that can of pineapple she remembered seeing on her pantry shelf. She would make that recipe with grated carrots and lemon Jell-O that everyone seemed to like.

Lou's eyes filled with tears. "Jordan is just heartbroken, and my heart goes out to him. They've only lived in our little apartment a short time, but I feel I've known him much longer." She frowned. "Now, Millie . . . I never could figure her out. She just didn't have a *place*, if you know what I mean. Have you ever known anybody like that? I can't think of a way to describe Millie McGregor except that she was always ready for a good time and the young people seemed to take to her. Why, Delia was so upset when she heard about it, she had to go to bed." Lou shifted her purse to her other arm and attempted to adjust her coat over her bosom. "It seems like we've been wading through a whole pile of troubles here ever since that woman's skeleton turned up back in September."

"Well, I happen to have some *good* news," Virginia said, lowering her voice. And she told her about the return of the War Bond money that morning. "I suppose it's all right to mention it," she added, "as I wasn't advised to keep quiet about it."

Minutes later at the library she noticed the obvious absence of Emmaline Brumlow and was momentarily taken aback as Emmaline didn't think any meeting could be conducted properly without her.

"I wonder if they'll release Buddy Oglesby now that the money has been returned," Emma Elrod suggested after Virginia told them her news. "He couldn't have been the one who returned it if he was still behind bars," she added, "unless, of course he did it earlier."

"I don't believe the person who returned it was the one who took it," Virginia reasoned. "Whoever it was didn't seem to be sure it was the correct amount that was missing."

"Where else could it have come from?" Ida Ellerby wanted to know. "I don't know of many people here who have thousands of dollars floating around."

Virginia thought of the conversation she and Dimple had had earlier. *If Millie had been blackmailing Phoebe, she might've been the one who stole the War Bond money as well, and possibly Jordan had found it and returned it.* However, she had been brought up to believe it was in poor taste to speak ill of the dead, so she kept her thoughts to herself. For now.

Later that afternoon Charlie and Annie sat at Phoebe Chadwick's dining room table, bare now except for writing materials and a scattered stack of reference books. Their principal, "Froggie" Faulkenberry, had assigned the two of them the responsibility of planning the assembly program to be held at the end of the month.

"We'll need music—definitely," Annie said, making a note in her composition book. "I'm sure Kate Ashcroft can get some of the children in her music classes to sing something appropriate . . . and Alice Brady might have some of her expression students perform a couple of skits. The children usually love—

"Aw—applesauce!" Annie stopped in mid-sentence when the lead broke in her pencil and sighed after erasing the mark it had made. "Look at the ugly black smear this old imitation rubber eraser made. I think I'd rather just cross something out than try to use one."

Annie's patience had worn thin because she had yet to hear from Frazier since he'd shipped out, and even small things seemed to annoy her more than usual.

"It doesn't matter," Charlie told her. "We're the only ones who'll see this anyway." She tried to keep her voice calm as she knew how Annie felt. Will would soon move on to the final stages of his training at Craig Field and would probably leave immediately afterward to become a part of the Eighth Air Force in England. It wasn't looking encouraging for the two of them to get together anytime soon.

"Froggie could've given us a little more time," Annie grumbled. "We've only about two weeks to work this out."

"It's almost Halloween. What about a ghost story?" Charlie suggested. "Something that won't be too scary for the smaller children. I'm afraid most of the ones I know would give them nightmares."

Annie smiled. "I think I know who could help us . . ."

"*Miss Dimple!*" they said together.

Dimple Kilpatrick deposited a neat stack of folders on the table and smiled. She had been waiting for this day. "I've collected these little stories over the years, and you're most welcome to browse through them and use the ones you like best. Frankly, I would find it difficult to choose as I'm fond of all of them."

Charlie selected a folder and ruffled through its contents. "*Hansel and Gretel*—one of my favorites, but isn't it a bit frightening for the little ones?"

"Ah, but you haven't read it," Miss Dimple said. "These are *revised* fairy stories, and some of them will make you laugh out loud. As we know, most fairy tales are rather violent and terrifying, so from time to time I have asked my classes for suggestions to change them in any way they like. I believe the results may surprise you."

Leafing through the stories, they laughed as they read.

Gretel put pebbles in the witch's stew and the witch became so heavy she couldn't move.

Instead of letting down her hair, Rapunzel slid down the drainpipe and landed in a mud puddle.

Cinderella put poison ivy in the beds of her stepsisters and they both broke out in a rash and couldn't go to the ball.

Snow White changed her stepmother's mirror for one that couldn't talk.

Red Riding Hood and her grandmother locked the wolf in the basement and wouldn't give him anything to eat but spinach and turnip greens. When they finally let him out, he ran away as fast as he could and never came back again.

(Charlie felt a little sorry for the wolf in spite of herself.)

"These are wonderful," Annie said, putting several stories aside. "I think they'll be even funnier if we let some of the children read them."

Charlie agreed and suggested a likely candidate. Willie Elrod would be perfect to take part if they could trust him not to embellish too much.

Miss Dimple nodded. "Don't worry. I'll have a word with our William."

Charlie sniffed as an appetizing aroma came from the kitchen. "Something sure smells good. What's for supper?"

"I think Odessa's warming up the leftover stew we had earlier," Annie said. "I'm sure there's plenty. Why don't you stay?"

"Can't." Charlie made a face. "Have to go home and think of something for supper. Delia's down in the dumps because of Millie's death, and Mama's supposed to be writing her obituary for the *Eagle,* so it's up to me. Guess it's going to be leftover meatloaf again." Everyone knew her mother didn't cook unless it was absolutely necessary, and Charlie really didn't mind. Her mother worked hard at the ordnance plant and in her job writing the society news for the local paper. Besides, Jo Carr's cooking left a lot to be desired.

"I really didn't know Millie well," Annie said, gathering up her papers, "and I'm sorry I didn't make more of an effort. I suppose Jordan gave your mother the information she needed."

Charlie nodded. "Not a lot. Just a little background information— where she was born, went to school, etcetera. Neither of her parents is alive, and I don't think she had any siblings. I was kind of surprised to see she majored in math. She always seemed like more of the artsy type."

Annie grinned. "Like me?"

"Not at all like you," Charlie told her. There was no comparison between the two women.

"And where *did* she go to school?" Miss Dimple wanted to know.

"Right over in Milledgeville at G.S.C.W.," Charlie said. Her own mother was a student at Georgia State College for Women in the day when women had to wear uniforms and were told to turn away when a young man passed by the window. Of course she doubted if it was that strict when Millie went there.

"Do you remember her maiden name?" Miss Dimple asked.

"Yes, it was Knight." Charlie had no trouble remembering because while she and Annie were at Brenau College they had lived down the hall from two roommates whose last names were Knight and Day.

"Millie Knight . . . or perhaps Mildred Knight," Miss Dimple murmured as she left the room. Phoebe's daughter Kathleen had attended G.S.C.W. at about the same time.

But Phoebe Chadwick shook her head. "Millie Knight. No, it doesn't ring a bell, but I'll ask Kathleen if she remembers her."

Dimple Kilpatrick stood in her friend's doorway with her hands clasped in front of her. "And are you planning to explain to her just why you want to know?"

Phoebe sat at her dressing table and tucked a stray strand of hair into place. She took her time in answering.

"I don't know, Dimple. I really don't know. If, as you and Virginia believe, Millie McGregor was responsible for blackmail—and perhaps other things as well—she's gone now. What good will it do Kathleen?"

"I wasn't thinking of Kathleen," Dimple said softly.

CHAPTER TWENTY-FOUR

*S*o the coach's wife was dead. Head hit a rock, they said. Well, that was a coincidence! And now rumor was the coroner believed it was likely Cynthia Murphy had died in the same way, probably from a blow to the head.

He knew from personal experience the woman could drive a man to violence; why, any of them might've done it. It would just be a matter of time now before somebody learned his secret and began to point fingers at him. Maybe he should leave town . . . but it was too late to run.

❧

It had to be her! Strange that she should end up in Elderberry when she'd made light of the little town back in college. Kathleen knew right away who her aunt Phoebe was talking about when she told her about Millie's death. Millicent Knight had lived in her dormitory during their first two years of college, but she didn't remain Millicent long. Petite and vivacious with long blond hair that had a tendency to curl, she earned the nickname Goldilocks, and eventually, Goldie, when she ate the cookies her roommate's mother had sent from home—the entire box. "I really didn't mean to," she'd explained, wide-eyed, "but before I knew it, I had eaten them all up!"

A keen math student, Goldie was in school on a scholarship, and for a while tutored Kathleen in the subject when she was having a difficult time in that class. Millie had seemed grateful for the small fee she collected from working with Kathleen and a few other students and often used it to supplement her meager wardrobe.

At the end of one of their sessions she had told Kathleen how she had been adopted after her parents died of scarlet fever when she was about seven.

"Sometimes I've felt like I might have been adopted," Kathleen told her, more to make her feel better about her situation than anything else. "I don't look or act like either one of my parents, but then I guess most everybody feels that way at one time or another."

Goldie only shrugged. "Maybe you were," she said. "I wish somebody with lots of money had adopted me." A year or so later Kathleen learned that although Millie's parents were older and lived frugally on the salary her father brought in as a telegraph operator, she was *not* adopted. It was one of the many lies she told to promote sympathy, or maybe she thought it would help her get some of the things she wanted. Millie didn't have money for frills, and she did love frills. There had even been a couple of instances of missing jewelry in the dorm, but nothing could be proved, and no one wanted to point a finger.

Kathleen remembered losing a ring her parents had given her for Christmas. It wasn't an expensive ring, a small sapphire set in gold, but she had loved it because they had given it to her and because it was her birthstone. Goldie had been in her room the night before it disappeared, but then so had several others, so she didn't pursue the matter.

Goldie had attached herself to Kathleen for a while, and then she moved on to someone else. She wasn't capable, it seemed, of maintaining a lasting friendship, but frankly, Kathleen was relieved when the girl tired of her. Earlier in their second year the school choral group had made a brief concert tour of several towns in the area. When they performed at the Methodist church in Elderberry, Kathleen's aunt Phoebe had invited the group over afterward for dinner. Of course she had gone to a lot of trouble to make everyone welcome, and Goldie was awed by the huge dining room table with its crystal chandelier, the lovely fragile china, and gleaming silverware.

"Your aunt Phoebe must be rich!" she'd whispered over dessert, and Kathleen explained that her aunt earned her money the hard way by taking in boarders and that several other people lived and ate there as well.

"Huh! If I were her, I'd sure get out of this one-horse town," Millie said. She had poked fun as well at the small business district and the modest church where they sang.

"I doubt if she would want to leave. This is her home—hers and Uncle Monroe's. They're comfortable here, Goldie, but they're certainly not rich."

"But she's always sending you money," Goldie pointed out. "Didn't she pay for your tutoring? And what about that expensive evening gown you wanted? She bought it for you—just like that!"

Kathleen laughed. "She spoils me, I know, but Aunt Phoebe wasn't able to have children and she's always been like a second mother to me."

Goldie narrowed her eyes and looked at her. "Maybe she's more than that," she suggested. "You look just like her."

Kathleen had always wondered, but didn't dare ask, especially while her parents were alive. She loved both of them, loved them dearly, but there was a bond, a closeness, between her and Phoebe Chadwick that she couldn't explain. While going through old letters after her parents died, she had discovered correspondence from

Phoebe dating from the time she was born, letters inquiring about her: Was she healthy? Did the formula agree with her? Has she smiled yet? That kind of thing. And then later, when she began school, her aunt wanted to know if she was happy there. Was she reading yet? What was her favorite book? Song? She also learned from the letters that her aunt had helped pay for her college education.

Kathleen had been born three years before her aunt married Monroe, and she had felt no kinship with Monroe Chadwick, although he had never been unkind to her. If she had been Monroe's child, surely the couple would have married earlier and she would have been brought up in their household.

But if Monroe was *not* her father, then who was? Kathleen decided it was way past time to find out.

※

"Kathleen! Honey, is something wrong? Is it Harrison?" Phoebe held out her arms to the woman who stood in her doorway. "Did you drive all the way here from Macon?"

Kathleen smiled and embraced the woman who called herself her aunt. "No, no, I'm fine. Harrison's all right. I rode all the way on the bus between two good-looking soldiers, but I would like to sit down. What about the kitchen? Or is Odessa still here?"

"Just left, and I believe there's a little taste of that cottage pudding left from dinner, but wouldn't you rather sit in here?" She motioned to the parlor. "Kathleen, is everyone all right? What's going on?"

"That's exactly what I came to ask you." Kathleen walked beside her into the kitchen that always enveloped her in its warmth and comfort, smelled of good things to eat and welcomed her home.

"You wrote me about what happened to Millie McGregor," she said when the two were seated at the table. "I did know her in college—but you probably heard me speak of her as Goldie. She even came here once when you entertained the chorus."

Phoebe nodded. "I remember, but there were so many, and I was busy seeing to the table . . ."

"What did she do, Aunt Phoebe? I imagine she was up to no good. And why was she killed?"

"It seems she was running and struck a tree limb in the dark. They say she hit her head on a stone when she fell, but it's all over now. I hope the poor woman is at rest, so let's don't worry anymore about it." Phoebe patted her hand. "More tea?"

"But there's more to it than that, isn't there?" Kathleen persisted. "You haven't been yourself since . . . well . . . It had something to do with *you*, didn't it, Aunt Phoebe?"

Phoebe Chadwick looked at her daughter's face, heart-shaped like her own. Her dark hair, beginning to gray a little now, was the rich chestnut brown hers had been when she was young; but her mouth, so ready to break into a smile, the dimple at the corner of her lips, was so much like her father's it took her breath away.

"Yes," she said finally. "It did." Phoebe told Kathleen about the blackmail and she told her why. "But I don't understand how she knew you were mine," she added. "Especially after all this time."

"There's no way she could know for sure," Kathleen said, "but I suppose she must have thought it was worth a try to get some easy money.

"And now," she added. "Tell me about my father."

And, taking her daughter's hands in both of hers, Phoebe Chadwick did just that.

⧈

The funeral service for Millie McGregor was brief and simple. The church, of course, was filled, and afterward those closest to Jordan McGregor gathered at Lou and Ed Willingham's for a quiet lunch, after which people whispered among themselves, offered handshakes and condolences to Jordan, complimented Lou on her Boston brown bread and dried apple pie, and went home looking as if they'd won a reprieve. Jordan, his eyes red and shoulders slumped, walked back to the empty garage apartment alone.

Lou watched him from her kitchen window. She wished she could tuck him in bed with ginger tea and hot chicken soup and make everything all right. But she couldn't. No one could.

"I've never felt such tension at my table before," she confessed to Ed. "Usually, someone will relate an anecdote or some warm, amusing story about the person who died to help us remember them in a positive way, but today everything seemed gray and cold. There was no hope, no light."

Ed put an arm around her and snatched up a dish towel to help out. "For Jordan right now, I don't believe there is."

Charlie stepped out of Lewellyn's Drug Store with face cream for her mother and a box of scented soap for Odessa's upcoming birthday. Lemon verbena was her favorite, Phoebe said. She had attended Millie's funeral that morning with her sister, leaving their mother to stay at home with Tommy, but neither had gone to the luncheon at her aunt's. Charlie had tried to get Delia to walk into town with her to pick up a few items she needed and perhaps stop at Lewellyn's for a limeade, her sister's favorite drink, but Delia would have none of it. A movie was out of the question as the only thing playing at the Jewel on Saturday was a western, *King of the Cowboys*, with Roy Rogers and Smiley Burnette. The theater would be filled with children, and the floor, sticky with chewing gum and who knows what else. A lot of the people from the country were in town as was their custom on Saturdays, and the streets were crowded with farmers in overalls, children with nickels burning holes in their pockets, and a few servicemen visiting with friends while home on leave. Most drove trucks or cars they had bought long before the war, but a few came to town in horse-drawn wagons, and these were hitched under a shade tree in front of the courthouse.

Packages in hand, Charlie turned toward Murphy's Five and Ten. Delia had always loved the coconut bonbons there, and maybe a treat would cheer her up a little. She had reached the corner when she saw Miss Dimple standing across the street in front of Brumlow's Dry Goods. She stood for a few minutes facing the door but didn't attempt to go inside, and as Charlie watched she felt a momentary chill, a premonition that something wasn't right.

"Miss Dimple!" Charlie called to her as she hurried across the busy street, and the older woman turned at the sound of her voice and started walking to meet her at her usual no-nonsense pace.

"I saw you in front of Brumlow's," Charlie began, "and thought—" She broke off at the look on Miss Dimple's face. *What else could possibly go wrong?*

"It's closed," Miss Dimple said, and her expression was closed as well. Charlie couldn't read it.

"Closed?" Charlie repeated numbly. *Brumlow's never closed on Saturdays!* "Do you suppose somebody's sick? Come to think of it, I don't remember seeing Emmaline or Arden at the funeral service this morning. Maybe I should call."

"No, wait." Miss Dimple touched her arm with a gloved hand. "Perhaps Bennie knows what's going on."

But Bennie Alexander, who owned the small jewelry store next door to Brumlow's, had seen neither Arden nor her mother since Thursday, he told them. Bernice Fox, who filled in for the Brumlows once in a while when one of the women was sick, had come in for a short time Friday morning, he said, but had closed the store and left around noon.

"Did she mention if anything was wrong or say when they would be back?" Miss Dimple asked.

"Only that there was some kind of family emergency," Bennie

said. "Bernice didn't say what, and probably didn't even know." He paused to point out a display of birthstone rings for Ida Ellerby, who was shopping for her granddaughter's birthday gift. "I'm sure you're aware of how reserved Emmaline can be."

"Stuck-up, you mean," Ida muttered under her breath.

Charlie didn't reply, and Miss Dimple acted as though she hadn't heard her. Emmaline Brumlow's lack of social skills weren't their concern at the moment.

"What should we do? Should we call?" Charlie asked as they stepped outside together.

"I believe in this case we might sidestep that courtesy and go straight to the house," Miss Dimple advised. Both women knew that Emmaline Brumlow would probably discourage them from coming, and they didn't mean to allow her that choice.

The Brumlows lived in a comfortable redbrick Georgian-style home a few blocks from town. Dimple Kilpatrick had often walked past the ivy-covered house that was surrounded by a wrought iron fence and almost hidden from the street by a grove of oak trees, now glorious in foliage of red and gold. Today she didn't pass by the house as usual but pushed open the front gate and walked boldly up the brick path. Charlie accompanied her, grateful for the older teacher's serene company, as she dreaded what they might find there. And as soon as she saw Arden's tear-stained face she knew something had happened to Hugh.

Charlie had gone through all eleven years of school with Arden Brumlow, and although they had never been close friends, she'd always liked Hugh's sister and even felt sorry for her for having to put up with her dictatorial mother. Today she didn't wait to be asked in, but instead pushed open the door and took Arden in her arms while Miss Dimple stepped inside behind her. "Is it Hugh?" Charlie asked, and Arden nodded. "Wounded—somewhere in the Solomons. We don't know how he is, or even where he is." She led them into a large parlor filled with stiff-looking Victorian furniture covered in a gray-blue velvet; heavy draperies in a gold brocade covered the windows. Although she had dated Hugh for several years and known him all her life, Charlie had never been inside the Brumlow home and found the room suitably depressing.

Arden sat between them on a most uncomfortable loveseat. "Oh, Charlie, this is the worst thing that's ever happened to us! How did you ever bear it when you went through this with Fain?"

"The same way you will, and you *will* get through it," Charlie assured her, thinking the news could have been worse. Hugh could have been killed. "How is your mother taking this, Arden?"

"Awful! I'm worried sick about her. She won't even come out of her room. I don't know what to do."

"I see." Miss Dimple stood and looked about. "Why don't you begin by telling her that we're here?"

"It won't do any good," Arden said, but she obediently went into a room down the hall, where they heard a door close softly. She returned shaking her head. "I'm sorry. She said she doesn't want to see anybody. She's been this way since we heard."

"Nonsense," Miss Dimple said. "There are some things one should never have to bear alone."

Charlie and Arden watched speechlessly as Dimple Kilpatrick made her way down the hall and opened the bedroom door. The two of them followed meekly and listened to the sound of the window shades swish up, one after the other, and flip-flop at the top. "I taught Hugh Brumlow and watched him grow into a fine young man," Dimple told Emmaline. "I can't imagine what he would think if he could see his mother making herself sick with grief. What good is that going to do? Now, I'm going to run a hot bath, and I expect you to be up and dressed when I come back with some of Odessa's vegetable soup. There are too many people who care about Hugh to let you do this to yourself, Emmaline, and believe it or not, we care about *you* as well."

Charlie heard the sound of water running, and soon afterward

Miss Dimple left the room. Without a word Emmaline Brumlow got out of her bed, walked into the bathroom, and closed the door.

The walk home seemed like a hundred foreign miles instead of a few familiar blocks. Charlie remembered how on their last picnic together before he left for the navy, the two of them had gone to Turtle Rock, which held so many happy summer memories for both of them, and Hugh had proudly pointed out the trail he'd helped blaze with his Boy Scout troop and taken a last look at the town he loved from the top of the hill.

Hugh probably hadn't had time to receive her last letter, Charlie thought. But she would write to him again as soon as she got home, and she would keep on writing, just as she had for Fain.

They had reached the middle of town before she realized she was crying. She didn't try to hide it. Miss Dimple didn't, either.

CHAPTER TWENTY-FIVE

*H*ow did you know?" Virginia asked.

Miss Dimple set the bag of Halloween decorations inside the library door. "How did I know what?"

"You mentioned earlier that you were almost certain Jordan Mc-Gregor never contracted malaria from fighting in New Guinea. How did you know that?"

"Remember the blood drive at the Baptist church?" Miss Dimple carefully removed her purple hat with the velvet roses and set it aside. "I gave blood, of course, as did Coach McGregor." She took time to tuck her hair into place before continuing. "The Red Cross would never have accepted blood from anyone who'd had malaria."

H. G. Dobbins had just finished his shift at the county jail and was walking to his truck, thinking of that good-looking little teacher who had helped with the follies. He couldn't get her off his mind. She pretended she didn't want to have anything to do with him, but he knew she'd come around. Most of them did. A new restaurant had opened a few miles north of town—had a dance floor and everything, and he'd heard the food was pretty good. Maybe he'd just drive by that place where she lived and see if he could talk her into going with him.

He was about to back out of the parking lot when a city police car pulled in beside him and Bobby Tinsley got out and flagged him down.

"Whoa there a minute, will ya, H.G.? I need a word."

H.G. rolled down his window. "Yeah? What's going on, Bobby?" Maybe he should go home and change, he thought, before trying to see Annie. A shave and a change of clothes wouldn't hurt.

Bobby Tinsley put one hand on the truck window and one on the door handle. "I'm afraid I'm going to have to ask you to come in with me, H.G. Shouldn't take long, but we need a few minutes of your time."

"What?" The deputy laughed. "Is this some kind of joke?"

But the police chief wasn't smiling. "Some questions have come up, and we just want to be sure we have everything covered," he said, opening the door of the truck and waiting for H.G. to step out of the vehicle.

"Questions about what? What's this all about?" H.G. got out of the truck and slammed the driver's-side door as hard as he could behind him. That little ass Bobby Tinsley had no right to treat him like this—no right at all, and he'd damn well better have a good explanation.

"Why didn't you tell us you'd had a relationship with Cynthia Murphy?" Bobby asked him later at the police station.

"Cyn— Who told you that? My God! I thought the woman left here years ago—well, until that skeleton turned up." H.G. looked about him. They had taken his revolver and had him sitting at a table in a little room not much bigger than a closet—like a common criminal!

"According to Reynolds Murphy, it hasn't been that many years," Bobby said. "Seems the two of you were seen together not too long before she disappeared. You wanna tell me about that?"

What H. G. Dobbins wanted to do was to take out a handkerchief and wipe his brow, but he knew that was a sure sign of guilt. "What makes you think I had anything to do with what happened to that woman?" he said.

Bobby smiled and shook his head. "A lot of folks call you Cowboy, don't they? I mean you wear those boots and all."

"So what? Is that some kind of crime?"

"Not that I know of," the chief said, "but a couple of times Reynolds said he overheard a phone conversation between his wife and somebody she called Cowboy. She led him to believe, of course, it was perfectly innocent—"

H.G. slammed his hand on the table. "It's been a long time since anybody called me that, and I'm not the only person with that nickname!"

"Probably not," Bobby said, "and I doubt if Reynolds would've thought any more about it if he hadn't learned recently that it used to be yours."

"Now wait just a minute!" H.G. started to stand and then thought better of it. A second policeman, Fulton Padgett, was right outside the door, and he weighed more than two hundred and fifty pounds if he weighed an ounce. "I thought you were questioning Buddy Oglesby in that case. Weren't he and Reynolds Murphy's wife a pretty hot pair off and on for years? And I still think he might've had something to do with taking that War Bond money. You're kinda wandering far afield, aren't you?"

"We let Buddy go this morning," the chief told him, "He said he was living in Savannah around the time Cynthia Reynolds disappeared, and the facts back him up. That doesn't mean, of course, that he couldn't have come back here and killed her. Right now we can't pinpoint the date, but he's not going anywhere. I can promise you that. As for the money, I don't see how in the world we can hold him on that."

H.G. forced a laugh. "So you plan to arrest me on the flimsy evidence that I'm sometimes called Cowboy! You'll have to do better than that."

"Oh, we can do a lot better than that. When Reynolds learned your nickname, he went to a few of those places outside of town he suspected his wife might've frequented, and a couple of people said the two of you were seen there together on more than one occasion—in fact, you were there with her just before she disappeared. They identified you by your picture in the *Eagle*. Remember? It was on the front page after they made that photo of all those folks in the womanless wedding."

H.G. laced his fingers together and clenched them tight. Damn that woman! Cindy Murphy had been some doll, and when she got all decked out she looked like a million dollars. At the end of a night with Cindy, he'd never been disappointed, but she wasn't worth this. Hell, no!

"I want a lawyer," he said.

❦

"I suppose that tale about her husband serving in New Guinea was just one of the many lies Millie McGregor told," Virginia said. "I wonder why she did that?

"Give me a hand with this, will you, please, Dimple?" She was determined to carve a jack-o'-lantern for her upcoming Halloween party for Elderberry's young readers. "You should be an expert at this you've carved so many. Should I draw the face on first?"

"I'm afraid the poor soul must have been a compulsive liar, and I suppose it made her feel important . . . such a shame . . . My goodness, Virginia, first, let's make sure all the seeds are out!" With a large spoon, Miss Dimple raked and scraped the inside of the hollowed-out pumpkin and deposited the few remaining seeds in a large dishpan with the others. The two were taking advantage of a Sunday afternoon while the library was closed to decorate the cabin, and Virginia had spread layers of newspapers on the large rectangular table to protect it.

"Should we make it scary or funny?" Virginia asked. "I vote for scary," she said, not waiting for an answer. "What about Adolph Hitler? He's the scariest thing I know of. I could paint on the hair and the black mustache."

"Good heavens, not *that* scary!" Dimple laughed when she realized her friend was joking. "How about a cat? We could use Cattus here for a model."

And after a half hour or so of carving, in spite of Cattus's refusal to cooperate, the pumpkin began to take on definite feline features, with long whiskers, slanted eyes, and sharp, pointed teeth.

Virginia dripped candle wax in the bottom to hold the stub of a candle and laughed as the jack-o'-lantern cast its flickering yellow glow about the dim room. "It does look like a cat, doesn't it? The children will love it!"

Miss Dimple smiled. Virginia's childlike delight in simple pleasures and her love of books and children were some of the things she especially liked about her friend because she shared them, too—although perhaps a bit more serenely. The smells of candle wax and pumpkin evoked happy autumn memories of her own childhood as well as the many years of Halloween festivities in her familiar classroom at Elderberry Grammar School, when grade mothers usually provided punch, candy corn, and cookies shaped like ghosts and goblins and entertained the children with games and stories.

"I think our children need a break from all the horrors of war, even if it's just pretend—we all do," Virginia said, as if she could read her mind. "I'll bring some fall leaves from the yard to decorate the mantel, and Harris Cooper said he'd let me have some cornstalks from his victory garden." She planned the party for Wednesday after school, and the children were invited to wear their scariest costumes.

Dimple scooped the pumpkin seeds into a pail to take back to Odessa, who would bake them slowly with oil and seasonings as a snack for everyone to enjoy, and they had finished cleaning up the mess they had made when someone tapped at the door.

Virginia frowned. She was in the process of buttoning her coat to leave. "Is that somebody at the door? Surely they know we're not open today."

"I'll see," Dimple said as the tapping came again. She opened the door to find Buddy Oglesby standing on the porch with a troubled expression on his face and a basket of apples in his hands.

"I was looking for Virginia, but I'm glad to see you're here, too, Miss Dimple. I saw your car out front, Virginia, and hoped I might catch you here."

"Come on in, Buddy," Virginia said. "The library's officially closed today, but if you came for a book I'll be glad to help you. Mind you don't bump into the skeleton there."

Buddy stepped hesitantly inside the door, ducking under a jointed cardboard skeleton suspended from a rafter. Virginia had bought it for a dime at Murphy's along with a ghost, a witch, and a haunted house, now scattered about the room. He didn't seem to know what to do with the basket of apples and finally walked over and set it on her desk. "These are for you," he told Virginia. "Winesaps. They're supposed to be good . . . Oh, hell, Virginia, I don't want a book. I just want you to forgive me. I did a stupid thing— well, several stupid things. I know I caused you a lot of grief. I didn't mean to, and I'm sorry. I am so sorry."

Dimple Kilpatrick walked quietly to a seat by the window, feeling very much the intruder. This was not her show. Virginia looked as if she didn't know whether to continue standing or to sit. She finally decided to sit and invited Buddy to do the same.

She spoke in a low, halting voice. "Well, of course I'm disappointed, but the bond money was returned, and I'm thankful for that . . . Buddy, what in the world made you do such a thing? Stealing from the United States government—and at a time when our country needs—"

"What? Wait a minute!" Buddy held up a hand. "I didn't take that money!"

"Then who did?" Virginia asked. "I thought you were trying to tell me you stole the money on the night you so conveniently disappeared."

Buddy went to the door and opened it to see if anyone was outside, then stood with his back to the closed door. "Millie McGregor took that money, Virginia. It had to have been her, but it was my fault for trusting her."

Apparently forgetting the presumed eavesdropper, he left his station by the door and began to pace. "Intermission was almost over, and you'd gone back to your seat when I—well—I had to use the bathroom. You and I had already tallied up the money, and Millie was keeping me company at the table in the lobby while we waited for somebody from the police department to come and collect it and put it in their vault until they could get it to the bank. She suggested I take advantage of her being there and take a quick bathroom break." He ran a hand through his hair and shook his head. "I got back in less than five minutes, I swear, so she had barely enough to time to take all the cash. It was already wrapped, labeled, and tucked neatly away in the bag. All she had to do was replace what she took with leftover programs from the follies."

Virginia sat with a dazed look on her face. "I wonder if Millie was the one who called in that false report to the police station to keep them from getting there sooner."

"Chief Tinsley thinks so," Buddy said. "He checked with Hoot Mullins over at that Pure Oil station across the road, and Hoot said a woman came in and asked to use the phone just as they were getting ready to close. She must've called from there just before the follies started."

"She planned it from the beginning . . ." Virginia Balliew looked as if someone had just told her the library was on fire. "Then it must've been Jordan who brought it back. Do you suppose he *knew*?"

Buddy frowned. "I really doubt it. Certainly not at first, and that must've been a difficult thing for him to do, don't you think? I believe he ran across it while going through her things. She probably had it tucked away in her closet or a dresser drawer—someplace her husband wouldn't ordinarily look."

Virginia nodded. "I imagine he was looking for something for her to wear in the hospital . . . what a sad, sad development! I wonder—will we ever get past this?"

"We will, I think, when they know for sure who killed Cynthia Murphy." Buddy turned and faced them. "And it wasn't me!

"I'll tell you why I left so abruptly the night of the follies," he said, finally allowing himself to sit. "I was helping out at the props table on stage left when the shot was fired, and I knew whoever fired it thought I was on the other side. I feel awful about Jesse Dean, but thank God he's going to be all right!"

Miss Dimple moved closer and took a seat next to Virginia. "Why do you think someone wanted to kill you, Buddy?"

His laughter had no humor. "Not *wanted*. *Wants*, because I think I know who killed Cindy Murphy, and I made the mistake of making him aware of it. Another stupid thing! If I'd just kept my mouth shut, he never would've suspected."

"*He? He who?*" Virginia asked him.

"Your friendly deputy, H.G. Dobbins, that's who. He and Cindy were seeing one another right up until just before she disappeared, and she was in love with him. I know because she told me."

"She *told* you?" Virginia took Cattus on her lap. She was soft and comforting and warm.

"That's right. We dated some in high school and college, and even after she married she'd write or call me once in a while when she felt like getting together, but that stopped after Ross was born. I came back to find out if she'd see me again—just for old times' sake, you know. You never got Cynthia Noland out of your system. I found that out the hard way, but she wasn't interested. Told me she was in love with that imitation cowboy. Said they planned to run off together."

"Frankly," he added. "I consider myself lucky."

"What about her husband?" Miss Dimple asked. "What about Reynolds? And Ross. The woman had a son."

"I don't think Reynolds ever had an inkling about what was going on. Oh, he knew she flirted. He'd have to be blind not to be aware of that, but she had him wrapped around her little finger, and, too, he had to work long hours at the store and would sometimes get home late. It's just as well, I guess, he didn't know she was carrying on, or maybe he just didn't want to know. I think the boy adored her, although she ignored him most of the time. I always liked Ross—seemed like an okay little boy. I felt kind of sorry for him."

Virginia sighed, wishing she could sigh away what she had just heard, but Buddy Oglesby wasn't through.

"I knew it was Cindy in that grave as soon as I saw what was left of her dress," he admitted. "I gave her that dress the last time I saw her—got it from Rich's Department Store in Atlanta. Lord, that woman loved clothes!"

"And had a closet full of them, from what I hear," Virginia said. "Eloise Dodd, who collects clothing for the British War Relief, said Reynolds brought over several boxes of Cynthia's clothing. Beautiful things, too. Eloise said she was tempted to keep some of them for herself."

Dimple Kilpatrick rose and walked to the door, desperate for fresh air. Virginia followed, and Buddy trailed after her.

"Well, Buddy, what now?" Miss Dimple said as they stood on the porch while Virginia locked the door after them.

He shrugged. "I'll stay and help out Aunt Emmaline at the store if she'll have me. She needs me whether she'll admit it or not, and frankly, I guess I need her, too. And I think Arden could use a break now and then. Maybe one day she and Barrett Gordon will marry if this war's ever over."

Miss Dimple agreed and hoped it would work out for all of them. "Have they heard any more from Hugh?" she asked.

"We know he was wounded at Vella Lavella in the Solomons and he's on a hospital ship somewhere, but that's all," Buddy told her. "Arden says her mother won't go in the front of the house because she's afraid she'll see the boy on the black bicycle. You know, the one who delivers the telegrams."

CHAPTER TWENTY-SIX

*M*iss Dimple rose early as usual. Today the sun was not as lively as she, and the sky in the east was lightly streaked with the soft gray light of a promised dawn as if the Creator had barely stroked it with a giant brush. Miss Dimple never tired of watching the earth slowly come to life with faint tinges of gold and rose, followed by a glorious burst of color no artist could reproduce, no matter how hard he tried.

Pausing to collect scraps of litter on her morning walk, Miss Dimple thought of her friend Virginia, her joyful self once again now that the missing bond money had been returned. The extra money that had been in the envelope was exactly the amount Phoebe had paid to the person who had been blackmailing her, and they were almost certain that person was Millie.

And if Millie McGregor was blackmailing Phoebe, was it possible she had been doing the same thing to someone else?

With the point of her umbrella, Miss Dimple speared part of a Hershey bar wrapper and a discarded paper bag that had probably held someone's lunch, and shoved them into the container she carried for *that purpose. Millie had been found in the vacant lot next door to the abandoned house that had been her "collection center." Had she been running from one of her blackmail victims when she collided with that tree?*

Phoebe Chadwick was having a wonderful day. Kathleen had written to tell her she and her husband were coming for Thanksgiving and if all went as planned, Harrison might be able to join them—for a day or so at least. She had also received a chatty letter from Harrison, who told her he would soon be sending her a photograph of himself in his uniform, and she could hardly wait. What a handsome soldier he would make! The photo would share the mantel in the parlor with his mother's wedding picture. She and Kathleen had decided to wait until they were all together to tell him the truth about his heritage. Phoebe's sister and her husband, who had raised Kathleen, had died fairly close together when Harrison was eight or nine, so Phoebe had become accustomed to the role of surrogate grandmother, but now it would be *different!*

Odessa, delighted that Phoebe's appetite had improved, was making her favorite chicken pie for supper, and the rich aroma made Phoebe's stomach growl in anticipation. Humming to herself, Phoebe went into the kitchen to see if she could help.

"Well, I got all this here grease that oughta go to the butcher if anybody's goin' to town." Odessa held up the can she kept to collect the used cooking grease that was employed in the manufacture of explosives; they turned it in to Shorty Skinner, the butcher, on a regular basis.

"I believe Miss Dimple said something about the post office," Phoebe told her as she plucked a used paper bag from the bin in the pantry and slipped the can inside.

"Be sure she asks for that can back," Odessa said. "You can't get one like that with a lid and everything no more."

Phoebe promised, and Miss Dimple did the same. She needed shampoo as well as stamps but would stop by the butcher shop first, she said.

She was leaving the butcher's a little while later when Dimple met Josephine Carr on the same errand, and the two women visited together for a few minutes under Shorty Skinner's green-striped awning, where they could be out of the afternoon sun.

"What a frightening experience that must have been for you and Louise when you discovered poor Millie McGregor," Miss Dimple began. "I think you were most courageous to stay and help."

"It was a little nerve-racking," Jo admitted, "but what else could we do? And Lou was the brave one. She insisted on staying behind while I went for help."

"She must've been looking over her shoulder the whole time," Miss Dimple said. "Charlie tells me you saw someone running away."

Jo nodded, frowning. "I wish I could've been more help with the description, but it was dark and I couldn't see his face." She hoped Miss Dimple wouldn't ask what she and her sister had been doing there.

"Could you tell if it was a man or a woman?"

"I'm not sure," Jo said, "but I think it was a man . . . and there was something else . . . something about the way he ran."

"What do you mean?" Miss Dimple asked, shifting the empty can to her other hand. She knew she must reek of stale cooking grease.

Jo hesitated. "It seemed . . . familiar somehow . . . distinctive." She shrugged. "Probably doesn't mean a thing."

"Perhaps it will come to you," Miss Dimple said. She thought of Buddy Oglesby's distinctive walk, but the police didn't seem to consider him a serious suspect.

Jo shook her head, frowning. "I hear they're questioning that deputy—the one who wears the boots. Seems he and Cynthia

Reynolds were . . . well, more than just friends. My goodness, that woman *did* get around, didn't she? Makes me wonder—did Reynolds have his head in the sand all this time?"

Dimple Kilpatrick had wondered the same thing, but she managed to maintain an impartial expression. "I suppose we can be grateful Reynolds's sweet tooth led him to Jesse Dean's neighborhood the night of the fire," she said.

"Sweet tooth? What do you mean?"

"If Reynolds hadn't been on his way back from the Super Service to buy ice cream, he wouldn't have seen the blaze," Dimple explained.

Jo stepped aside to make room for passersby. "I see," she said, nodding. But she didn't see. Something didn't seem right.

"I get shivers all over every time I hear her sing!" Lily Moss said, hugging herself. Charlie had dropped by Phoebe's after supper that night to finalize plans with Annie for the school-assembly program, but they became sidetracked when sounds of *The Bob Hope Radio Show* came from the parlor. Kate Smith had just finished singing Irving Berlin's "God Bless America," and Charlie had to agree with Lily. The song inspired her, too.

"Heck, if I weren't so dad-blamed old, I'd enlist right now!" Velma said. "Bless his heart, Bob Hope does his best to keep the boys' spirits up with these USO shows, doesn't he? He and Dorothy Lamour and Frances Langford—it sounds like they have a lot of fun doing it, too."

Annie laughed. "Spike Jones was on there not too long ago. Have you heard his crazy song, 'In Der Fuehrer's Face'?"

"I'd like a chance at the fuehrer's face," Phoebe said. "The garbage can's just about full—can't think of a better place to put it."

Sebastian smiled, Charlie noticed, but didn't enter the conversation.

"What's this I hear about that deputy being questioned?" Velma said when the program was over. "What's his name? R.G. or J.T.—something like that—the one who was in the womanless wedding."

"H. G. Dobbins." Annie made a face. "He gives me the willies. I wouldn't be surprised at anything he did."

Peering through her bifocals, Miss Dimple worked at patching the elbow of a small blue jacket that obviously belonged to one of her students. Some of the children came from families where the mother didn't have the time, inclination, or skills to mend a tear, and from the look of this garment, it had led a rough existence. "They must not have had enough evidence to hold him," Miss Dimple said. "I saw him in town this afternoon. Naturally, if anything comes of it, that would be under Sheriff Holland's jurisdiction."

"From what Aunt Lou tells me, Reynolds Murphy found out he'd been having an affair with his wife and said something about it to Bobby Tinsley, but I don't know if that's true." Charlie shrugged. Everybody knew her aunt exaggerated, but that particular bit of information had come from Uncle Ed, whose dental office was right across from City Hall.

"Oh, my!" Lily said. "But if he knew that, why did he wait so long to say something about it?"

Charlie told them what she'd heard about Reynolds's finding out the deputy's nickname was Cowboy. "He didn't really know the man until the two of them were in the follies together."

"Still, that doesn't seem like enough to make them suspect the fellow," Sebastian said, frowning.

"Yes, but she'd also been seen with H.G. at some of those road-houses outside of town, and that was not too long before she disappeared," Charlie explained.

"I think she'd been seeing Buddy Oglesby some, too," Annie said. "Reynolds must've been blind not to realize what was happening right under his nose."

Phoebe looked up from hemming the skirt she had made for Odessa's birthday. "I think he's always been that way about Cindy's goings-on," she said. "I remember how Reynolds grieved when she disappeared. He absolutely adored her."

Sebastian folded the newspaper he'd been reading and set it aside. "I believe there are some men—and women, too—who will put up with almost anything rather than lose the person they love."

Charlie looked at Annie. As much as she loved Will, she could never ignore something like that, and she didn't think Annie could, either. "I'd feel better believing he *didn't* know," she said.

Lily spoke up. "Well, it makes me feel uneasy. That deputy is running around free as a bird, and they've let Buddy Oglesby go, too. How do they know one of them isn't responsible for what happened to Jesse Dean? And I shudder to think about poor Millie McGregor."

Velma nodded. "And don't forget Cynthia Murphy. She might've been wild as a haint, but she didn't deserve what happened to her."

"At least the bond money's back where it belongs," Annie said. "I wonder if Buddy did take it."

Miss Dimple looked up from her darning. "Buddy Oglesby has made some unwise decisions, but he isn't a thief."

"Well, if he didn't take the money, who did?" Velma asked.

"Perhaps time will tell." Miss Dimple went back to her stitching.

"I feel I owe you an explanation." The car slowed beside her as she walked home from school that afternoon, and Miss Dimple stopped and stepped closer to see who was speaking. Jordan Mc-Gregor reached across and opened the door on the passenger side. "Could I treat you to a Co-Cola at the drugstore or someplace? I hope you have a few minutes to spare."

Dimple Kilpatrick was so well organized she had her lessons

planned through the month of December, and she certainly had a few minutes for this heart-wounded fellow. Also, he intrigued her. "Of course," she said, getting into the car. She didn't care for carbonated soft drinks, but that wasn't important. Lemonade would be fine.

"I hope you'll excuse my rudeness for not coming around and opening the door, but there seems to be a lot of traffic at this hour," he said. Miss Dimple smiled and agreed. It was almost five o'clock, and those who had cars were driving home from work.

"I understand Ray's Café sometimes has passable coffee," Miss Dimple said, "if that suits you just as well."

Jordan McGregor nodded and turned left on Court Street. "That would be fine," he said. He seemed relieved, and Dimple thought she understood why. Lewellyn's Drug Store was usually crowded, and after what the poor man had been through, she felt that even though most would be thoughtful enough to give them some privacy, others might interrupt to express sympathy and concern.

"I believe Ray's is usually fairly quiet this time of day," she said. "Their biggest rush is at lunchtime, and those who come for supper don't arrive until later."

Two middle-aged men were in deep conversation over pie and coffee at a table in the window when they entered the restaurant. Dimple recognized one as Clyde Jefferies, who owned the local feed and seed store, but she didn't know the other fellow. He wore overalls, so she assumed he must farm in the area. She and Jordan took a table in a far corner of the restaurant so they would be less likely to be disturbed.

Jordan McGregor didn't waste any time. "I suppose you've guessed that Millie took that bond money?"

Dimple, who took pride in her composure, felt as if she'd had the wind knocked out of her. What he had said was true. She did think

Millie had taken the money, but she didn't expect him to greet her with the admission.

They ordered coffee and, at Jordan's insistence, apple pie. Dimple knew it wouldn't be as good as Odessa's, but it proved to be a fair competitor. She told him that, yes, she had come to the conclusion that Millie had taken the money while Buddy was in the restroom, and they were relieved to have it returned.

Jordan put down his coffee mug and stared silently at his plate before continuing. "There's a name for what Millie had, Miss Dimple. It's called kleptomania. She took things that didn't belong to her."

Miss Dimple was familiar with the term and nodded sympathetically.

After a minute, Jordan continued, and it was obvious he was having trouble with his emotions. "Earlier, you asked me about my time in New Guinea, and it led me to believe you might've been misled." Flustered, he paused and ran an index finger around the rim of the mug. "You see, my wife . . . well, sometimes Millie exaggerated. She'd enlarge on a story if she thought it would bring more attention. In this case, I'm afraid she did, and I have no idea how many other tales she embroidered. It was an illness, and I know now she needed help, but she resisted that, and I was afraid I would lose her if I persisted . . . of course, in the end I did, didn't I?"

Dimple Kilpatrick knew what it was like to lose someone you loved, no matter the situation. Such a long, long time ago in another war she had lost someone, too. Reaching across the table, she took his hand. No words, just a brief gesture, but Jordan's face softened. "I was never in New Guinea, Miss Dimple. My unit was scheduled to go there, but there was an accident at the base— nothing dramatic or heroic. We were on maneuvers and the truck we were in turned over and crushed my leg. Frankly, all of us were lucky to get out alive, but it finished me for the army, I'm afraid."

Jordan took a swallow of his coffee and faced her across the table. "Others have told me they heard the same story from Millie. I'm sorry. I guess I wasn't enough of a hero to suit her."

"Sometimes it takes a hero to admit the truth," Miss Dimple said, "and to deal with our troubles during difficult times. I think you're doing just that. Our young boys need you, Coach McGregor. Our town needs you, and I hope you'll come to call Elderberry home."

"Thank you." The coach's smile was brief. "I hope the money was all there."

"That and more," she told him. "Virginia found seventy-five dollars over what had been missing. Do you have any idea where that might've come from?"

He frowned. "I have an idea, but I don't know what to tell you to do about it. I suppose I'll just have to leave that up to Virginia."

During the drive home Miss Dimple was pleased to hear Jordan McGregor relate how supportive his fellow faculty members had been and how touched he was by the comfort he'd received from members of the high school football team. "Already some of the boys are talking about enlisting," he said. "Such fine young men! I just hope this war will be over by the time they're old enough for the draft."

Jordan didn't mention the manner in which Millie had died until they drew up in front of Phoebe's home and he walked with her to the door. "I don't know what Millie was doing in that empty lot that night when she fell and struck her head, but from what I've heard, it seems she was being pursued. It drives me crazy wondering why and by whom, yet there's nothing I can do but hope and pray the police will deal with it soon. First I think it might be one person, then another. It just doesn't make any sense!"

Miss Dimple agreed. "Everything seems to have come to a boil all at once," she said. "I hope we'll have some answers soon."

The coach paused as they reached the door. "There's one more thing that bothers me," he said before leaving, "Unfortunately, my wife was in the habit of saying things that weren't true, but she did tell me something that has since caused me to wonder. Millie said she saw the person who put that rifle in Reynolds Murphy's car the night of the follies . . . it wasn't the one I might have suspected."

CHAPTER TWENTY-SEVEN

*H*arris Cooper's wife, Angela, stood in the bedroom doorway watching Jesse Dean pack his bag. "Are you sure you're ready to leave?" she asked. "You know you're welcome to stay as long as you want."

"I can't thank you enough for your kindness," Jesse Dean said. "You've both been so good to me, but it's time to go home. I can't stay here forever, and my neighbors tell me the damage to my roof has already been repaired." Jesse Dean closed the suitcase with a feeling of finality. He didn't want to leave this safe place and these loving people who had become like parents to him, but it was time to face his fears. "Doc Morrison says I can even come back to the store next week," he added, smiling.

He flushed as Angela gave him a parting hug. "Harris is waiting in the car," she told him. "And I think you'll find a surprise there as well."

The surprise waited on the front seat, but happily moved over to make room for Jesse Dean. He had brown floppy ears, a wet pink tongue, and a tail that wouldn't stop wagging.

"His name's Jake, and don't ask me what breed he is because I don't know, but he's all yours," Harris said.

And Jesse Dean enfolded the puppy in his arms and laughed. Now he wouldn't be alone.

❧

Shame on you! Josephine Carr told herself. She had been putting off going to see Emmaline Brumlow, when she, of all people, knew only too well the worry and uncertainty a mother endured after receiving tragic news from the front. Charlie, her own daughter, had called on the family twice and said Emmaline was beginning to face what had happened and was attempting to come to terms with it. That morning Jo had made up her mind to do her duty and was on her way with a loaf of cheese bread she'd made with Charlie's help from a recipe they'd clipped from *Good Housekeeping*.

She remembered the sympathetic looks, the clumsy words of comfort, the hugs and the tears she had received from well-meaning friends when they learned Fain was missing, and she remembered how she'd wanted to run away; hide in some dark, quiet place and shut out the world. Above all she remembered the agonizing hurt and the near-impossible challenge of going on with her life.

Emmaline was a royal pain in the rear, but she was a mother and she was suffering. Bread in hand, Jo knocked at the door.

Arden, looking flushed and prettier than Jo had ever seen her, answered the door. "Mrs. Carr, please come in. I think there's still some coffee left from breakfast. Why don't I pour us a cup?"

Jo followed her into the kitchen, looking around for Emmaline. "Your mother? How is she, Arden?"

"Oh, she's at the store." Arden indicated a chair and turned a flame under the coffeepot. "I don't guess you've heard, but we got some wonderful news late yesterday—well, maybe not the best news, but Hugh's going to be all right, and he's on a hospital ship on his way back to the States! They're sending him to the army hospital at Camp Shelby in Hattiesburg, Mississippi, and if we're lucky he

246

might even be home for Christmas!" Arden sat across from Jo at the kitchen table, her expression now serious. "Hugh lost a leg, Mrs. Carr, but he could've lost his life. They say they can fit him with an artificial limb and he'll be able to walk again . . . he wants to study medicine, you know."

Josephine Carr did know, because for a time she thought perhaps Hugh might become her son-in-law and Charlie had continued to correspond with him. She opened her mouth to tell Arden how glad she was to hear the news, but instead began to cry.

"I'm so sorry! I don't know what made me do that," she said after wiping her eyes. "I guess those were tears of relief."

Arden stood and put her arms around her, and Jo saw that she had been crying, too. "I'm used to it," she told her, laughing. "I never know when it's going to happen.

"I have some other good news as well," Arden added as she filled their cups. "I can finally plan my wedding. I wrote to Barrett last night and told him that as soon as he comes home after this war, we're going to walk down that aisle." She paused. "Or, at least I'm going to walk down it. I guess the groom just waits at the altar, doesn't he? And Hugh can give me away. I don't care if he has to escort me on crutches as long as he's here for our wedding."

Jo thought of Barrett Gordon, who was on a ship somewhere in the Pacific, and prayed that Arden's wishes would be fulfilled. "Oh, Arden, how exciting for you! It's never too soon to plan a wedding," she said, not wanting to dampen the young woman's enthusiasm. "And just think—since you're in the retail business, I imagine you'll be able to have your choice of wedding gowns."

Arden nodded. "Maybe after the war. There's not much to choose from now. I thought I'd have my bridesmaids wear yellow. It's such a cheerful color, and my college roommate promised she'd be my matron of honor. She's expecting her first child around Christmastime, and if the baby's a girl, maybe she'll be old enough to be my flower girl—but heavens, I hope we don't have to wait that long!"

"You might want to change your mind about having a flower girl," Jo said, and told her about a wedding she'd attended where that young member of the wedding party wet her pants on the way down the aisle and left a puddle at the altar.

"Oh, dear!" Arden said, laughing. "That sounds almost as outlandish as those nutty men in the womanless wedding."

Coffee sloshed into the saucer as Jo abruptly set down her cup. The womanless wedding . . . of course! Now she remembered where she had seen the man with the peculiar loping gait.

So Millie was dead. And they said she was the one who had taken the War Bond money, and she'd probably done other terrible things, too. Delia had a hard time believing it, but she knew it was true and it left her with upside-down emotions. She had liked Millie McGregor, really liked her, or she had liked being with her because she was fun and Delia was lonely and bored, but when it came right down to it, she had never felt she'd known the *person* who was Millie. She was sorry Millie had died the way she did and hoped she hadn't suffered. Her mother had tried to assure her that she hadn't, at least not for long; and she sympathized with the husband she'd left behind, but Delia Varnadore felt used, cheated. The woman she'd thought was a friend was not only a liar, but also a thief who had schemed the whole time to cheat the people who had been kind to her, and then she would move on. Charlie and her mother—and Aunt Lou, as well—seemed to think Millie McGregor was saving up to leave them all behind—husband included. Of course they would never know for sure.

As she walked to town pushing little Tommy in his carriage, it occurred to Delia that she had used Millie as well. Would the older woman still have seemed fun and appealing when her old friends came home from college? Delia drew in her breath. *I don't want to ever be like that!* Steering the carriage around a rough spot in the sidewalk, she began to walk faster.

"Hey there! What's the rush?" Leaning on his rake, John Mote waved to her from his front yard. "Isn't that boy walking yet?" he joked.

Delia liked both the Motes, and it made her sad to see the gold star along with the blue one in their window. Their son Chester had been killed earlier in the war, and their other one, Jack, was somewhere in Italy. She smiled and wheeled the baby closer. "I see she has you working today, and I must say, it's about time." Mrs. Mote was usually the one outside working in the yard. She said it soothed her mind.

"No rest for the weary," he said, mopping his face. "Marjorie fell and broke her wrist the other day, and she's had me hopping ever since."

Delia was sorry to hear that as she was especially fond of Marjorie Mote. "What can we do to help? What about supper? Don't tell me she has *you* cooking?"

He laughed. "The church circle's taking good care of us in that category, but if you're going near the library, you might pick her up a couple of books. Virginia knows what she likes."

"I'll be glad to," Delia promised, and decided to go there first. The night before she had heard Charlie and her mother laughing in the kitchen as they made cheese bread for the Brumlows. They seemed to be having fun, and Delia had mentioned that maybe it was time she helped out more with meals. During the first few months she and Ned had been married she'd learned to prepare the basic foods, but was afraid to try anything too difficult or fancy. At the time, Ned was too in love to care, but you couldn't live off hamburgers and canned peaches forever, and this morning after Charlie left for school, Delia had found the cookbook open to a recipe for gingerbread at her place at the table. Well, how hard could that be? And if it turned out good, she'd take some to the Motes.

"I don't know what to do. What if I'm wrong?" Jo had stopped by her sister's on her way back from visiting with Arden and, although she had thought twice before telling Lou what had been worrying her, the burden of it was more than she could bear alone.

"Maybe we should go to the police," Lou suggested, tossing her apron aside.

"And what would we tell them, that we suspect Reynolds Murphy of lying about buying ice cream and that the person I saw running away ran like one of the bridesmaids in the womanless wedding? They'll laugh me out of the building."

"Then we'll confront him together. I'll go with you. What can he do in broad, open daylight right there in the middle of town?"

"No, wait. Let's think." Jo was beginning to regret sharing this with her impetuous sister. "This will keep a few hours longer. Jordan McGregor told Dimple Kilpatrick that Millie said she'd seen the person who put the rifle in Reynolds's car the night of the follies but he didn't say who it was. She might have been trying to blackmail that person, too."

"Why didn't he tell Miss Dimple who it was?" Lou wanted to know. "And have you thought it might have been Jordan himself? He has a limp due to an injury—*and* he was one of the bridesmaids, too."

"From what I understand, Miss Dimple tried her best to pry that out of him, but he said he wanted to be sure before he made an accusation. Jordan knows very well Millie's tales weren't always true. Besides, he was at a meeting of the school board that night, wasn't he?"

"Well, at least for *part of the time*." Lou's eyes gleamed. "Just think, Jo, if we can find out who *that* was, we'll know who Millie was running from when she fell—and maybe even who killed Cynthia Murphy!"

"Jordan should be home from school in a few hours. Let's see what he has to say." Jo loved her sister—if only there were some way to dampen her reckless enthusiasm.

Twisting her dish towel, Lou walked from one end of her kitchen to the other. "I don't know. That's a long time to wait, Jo. I think we need to set up a trap."

Jo sighed. "What kind of trap?"

Lou thought about that for a minute. "Well, one of us could call Reynolds on the phone—tell him we know what he did—that we have proof . . ."

"What kind of proof?"

"It doesn't matter what kind of proof, Josephine. He won't know we don't have any. Anyway, you'll arrange a place to meet him—someplace private . . ."

"*I'll* meet him? What about you?" Jo demanded.

"Silly, we'll all be there—the police, too," her sister explained, "but he wouldn't be aware of that yet. Then when he makes a move toward you, that's when we step in."

They heard the front door close just then and Ed Willingham hollered, "Dinner ready? I'm home!"

"Oh, lordy! Don't let on to Ed," Lou said. "He'll never understand.

"Back here, Ed!" she yelled.

"I have to get home. Talk to you later," Jo told her. On the way out she gave her brother-in-law a resounding kiss on the cheek. She had never been as glad to see him.

The spicy aroma of gingerbread greeted her when she got home, and Jo was delighted to find her younger daughter peeling potatoes for supper.

"I told Mrs. Mote I'd come back and read to her this afternoon," Delia said. "She's broken her wrist, and it's hard for her to hold the book. Besides," she added, "I think she likes being around my little Pooh Bear."

Jo smiled. "And who wouldn't?" she asked, giving the baby a kiss. "Smells like gingerbread. Is that for Marjorie?"

"And for us, too, if it turns out all right." Delia frowned. "What's wrong, Mama? You look worried. I'm not going to burn down the house—I promise."

Jo laughed. "It's just something I have to think about, but it will keep, and if your aunt Lou calls, tell her I'm not here."

CHAPTER TWENTY-EIGHT

*M*iss Dimple stood on the corner watching the convoy of trucks passing by, each khaki-colored vehicle filled with soldiers wearing the same drab color. Most smiled and waved back at the people who had gathered to wish them well. Across the street Marjorie and John Mote stood together on the curb with hope on their faces and the worst kind of hurt in their hearts. Some of the soldiers laughed and called out, and a few threw chewing gum and hard candy for the delighted children, who hustled to collect it. Most of the men looked young; they had probably finished their basic training, she thought, but had not yet seen war. How many would come back?

Beside her Willie Elrod stuffed a stick of gum into his mouth and waved a small American flag as high as his slender arm could reach. "One of these days," he said proudly, "I'll be on one of those trucks. I'm going to be a soldier, too!"

Dimple Kilpatrick drew in her breath, closed her eyes, and said a silent prayer.

What to do? If she brought her concerns to the police and they turned out to be wrong, not only would she be a laughingstock, but she would also hurt an innocent person. But, Jo wondered, what if she was *right?* Cynthia Murphy had been killed, her body buried in a shallow grave; someone had to have pulled the trigger that injured Jesse Dean and then tried to burn down his house; and now Millie McGregor was dead, and she suspected it was all by the same hand. Who would be next?

Jo didn't mention her concerns to Charlie when her daughter came home from school that afternoon. It had been several days since Charlie had heard from Will, and she was in a foul mood. Two of the boys in her class had gotten in a fight at recess, and she had been compelled to send them to the principal; a window shade in her classroom had fallen on a goldfish bowl in the windowsill, and not only did she cut her finger cleaning up the broken glass, but the surviving fish was now swimming around in an old metal candy box they'd used for crayons until they could replace the bowl. Charlie didn't have much hope for its chances.

"And I know I shouldn't be resentful, Mama," she added, "but Annie got *three* letters from Frazier all at the same time yesterday and she's been reading me parts of them all day. Doesn't she know I haven't had a word from Will all week? What's the matter with him? You'd think he would at least call!"

Maybe the convoy passing their house that afternoon had increased her worries over Will as it had reminded all of them of the casualties of war. Jo tried to soothe her ruffled offspring as best she could. "Charlie, you know very well how it is with the mail. I'm sure you'll hear something soon. Why don't you see what's on at the picture show this afternoon? Get your mind on something else."

"Huh!" Charlie said, and disappeared into her room.

With one daughter out and the other in her room sulking, Jo took advantage of the opportunity to telephone Dimple Kilpatrick and was relieved to find her in. She needed someone with a level head.

"Coach McGregor should be at home by now," Miss Dimple said when Jo explained the situation. "I'll try again to convince him to tell me who Millie claimed she saw. He told me he wanted to be absolutely sure before he said anything as he plans to do some investigating on his own. I don't think it would be a good idea, however, to tell him who you suspect. We don't want to upset the apple cart."

Jo Carr agreed and waited by the telephone for Miss Dimple to call her back. It didn't take long.

"Your suspicions are correct," Miss Dimple told her. "Could we meet somewhere and talk about this? There's no privacy here or I'd invite you over."

"Then I'll come by for you," Jo said. They seldom used the car in their garage, and as far as she knew it still had gas in the tank.

She found Miss Dimple waiting by the curb, her purple coat buttoned to the chin as the afternoon had turned much colder. "I do believe we might be going to have our first frost," Miss Dimple said.

Jo didn't answer. The weather wasn't her main concern just then, but she knew Miss Dimple was mulling the problem in her mind and would eventually come up with a practical solution. At the older woman's suggestion, she drove into town and parked on one of the less crowded streets.

"I don't believe your sister's idea of a trap is the best way to handle the situation," Dimple said after a time.

"Then how?" Jo shivered. She wished she'd parked in the sun.

"First, I believe we should speak with Cyrus Stone at the Super Service. If it's true that Reynolds did, indeed, indulge in a longing for ice cream, it would prove most embarrassing for all of us."

Jo agreed. Why hadn't she thought of that?

They found Cyrus behind the candy counter, treating himself to a bag of peanuts and a NuGrape soda. Why, of course he remembered the night of that fire at Jesse Dean's, he told them. He'd had a heck of a time getting past the fire truck and all that commotion on his way home that night. Cyrus frowned. Good gracious! The last time Reynolds Murphy had been there was sometime back in the summer when he came in to get a tire patched.

"Now what?" Jo asked as they drove back to town.

"I think we should confront him all together." Dimple looked at her watch. "Most of the stores close at six, and he always stays after to take care of the accounts and to lock up."

Noticing Jo's doubt, Miss Dimple continued. "I know this man. I've known him for a long time, as have you. I don't know how this all started, what made him do the things it looks like he's done, but I can assure you that he's suffering. That's a lot of guilt to carry around. It must be a terrible burden. I think it would be a relief for him to finally face the truth."

"But he shot Jesse Dean! And look what happened to Millie McGregor."

"Reynolds Murphy is a crack shot, Jo. Why, he instructs the Home Guard in riflery. I don't think Jesse Dean was his intended target, but I do think he wouldn't be alive today if Reynolds had wanted to kill him.

"As for what happened to the coach's wife," she continued, "that might have been an accident, although I don't think there's any doubt he was responsible for it."

Jo drew in her breath. She wanted to put an end to all the questions, the fears, the doubts they had lived with for the past several weeks, but she also wanted to live to welcome their sons home from the war, to see Charlie happily married, and to watch her grandchildren grow up. "And what if he isn't all that eager to confess?" she asked.

"Then that would be Bobby Tinsley's problem, and Sheriff Holland's, too, of course, as Cynthia Murphy was probably killed out in the county. Naturally, I intend to ask Bobby to come with us."

Jo frowned. "Do you believe Bobby will go along with it? What makes you think he'll take our word?"

Miss Dimple smiled. "Let's just wait and see."

Jo insisted that Lou be included in the plan as she wanted to be able to exist peacefully with her sister for the duration of their lives, and they agreed that the two of them would wait in the car while Dimple went in to talk with the police chief. When she came out she wasn't exactly smiling, but she did look a bit pleased with herself.

"We're to meet Bobby at the end of the alley that runs behind the store promptly at six thirty," she told them. "That will give Reynolds time to account for the sales they took in today and put the money in the safe. His office opens onto that alley, and I'll knock on the door and call to him so he won't be alarmed. Bobby thinks he'll be more likely to open the door to me, but of course he'll be right there with us."

Jo gasped. "What if he has a gun?"

But Miss Dimple only frowned and shook her head.

"And then what?" Lou asked.

Miss Dimple took time to tuck a soft gray strand of hair under her violet knitted hat. "Then we tell him what we suspect he did, that we know from Jordan that Millie saw him put the rifle in his own car the night of the follies and we believe she was trying to blackmail him for that reason."

"And I'll tell him I recognized him from the way he ran the night Millie struck her head," Jo said, "and we know he wasn't at the Super Service the night of Jesse Dean's fire."

"What do I tell him?" Lou wanted to know.

"You tell him that it's time for him to admit his mistakes and make a clean breast of things. Tell him that no matter what he's done, he's still one of ours, but it's time for him to pay the price." Miss Dimple might have been speaking to one of her students.

Lou brightened. "I'll try, but I'm not sure I can remember all that."

She did, however, and said it most convincingly with only the slightest tremor in her voice.

After a brief pause, Reynolds Murphy had opened the door at Miss Dimple's request to find the four of them standing there, and at first he didn't seem to notice Bobby Tinsley in the background. When he did, he stepped back and let them have their say, and as Miss Dimple had predicted, he didn't deny their accusations.

"I didn't mean for that to happen to Millie McGregor," he said later. She had attempted to blackmail him, he said, and he had waited that night to see who would show up to collect the money. "When she saw me, she ran, and I ran after her. I don't know what I meant to do—frighten her, maybe—but I certainly didn't intend to kill her," he told them. "It looked like she ran into a tree and fell. I didn't know until later she'd hit her head on a rock. I ran, of course, because I didn't want anyone knowing why she expected me to pay her. It's true she'd seen me put that rifle in my own car," he admitted. "I did it to confuse them after what happened to Jesse Dean, but Millie threatened to tell everyone what she'd seen. I only wanted to try and reason with her. You have to believe me—I wasn't planning to hurt her."

"What about Jesse Dean?" Jo asked. "He could've died, you know. And you were the one who set fire to that trash can, too, weren't you? What has he ever done to you, Reynolds?" Jo was fond of Jesse Dean Greeson, and it saddened her to think how he must have suffered.

Reynolds shook his head and sighed. "Nothing! Absolutely nothing! I only set that fire so everyone would believe Jesse Dean was the original target, and I made sure he got out before it did much damage."

"So convenient, your being there," Miss Dimple commented, forcing him to meet her eyes.

"Buddy Oglesby was supposed to be on that side of the stage—not Jesse Dean, and I only meant to frighten him."

"Why?" Miss Dimple wanted to know.

"Because he'd said earlier—back when rehearsals first started—that even though he had nothing to do with my wife's death, he insinuated that he knew who did. Cynthia had told me the two of them had been sweet on each other years ago, and I knew they'd kept in touch. I didn't know how much he knew or thought he knew . . . I'll admit I can't bear to look at the man, but I just meant to scare him into silence, that's all."

"You scared him, all right," Bobby Tinsley said. "He took off and didn't come back until we dragged him home."

"He wasn't even talking about you," Jo told him. "Buddy thought H. G. Dobbins was responsible for Cindy's death."

"Still, he had no business keeping after Cindy. They'd been a couple in high school—*high school,* mind you! Why couldn't he leave her alone?"

Bobby Tinsley didn't tell him that from what he'd heard, it was Cynthia who wouldn't leave Buddy alone. "Do you want to tell us how your wife ended up buried next to the Hutchinsons' cotton field? Was that an accident, too?"

Reynolds Murphy didn't try to stop the tears. "It *was* an accident! I didn't mean to kill her. I loved her, and I don't think anybody who knows me would argue with that. Cindy was my world—she and Ross." He paused and shook his head. "*Was,*" he repeated.

He sank into a chair. "I'd been on a buying trip to Atlanta, but I came home a day early and found my wife had been with another man. I didn't know who, because he left as soon as he heard my car, but I'll swear on my mother's grave it was H. G. Dobbins, except at the time I had no idea he was the one. I'd heard her talking to somebody named Cowboy a couple of times on the phone, but she said he was just an old friend. I should've known better, but I wanted to believe her—oh, you just don't know how I wanted to believe her!

"Cindy said she didn't love me, that she wanted to be with somebody else and they were going away together. *And she told me Ross wasn't even mine!* That's when I hit her—hit her hard. She fell, and her head struck the marble slab that was in our kitchen, the one my mother used to make yeast bread. I've since had it removed—had new cabinets put in and everything. I couldn't bear to look at it."

"And then what?" Chief Tinsley asked.

"She wasn't breathing! I tried to revive her, but it was too late. Oh, God, she was dead! Cindy was *dead.* I didn't know what to do, so I put her in the car and drove all around the county for I don't know how long. I'd brought along a shovel, and I buried her somewhere on the Hutchinsons' property. Hell, I didn't even know where I was! Ross was on some kind of camping trip with the Scouts, and as soon as I could arrange it, I enrolled him in that military school. I didn't even want to be around him."

Dimple Kilpatrick had never taught Ross Murphy as he'd attended one of the schools in the county, but she could imagine how the young boy must have felt at being abandoned by the only parents he ever knew, and she had to use every bit of her willpower to keep from leaping across the table and shaking Reynolds Murphy until his brains rattled. *It didn't matter now if he was the boy's natural father or not. The young man deserved better. Buddy Oglesby had professed a liking for Ross, and she thought he just might need company on the road he had chosen. Well . . . time would tell.*

The sky was turning dark as Charlie raked crab apples into a pile in the backyard and tossed them into a bucket. The tree made a mess every fall, but it was beautiful in the spring, and if they could get enough sugar they made wonderful jelly.

Delia was upstairs putting Tommy to bed, and her mother had called from Aunt Lou's to say she might be a little late and would tell them all about it when she got home. She and Delia had eaten a light supper of scrambled eggs on toast and some of the apple-sauce from last fall's crop. Maybe raking up crab apples would keep her from thinking of Will. Had he been transferred to Craig Field or some other base before he could let her know? Or worse, maybe there'd been an accident with his plane! Things like that happened. She'd heard all about them. Charlie reached for another crab apple with her rake. She wasn't going to think about that.

Her mother had sounded excited over the phone, and she was rarely late for supper, so something must have been going on. Between Jo Carr's routine work at the ordnance plant and her hum-drum job writing society news for the *Eagle*, Charlie couldn't imagine what it could possibly be. Probably some wild scheme of Aunt Lou's . . . Well, she would just have to wait to hear about it later. She tugged her hat over her ears against the cold and wished she'd thought to put on gloves. It was getting dark and Charlie could hardly see, but still she raked until the bucket was so full she could barely lift it.

Hearing footsteps on the driveway behind her, Charlie thought at first it was her mother returning until she heard his voice.

"Can I give you a hand with that bucket?"

Turning, she saw Will standing less than three feet away. *Will Sinclair was real and he was here—right here in her own backyard!* Charlie closed the gap between them in less than a second.

"I didn't want to call because I wasn't sure I could get a pass until the last minute," he said between kisses, "so I thought I'd just surprise you."

"Well, you did," Charlie admitted. "How long will you be able to stay?" The touch of him, the smell of him, the warmth of his arms around her—if only she could keep it forever.

"Just until tomorrow," he murmured into her hair. "What time does the jewelry store open in the morning?"